FRAGILE DARKNESS

ELLIE JAMES

FRAGILE DARKNESS

ELLIE JAMES

Quercus

First published in the US in 2012 by St Martin's Press,
175 Fifth Avenue, New York, N.Y. 10010

First published in Great Britain in 2013 by Quercus Editions Ltd

55 Baker Street
7th Floor, South Block
London W1U 8EW

A CIP catalogue reference for this book is available
from the British Library

ISBN 978 0 85738 826 1

1 3 5 7 9 10 8 6 4 2

Printed and bound in Great Britain by Clays Ltd, St Ives plc

For Holly,
for everything

Acknowledgments

Writing a book is a solitary experience, but creating one is not. Exploring Trinity's world has been a fascinating experience, one of adventure, research, travel, and possibility. I've learned things I never anticipated learning, crossed lines I never planned to cross, and dreamed increasingly fascinating dreams. I walked the streets of New Orleans, both among the living and the dead. I slipped between darkness and shadows and light. And in the process, I've spent countless hours with friends both old and new. Without them, the Midnight Dragonfly series would not be what it is today.

A special thanks to my wonderful editor, Holly Blanck, for sharing my love of the unexplained, never being afraid of dark places, and loving Trinity as much as I do. For your vision, your patience, and letting me make you cry. For being you.

My wonderful agent, Roberta Brown, for your continued wisdom, belief, and energy—*especially* your energy.

My amazing and talented soul-sisters Catherine Spangler and Linda Castillo, for the friendship, the support, the ruthless red pens, and the hours on the phone. I really worked you hard with this one!

Faye, for all things New Orleans.

Wendy, for not being afraid to go on an adventure with me.

Luisa and Jamie, for the early reads.

The Afternoon Gang, for smiling kindly when I talked about another world.

My AWESOME Facebook community, especially Terri, for patiently answering questions, and sharing my excitement.

And as always, my husband and children, for letting me play in Trinity's world, and not taking it personally when I forget to wash the clothes. Or fix dinner. Or about that school project or what day of the week it is . . .

You have my deepest, sincerest thanks.

I will love the light for it shows me the way,
yet I will endure the darkness because it shows me the stars.

—OG MANDINO

FRAGILE
DARKNESS

FRAGILE
DARKNESS

Prologue

I ran.

Darkness bled from all directions. Nothing moved. There was no sound, not even the breath of the night.

"Where are you?" I shouted, or maybe it was a whisper. I didn't know, it didn't matter. *"Why can't I find you?"*

Around me the stillness deepened, the echo of my own heartbeat blasting against the silence.

I had to find him. That's all I could think. He couldn't be gone.

Not forever.

Faster now, I ripped through the nothingness, knowing—

I went down without warning, sprawling against something hot and warm and sticky. I tried to scramble up, but a sudden, rhythmic thudding stopped me. Footsteps. In the distance. Behind me?

I twisted around—

Louder, closer.

I pushed to my feet, but no longer knew which direction I'd come from, or in which direction I should run. A dark vacuum swirled around me, closer. I took off anyway, stumbling as the sound of my name ripped into the stillness.

"Trinity!"

I stopped as the night stirred, and a sudden gust tore through the trees. Stars exploded against the inky sky, glimmering together, until there was only white, a white so bright and pure I had to look away. I swung around, but then the white was dripping, huge globs sliding against the horizon to reveal the silhouette in the background, dark and curved and intricate. . . .

I came alive hard and fast, jerking upright to the steady glow against the shadows—the unblinking yellow of Delphi's eyes, and the green numerals of my bedside clock. 5:21.

And I knew he was gone.

I hung there tangled in the sheets, trying to breathe, to understand, but the slippery images receded like silent waves into the cold, dark ether of the unseen.

"Come back," I whispered. *"I need you."*

But that's not the way it worked.

I had no memory of falling asleep, only of sitting in my bed reading my mother's journal. Now the notebook lay on top of the bright pink T-shirt on the floor, hiding the single word rhinestoned across the front: *Fleurever.* I reached down, but instead of soft cotton, something cool and smooth slipped beneath my fingers.

I froze. There in the soft glow of the nightlight, the iridescent dragonfly—the one that belonged on the trunk across the room—shimmered, its glued wing lifted, the other resting against the card I'd thrown away the night before.

It was the third time I'd found the blown glass on the floor since coming home from the hospital.

A few inches away my mother's journal lay open to the last page I remembered reading:

The danger does not come through hearing the shadows, and it cannot be avoided by ignoring them. That would be like pretending your heart doesn't beat or trying to stop it. The silent whispers come to me for a reason, crying out through the gossamer bands of time and space, warning me to pay attention. To open my eyes and see what no one else does. What's not there yet, in this world, this life.

But will be.

Sometimes I am meant to intervene. Sometimes I'm not. I never know beforehand. I never know when it's about the journey, or when it's about the destination.

When it's about me, or a stranger.

When the two are the same.

Once I didn't want to know. Once I wished the shadows would go away, and take the previews with them. That I didn't have to know, to see, to live things over and over.

Wish that I didn't have to feel, to hurt.

But then my wish came true, and I realized how fragile darkness can be.

ONE

The old house glowed in the moonlight.

With Spanish moss whipping against my face, I slipped from the flagstone path to the shadow of the huge oaks, and lifted a hand to my throat. *Breathe,* I told myself. *Just breathe.*

It was March. Spring Break had started with the afternoon bell several hours before. Mardi Gras was in full, crazy swing. Two hours earlier I'd stood among thousands in the rain of doubloons and beads from the Krewe of Morpheus parade. Another six would roll tomorrow, all building to Fat Tuesday in four days.

And yet it was impossible to walk through the old Greek Revival without remembering the night last fall, when the first breath of evil whispered against my soul.

But a respected family lived in this house, a professor at Tulane and an antiques dealer, their five sons ranging in age from twenty-seven to sixteen. Thousands of twinkling lights turned the big white columns into candy canes of green and purple.

Light shone from every window. Music blasted. Almost everyone I knew was inside. A nightmare was not about to unfold, only a party. My first since the rhythmic beep of hospital machines had gone quiet.

I needed to go back inside. Victoria or Deuce would notice I was gone, and they'd come looking for me.

After a quick check of the porch, I looked up through the swaying branches toward the sprawl of the sky. There the moon hung like a glowing crescent ornament against a glittering panorama of inky velvet.

Twenty-six days. Sometimes it seemed like only the blink of an eye since that final kiss in the shadow of the roller coaster. Other times it was like the whole world stood still, each moment, each breath, carved in its own eternity. I kept waiting to wake up, to pull myself from the nightmare and find everything as it had been before: my aunt dancing around the kitchen and Chase waiting by the fountain at school, Grace reading palms at her table in Jackson Square and Dylan—

That was where the rewrite stopped, the second his name drifted into the illusion.

"Trying to count the stars, Mile High?"

Turning, I found Deuce slipping between the big old trees, as if his body moved to a hip-hop rhythm only he heard.

"I always like nights like this," he said, and with his voice the memory returned to the shadows. "When the sky's so clear it's like a window to another world."

At a little over six feet, Deuce had the well-muscled body of a lightweight boxer. He wore his black jeans tight and his button-downs slim-fitting. Tonight's shirt had a tribal pattern. His ebony hair was closely cropped. Long, thin sideburns angled down into a chinstrap. A thin scar streaked above his upper lip and another through his right eyebrow. On first glance, no one would guess that his soul was that of a poet, and that with only a few notes of his sax, he could stir emotions you didn't know you had.

Only a few minutes before he'd stood on the steps, surrounded by girls in micro-dresses and knee-high boots.

"Escaped your fan club?" I asked.

He grinned. "They're recruiting new members."

My own grin just kind of happened. Deuce had that way about him. In those first few days after waking up in the hospital, riding waves of numbness and grief, I'd never imagined I could smile again. Then he showed up one night with a carton of ice cream. I told him I wasn't hungry, but he said it didn't matter.

Ten minutes later we were both covered in multicolored sprinkles and chocolate syrup, while my cat licked anything she could find, and I smiled.

Then I cried.

And there on the hard, cold wood of the kitchen floor, Deuce drew me into his arms and started to sing.

I have no memory of the words, only the feeling of being safe.

A long time passed before he let go.

"I know this great spot south of town," he said as the back door fell open and music throbbed into the night. Laughing, a group of girls in baby-doll dresses climbed onto the porch rail and started to dance.

The Friday before Mardi Gras, the annual Greenwood bash was revving crazier by the minute.

"It's down by the river," he said. "What do you say we get out of here and—"

I realized where this whole conversation was going. "Deuce, no. You've got a gig."

"And you're standing out here by yourself, while everyone you know is inside."

I hadn't meant for anyone to see me.

"I saw, Mile High," he said. "I looked up and saw you out here in the shadows, like you wished they'd swallow you, staring at your phone. You can't tell me you really want to be here."

Want. It should have been an easy word. Seven months ago, when I first came to New Orleans, the city where I'd been born but didn't remember, it was. I wanted to meet people and make friends, go out and be like everyone else. I wanted an awesome pair of low-rise jeans and a new phone. I wanted my lab partner to—

The memory brought the stabbing feeling back all over again. I'd wanted Chase to look at me and smile, to feel the same awareness that rushed through me.

Back then I hadn't known about the shadows waiting, or strangers who knew more about me, my life, than I did, who could heal with a simple touch, and devastate without lifting a hand.

Now I wanted the horrible things I saw to never come true, the fact that I saw them to never touch anyone I cared about.

Looking at Deuce, there was only one way to answer his question.

"I *want* you to have this gig," I said. Playing the Greenwood party was a huge deal. "And I *want* Victoria to hear Trey sing." Because whenever she did, my best friend lit up like a thousand-watt lightbulb.

And my aunt. I wanted her to be okay again.

And Grace. I wanted her to come back to New Orleans, for her to be okay, too.

But neither of those had anything to do with Deuce's question.

The word I'd found scribbled in my journal that morning did.

Tonight.

I didn't remember writing it, but the therapist I saw every Friday said that was normal, good even. That things locked inside me were finding ways to get out.

But the seven scrawled letters had sent something cold swirling through me.

Running through the dark. That's all I'd seen since the afternoon I slipped inside a killer's mind and discovered a deception that left the community in shock.

After that, it was hard not to jump at shadows.

But the word *tonight* didn't mean anything ominous. I knew that. It wasn't from somewhere unseen. It was merely confirmation that spending the evening with friends was the right thing to do.

That was all.

"So yeah," I said, pushing aside the memory. I'd been here over an hour. Aside from some dizziness, nothing had happened. Nothing was going to. "This is where I need to be."

Even if the thought of walking back inside the loud crush of people from every high school within thirty miles had my chest tightening all over again.

The charcoal of Deuce's eyes gleamed. "Needing is a start," he said all quiet, soulful. "But someday you'll *want* again." Watching me, he slid an arm around my waist. "You'll want something for *you,* not only other people. It's Deuce 101, the law of jumper cables.

There may be nothing inside right now, but that doesn't mean it'll always be that way."

I leaned into him, holding his gaze longer than normal before turning back to the oak-shrouded mansion.

"Come on," I said, sliding my phone back into my hoodie. "Let's go find Victoria and Trey."

Through the frantic fusion of music and light, we made our way to the elaborate home theater. Three rows of cushy media chairs faced the giant screen framed by dark velvet curtains, while oil-painted movie posters lined the walls. In every space in between, guys and girls danced, oblivious to the muted movie playing in the background.

I found Victoria immediately, thanks to the bobbing purple feathers of her showgirl headband. I'd done a quick double take when she showed up at the shop in her little black dress and mismatched stilettos, not only in different sizes, but different heights, too. She'd scored them at the Muses parade, one covered in pink and purple feathers, the other shimmering with glitter. In total she'd been awarded seven, all because of a glitter-drenched sign proclaiming herself the founder of Glitterholics Anonymous.

She'd given me a clog and a mule, both the same height thankfully, one with thick purple and pink rhinestone stripes, the other covered in orange sequins.

Now with her back to me, she was absorbed in Trey's orbit, their bodies pressed tight as they moved in slow, almost nonexistent, motion. If Deuce was the boxer, his Blood Brothas bandmate was pure California beach boy, with sun-kissed brown hair and a lazy, steal-your-breath smile.

He and Victoria, with the pink streaks in her bright blond hair and her tilted green eyes, her compact gymnast's body, made a knockout couple. Hip to hip, he held her close, his arms slung around her waist. And as I moved closer, I could see his eyes were closed.

The tight feeling in my throat loosened a little.

Their flirting had turned serious the past few weeks. She insisted they were only friends, but I saw the longing in the way she looked at him, and in the way he looked at her. The way he touched her. It was no secret how into each other they were.

It was part of my agenda for the evening, to show her it was okay for her to be happy.

Deuce started toward them, but I caught him by the arm and pulled him back. "Not yet."

Habit made me glance around, searching the dimly lit sway of grinding bodies for her ex. I hadn't seen Lucas yet, but knew he was probably around. Everyone at school had been buzzing about the party, with the exception of Drew, whose family was joining Chase's at the New Mexico cabin where they'd been since late February.

"Give them a few more minutes," I said, stepping back against the wall. "Why don't you go set up," I suggested. "I'll send Trey out in a minute."

He hesitated. I could tell he didn't want to leave me alone.

"It's okay," I assured him with an overly bright smile. "No more wandering off. Promise."

It took another minute or two, but finally Deuce glanced at his watch and relented. "I'll be out back if you need me."

I shook my head, sending a few long, curly tangles against my face.

He slid them back and reluctantly turned away.

With two steps, the crowd swallowed him, and I was alone.

The song ended. Another blasted from the speakers.

Slipping against the wall, I watched the sweaty, energetic danc-ing and the groups standing around laughing and drinking, the couples wrapped around each other in the big chairs, not spending too much time on anything, not the girl in a blue butterfly mask or the one with the short pixie hair standing on a media chair, crying, nothing until the velvet drapes swayed.

He stood in the shadows, tall, apart from everyone else, his face concealed by a half-gold/half-white Venetian mask. But I didn't need to see the hot burn of his eyes or strong line of his cheeks, not when the quiet, guarded intensity slipped through the frenzy, as if instead of watching, he'd lifted a hand, and touched.

Because he'd never needed that, a hand to touch me.

Dylan.

My heart slammed hard, and a thousand little pieces started to scatter. The hair was the same, maybe a little longer, but the same sharp curtain cutting above his jaw. But it was the unmistakable stillness to him that fired through me, the way he watched, ex-actly like that very first day from the shadows of his father's porch. He wasn't a come-over-and-say-hi kinda of guy.

The party fell away, taking with it the blast of music and crush of bodies, leaving only the shadows, and the remains of the dream I'd wanted so badly to believe. He watched me breath by breath, each deeper than the last, slower, until even that fell away.

Four weeks had passed. Four weeks since I'd opened my eyes in an unfamiliar hotel room to find him leaning over me. Four weeks since he'd dragged me from a fire and held my hand as I ran through a killer's mind. Since I'd heard him shout my name.

Four weeks since I'd let fantasy carry us past the point of no return, since one second, *one mistake,* changed everything.

"Say yes."

The voice registered, echoing in through some distorted tunnel, but I didn't turn around, couldn't turn around, not when everything inside me rushed.

He didn't belong here. That was all I could think. Dylan Fourcade did not belong at an ordinary Friday night party.

"Hey, you okay?"

This time the voice ripped in closer, more urgent, and with it a guy blasted in between us, tall and thin with dark, chin-length hair tucked behind his ears and narrow eyes. He stood close, the way friends did, even though I'd never seen him before.

I took a quick step back. "Yeah," I said, glancing from him to the sea of dancing beyond.

My view of the curtains was gone.

"You scared me for a sec," he said. "You were really pale."

I blinked, bringing everything back into focus. "I'm good," I assured him.

The music changed, faster, more frenetic, everyone lifting their arms in the air, everyone except Victoria and Trey, who drifted in their own little bubble.

"Awesome," the guy said, stepping me against the wall. "Then say yes."

I kept glancing around. "Yes?" I hadn't heard a question.

His eyes met mine. "Awesome." With a this-is-gonna-be-good smile, he pressed a purple cup decorated with gold comedy and tragedy masks into my hand. Inside, something dark fizzed.

"Come on," he said, sliding an arm around my waist. "I've been waiting all night to get you to myself. Let's dance."

I stiffened. *Normal,* I told myself. This was what happened at parties. But I didn't want some random guy's arms around me, didn't want to feel his body pressed to mine. The last time some-one had held me—

I didn't want that memory, either.

"Not now," I managed. My hand tightened against the cup. "I'm waiting for a friend."

"Your bodyguard guy?" he asked with a slow, knowing smile. "Yeah, he went out back."

Bodyguard guy.

More memories surged, memories I didn't want.

"So, what? He appointed you my bodyguard?"

"I wish it was just your body."

But the narrow-eyed guy didn't mean Dylan, I realized, re-fusing to look back to the curtains. There was no way a stranger could know about that. He meant Deuce.

"He's not my bodyguard," I said, pulling my arm away.

"S'okay." He swayed. "I get it. If I were you I wouldn't go any-where without a bodyguard, either."

I slid along the wall, not wanting to draw attention by pushing him away and bolting like a freak, but more than ready to be rid of him. "I really gotta go."

"It must be hard, living with what you know," he said, closer now, so close I could feel his breath against my cheek. "That's why you went outside by yourself, isn't it?"

Then I realized this wasn't normal at all. I jerked back.

He stopped me with a hand to my forearm. "You're that girl everyone's been talking about." His eyes, suddenly dark and in-tense, met mine. *"The prophet."*

TWO

The word crawled over me.

I'd grown up fascinated by people like Nostradamus, who foretold future events. *Prophet* made me think of wisdom and big predictions, cultures like the Mayans and their knowledge of the universe.

Hearing the word used in reference to me by some random guy I'd never seen before made me feel like I stood there naked for the whole world, or at least the whole party, to see.

I wasn't a prophet.

"Trisha?" he muttered, watching me expectantly. "Trina? Munson?" Stepping closer, he shoved a phone into my hand. "That's you, right?"

With the party swirling around me I glanced down to see my own face staring up at me, a picture I'd had no idea someone was

taking, of me standing in the shadow of a crumbling angel. My
hair was loose and blowing, my eyes fixed on some point in front
of me. And the headline: A PROPHET AMONG US.

I'd seen the blog before, but seeing the words again, here,
made me want to hurl the Droid across the room.

Instead I mechanically arrowed back to the main browser,
where he'd entered the search terms "New Orleans teenage psychic," to see what else his search had pulled up.

PSYCHIC TEENAGER TAKES DOWN PSYCHO COP.
TEEN SEER SEES BOYFRIEND'S DEATH—WHAT WILL
SHE SEE NEXT?
VOODOO ALIVE AND WELL IN THE BIG EASY

At first the police and media had tried to conceal my identity,
but the kids at my school knew too much, and within hours "un-
identified teen" turned into Our Lady of Enduring Grace junior,
Trinity Monsour. The stories went viral. My picture had been
everywhere—my school picture, candid shots I'd never seen, and
some that I had, such as the ones from last fall, when I'd run from
the darkness of the old abandoned house, along with wild specu-
lation and outright lies.

I saw through a killer's eyes.

I dreamed the future.

I could read minds.

I knew when the world was going to end.

I was an angel, a demon, a time traveler, marked, cursed . . .

"Is that why you're here tonight?" the guy asked, dragging me
back into the moment. "Because you think something's going to
happen?"

A dull ache started at the base of my skull, fraying the edges of my vision. "No."

"So how does it work?" He kept on, like it was a trick or game. Swaying, he shifted, revealing a bold "A" inked inside a dark circle against the bottom of his neck.

I tried to jerk back, but the wall stopped me.

"I mean, the stuff you know, where does it come from? Is it like a Ouija board or a séance, or do you go into a trance?"

Yanking my arm away, I shoved the phone and drink back into his hand and turned to leave, but before I could, a blur of pink staggered in, and cold, wet hands grabbed mine.

"Omigod! Trin-Trin!" Amber slurred, steadying herself against me. Droplets of mascara-smeared water slid down her face, dripping from her jaw to the pink feather boa wound around her neck—the *very wet* pink boa. She held on to me as if she would fall over if she didn't.

"I can't believe you're here!" she gushed. "Isn't it *amazing*?"

A few hours before, she'd looked at me from within her circle of friends in the cafeteria, held up a voodoo doll, and driven a needle right through its heart.

Yeah, that was Amber.

Now she clung to me, her tank top and micro shorts plastered like a swimsuit to her sickly thin body, courtesy of the hot tub, while her long dark curls hung like limp pasta.

"Whazgoingon?" Her words ran together as her teeth chattered. "Whatareyou*doing*here?"

I sucked in a deep breath, grateful at least that the guy in the orange shirt had taken a step back for the Amber show.

"Okay, so this is wild," Amber was saying, "but I have dreams, too, sometimes, and last night it was really *crazy*."

I turned back to her, the unfocused look in her eyes confirming she was beyond gone.

"We were at this party," she slurred, "me and Lucas and Jessie and V'toria, you and Chase and even Pitre."

I winced.

"We were all laughing and dancing, getting ready to do one of those séance thingies you do . . ."

Everything around me swayed.

"And then it started to rain!" Amber exclaimed. *"Inside."*

The party revolved around me—the girl who'd been crying, with the short hair and sad eyes, standing near a corner now, in front of a guy in a beanie with a blanket wrapped around him. He looked around wildly, as if watching a movie he didn't understand.

"So we ran outside and the sky was all blue." Amber kept on as the girl in the butterfly mask slipped back into view. "And then we were all flying, and the stars were all melting into each other."

Another wave of dizziness swirled through me.

"Look, I gotta go," I said with a quick check for Victoria, but Amber's bizarre grip on me tightened.

"Not yet," she gasped. "Not until you tell me what the dream means."

She was breathing faster now, harder, and I realized she was dead serious.

"Amber," I started, but then the blood was draining from her face and she took a jerky step back.

"Omigod," she whispered with a clumsy sign of the cross. "It means something, doesn't it? That's why you're looking at me like that. *I'm next."*

The words went through me like hot, boiling acid. Realizing where this was going, I turned.

"Tell me!" she screamed. "You can't just let me die like you did Chase!"

I froze, the loud roar rushing through me and throwing me back to the shadow of the old roller coaster.

"It wasn't her fault."

The deceptively quiet voice, *his voice,* slipped in through the vortex and pulled me back. Everything blurred, Amber's eyes blanking as Dylan broke between us in that predatory way of his, stepping her back to the wall until there was nothing except her and him, and me.

"Who are you?" she asked with a birdlike blink.

But already he was turning as if she wasn't worth his time, and taking me by the arm. "Come on."

"Holy effin' crap, you're that guy," she was saying, but then she was gone, and Dylan had me in the shadows of the next room, where a single Tiffany lamp glowed, and no music blasted.

He watched me. I could feel him, the familiar, hot burn of his eyes concentrated on me, but I didn't want to look, didn't know how to be in that moment, not after all that had gone down the last time we were together. The fear and the desperation, the stark, jagged point of no return. The memories hovered like poison, choking out everything else.

"Hey," he said. His voice was quieter now, without the edge from a few minutes before, and I knew that if I looked . . .

I made myself. No matter how much I didn't want to be alone with him, staring at the Oriental rug wasn't going to end things any faster.

Different. That was all I could think. There was something

different about him. This wasn't the guy who'd taken my hand and run with me through the darkness. His eyes were harder, darker, his body more contained. It was like an invisible wall surrounded him, cutting him off from the world around him, as if he were the witness of a terrible holocaust—or the sole survivor.

"You okay?" he asked.

And I couldn't do it, couldn't stand there and make small talk, not with everything we'd been through.

"What are you doing here?" I asked against the burn of my throat.

His shoulders rose, fell. "It's a party."

I couldn't stop the quick flare of my eyes. "You're hardly a party kind of guy."

"Depends on the party."

I pushed out a hot breath. There'd been so many big, intense moments between us, but none like this, normal, ordinary, in public at a party.

But this wasn't normal, either, I realized. It wasn't ordinary. It was like lightning from a clear blue sky. You knew it made no sense. You knew it shouldn't be there. *And you knew it was wrong.*

"You were watching me," I reminded him.

A quiet apology shadowed his eyes, but he said nothing. There was only the way he looked at me, the unsettling stillness that made everything inside me lock up.

"My friends are waiting," I said, and with two steps I really did see Victoria standing in the doorway with her feather plume and pink highlights falling against her face, her mouth hanging open.

"Trinity."

My name, that was all he said, but the rough edge to his voice stopped me. With Victoria's eyes going wide I turned and found the same rough edge to every line of his body.

"I meant what I said in the card," he said, keeping his gaze steady on mine.

The simple envelope had arrived the day of the funeral. I'd waited a week before opening it.

"I'd change it all if I could."

Seven words. That's all he'd written, followed by the scrawl of his name. But suddenly, with no more than that, the words and the memory, I was there all over again, running, screaming—seeing Chase fall.

Trying to breathe.

"I gotta go," I murmured, and this time I didn't look back, not even when his voice, quieter now, followed me.

"I know."

I kept walking, past a massive antique armoire and a life-size family portrait, past a marble statue of a nude woman, past Victoria. She scrambled after me, grabbing my hand and tugging me into the rush of music outside.

"This way." Wobbling on her uneven stilettos, she guided me away from the stage where Trey and Deuce played, toward the last green- and purple-wrapped column before the porch curved to the front of the house.

"Take a deep breath," she said all serious, but when her eyes met mine, questions danced faster than the crowd swarming the stage. "And tell me what *that* was all about."

"There's nothing to tell," I said.

"That was Dylan," she said, and though she phrased it as a statement, I knew it was a question.

"Yeah." He'd saved my life three times, but never met my best friend, because our paths had only crossed twice: two weekends, four months apart.

She watched me very carefully. "He's even more intense in person than the pictures I found on the Internet."

I looked away, toward the stage where Deuce stood with the mic wrapped in both hands, close to his mouth.

Last fall, after Dylan dragged me from the river, I'd looked for pictures, too. But I didn't need them anymore, not with the scrapbook etched in my mind: him watching me from the shadows of his father's porch and leaning over me beside the river's edge, with his clothes wet and his hair falling into his face; statue still in the morgue with a gun trained on the vagrant who held a knife to my throat and holding me in the darkness while a fire raged behind him; sliding down the brick wall of an alley; running, shouting my name . . .

I slammed the album closed before I reached the final picture, the one I would give anything to erase.

"What's he doing here?" Victoria asked. "Is something wrong? Isn't that when he shows up?" She grabbed my arm. "Is *it* happening again?"

I turned back to her. *It,* of course, meant premonitions.

"No," I said.

"Then what'd I walk in on?"

"Nothing."

She gave me one of those looks. "Trin, come on, I saw the way he was looking at you."

I shook my head, feeling it all over again, that horrible crushing pressure in my chest, as if air was being sucked out of me.

"We barely know each other," was all I said. Three days. If

you added up all the minutes and hours we'd spent together, that's what you'd get. And those days had been as far from "Hey, how you doing, let's hang out and get to know each other" as possible. They'd been big and blown up, magnified, isolated moments carved out on a razor's edge, when life and death had blurred and I'd needed something to hang onto. *Someone.*

"Just because we played together as kids," I started, but Victoria didn't let me finish.

"You played together as kids?" Sliding a pink streak from her mouth, she looked like I'd just disclosed some major state secret. "You never told me that."

"Because I don't remember." I'd only been two, then six. No one remembered stuff from that long ago. "Let it go," I said. "I have."

I broke off as the back door swung open and the party emptied onto the porch, girls racing down the steps to the backyard while guys shoved and vaulted over the rail.

"Fuck, who called the cops?" someone shouted as Victoria and I hurried to see what was going on.

The guy in the orange shirt stared at me as if I was making it all happen, while Amber danced in her own little world and the guy with the beanie and the blanket ran toward us.

"Will, no!" the girl with the short hair cried, following him. "We just want to help."

Several adults rushed past the girl in the butterfly mask, adults I hadn't seen all night—Mr. and Mrs. Greenwood, who I recognized from pictures inside, and another man, slightly younger with alarmed eyes.

The hum started without warning, not from the party but

inside of me, somewhere deep and dark and dormant, ripping through me with another swirl of vertigo. Dizzily I glanced from face to face, but they all seemed to revolve around me. Victoria and Amber and the guy in the orange shirt, the guy in the blanket and the girl with the short hair, the adults. And with the blur came the quick sweep of cold, and the world flashed white.

THREE

I couldn't move. I couldn't breathe. I hung there as frozen as the bleached-out night, waiting.

I knew what came next, what always came next, the streaks of invisible lightning giving way to the slide show from some other time and place, a slide show that had been absent for weeks.

A slide show that always previewed something bad.

"Trinity!" someone called, but the drone of the vortex made it impossible to know who. *Victoria,* a little voice inside me whispered. She was there, beside me, exactly like she'd been the night evil swept in from the open portal of the Ouija board, and warned that it was too late to stop destiny.

But I couldn't see her, only the white spilling from all directions, like a blizzard from the unseen, pure and pristine and shocking. Everywhere. Without form or texture, without the shadows from before. There was only the clawing from deep inside, something trapped and trying to get out.

Then I was falling, could feel myself falling . . .

"Quick, call a priest." I heard someone laugh.

"Holy eff'in crap, *Mile High*!"

Hands curled around my arms, dragging me back.

I didn't want to go. I tried to stay in the moment, in the white, so that color could meld into shape and the images would form. But the buzz dropped into silence, and the white faded, leaving not a premonition of something horrible, but my friends crowded around and staring like they wanted to throw up.

"Get the fuck away from her!" Deuce growled.

The moment held, frozen, Victoria and Deuce crouched over me and people I didn't know gathered close, the guy in the orange shirt and Amber with her phone held up, Lucas trying to drag her away.

But not Dylan.

Just as quickly everything lurched, timing jumping forward as the people around me scattered like ants, and I could feel myself trying to move, could hear the roar inside me, but it was like it was happening to someone else, that I watched from afar.

"Someone call an ambulance!" Mrs. Greenwood screamed.

"What's going on?" someone else shouted.

"Crap, is that the LaSalle girl?"

"Mile High, come on, baby sis. Don't do this."

The fear in Deuce's voice registered. Dizzily I pulled myself back from that odd, detached place and grabbed onto him, looking around, but it was like I turned one way, and the world spun the other. Almost everyone was gone now, everyone but Deuce and Victoria and Lucas and Amber, the adults and several uniformed cops.

Mrs. Greenwood kneeled beside us. "Is she okay?"

"Maybe we should call DeMarcus," one of the cops said.

I blinked him into focus. "No." There was no reason to call Detective Jackson. Standing, I fumbled for the porch railing, searching for—

I didn't know. I didn't know what I was searching for, only that something horrible and cold had brushed against me.

"Trinity?" Victoria asked, stepping into me. "Omigod, you're like ice." Her eyes, the green so dark it looked black, met mine. "Like when we did the Ouija board," she whispered. "Maybe that really *is* why he was here. Did you see something?"

"No." To both questions. "Nothing," I said.

"Here, sweetie," Mrs. Greenwood said, draping a blanket around me.

"I don't understand," Victoria stammered. "If you didn't see anything, what happened? It's like you weren't even there."

I didn't understand, either. It was like sitting down for a movie to start, but the screen going white before anything happened.

"You're Trinity, right?" one of the uniformed officers asked. "Monsour?" He was tall and thin, with military short hair and sharp, never-miss-anything eyes. He looked from me to Victoria to Deuce, then back to me. "I need you to tell me what happened. Do you need an ambulance?"

"No," I whispered. "Nothing happened."

He so didn't believe me.

"Is something going on?" I asked. The house that had been swarming not that long ago stood empty now. Mr. Greenwood, all tall and distinguished and antique-dealer looking, stood with two other cops off to the side. He looked like a dad about to ground his kids for life.

"That's what we're trying to figure out," the officer who'd

approached me said. "We got several back-to-back nine-one-one calls saying something bad was going down."

"I didn't see anything," I said. Not at the party, and not when the world flashed white.

He handed me a card. "If that changes, let me know," he said. "You want me to call someone? DeMarcus? Your aunt?"

I shook my head.

"How's she doing?" he asked, reminding me of the other cops who walked by the shop, glancing in with the same stunned, apologetic expression. "I know it's been rough."

That was one word, but there were tons of others for discovering your boyfriend was really a psychic psychopath. "She's okay."

The cop nodded, again like he didn't believe me, then walked over to the Greenwoods.

"Here," Trey said, sliding in next to Victoria and handing me a cup of water.

I lifted the glass to my mouth, sipping deeply.

Victoria lowered her voice. "You really didn't see anything?"

"No." But the disruption reverberated through me, like it had last fall with Jessica, a jittery residue in every cell of my body. "It's like one was trying to form, but there was too much white, like an overexposed picture."

Deuce frowned. "That ever happen before?"

"No," I said, confused.

Victoria shoved pink streaks of hair from her face. "Then it's probably nothing, right?"

Another roll of cold moved through me, but before I could say anything, a quiet, thready voice came from the backyard side of the porch.

"I think it was my boyfriend."

We all turned at the same time.

The girl with the pixie hair stood there, the one who'd been running after the guy in the beanie. Now she stood ghostly pale among a sea of heavily budded azaleas, staring at me through wide, tearstained eyes. She had her hands together prayer-like, pressed to her mouth.

"What?" I asked.

"I saw you," she whispered. "And I heard you just now, about the white." Nervously she glanced to the far side of the porch, where the cops and the Greenwoods were still talking, and lowered her voice. "You were looking at my boyfriend when it happened."

I frowned, trying to remember. "There were a lot of people there," I murmured, but I *could* see the guy in the blanket again, running toward me.

"He was looking at you, too," she said, stepping closer. "And . . ." Tears flooded her eyes. *"He kept saying something bad was going to happen."*

I saw Deuce stiffen, but stepped closer anyway. "When? To-night?"

"Earlier," she said, with a quick nod. "Inside." She kept glancing around. "He disappeared for a little while, and when I found him, he was different, like he was upset or scared. He told me I needed to go, that I didn't belong here, that something bad was going to happen."

"Bad how?" Deuce asked, inserting himself between her and the cops' line of view.

"He wouldn't say," she said. "He just pulled me into a corner and kept looking around, like he was looking for someone."

If he was scared, why hadn't he left? "Where is he now?" I asked.

"His dad came and got him."

"His dad?" Victoria blurted out, echoing my own thoughts.

The girl looked embarrassed, and, I realized, incredibly upset.

"I called his mom," she said quietly, sadly. "We're really close and I wasn't sure what else to do . . ." Her words trailed into a frown. "But then everything got crazy and then his dad got here, and the cops, and Will started running with everyone else. That's when we came outside, and he was running toward you and you got real still, like you were in a trance."

Trance?

"He was terrified," she whispered.

Deuce and I exchanged a quick look. "Sounds like he's on something," he pointed out.

The girl shook her head. "Not the Will I know. He had a beer or two, but that was it."

She swiped at her tears, stepping up to curl her hands around the twinkling railing. "Do you think I'm right? Could your trance have been about him?" she asked, real quietly. "The way y'all were looking at each other? Do you think that means some-thing?"

Fear and love and desperation clashed in her eyes, throwing me back to those final moments in Chase's hospital room.

"It's possible," I whispered.

"Then . . ." She cut a quick, desperate glance at the cops before continuing. "What if you, like, talked to him? Would that work? Could you do a reading or something, like they do on TV?"

Around us the night stilled, the sudden blast of hope in her wide, tear-drenched eyes glistening against the shadows from before.

Could I do a reading, like they did on TV? Like my mom had done?

I'd never tried, not like that. Not cold, like a pursuit. The images had always *come to me,* faces and places, something tangible to grab onto. I'd seen my dog lying in a clearing and my grandmother on the kitchen floor, Jessica on a mattress and Chase . . .

I pushed at the memory, but my eyes filled anyway, and when I looked at the girl, the dark swirl of desperation and love, I knew there was no way I could say no. Because the harsh flash of white meant something, too.

The things I saw, the things I felt, always did.

"Yeah," I whispered, sliding a hand to the soft leather curled around my left wrist, the bracelet Chase had made for me because I was me, and no one else was. "I'll talk to him."

"I still don't like it," Deuce said, stepping into the elevator of the sugar factory turned condo building an hour later. "Real life's not like those TV shows."

He thought I should wait and see if the vision finished forming on its own, that I was probably barking up the wrong tree, and that the girl—*her name was Kendall and she and her boyfriend were both juniors, like me*—was creating a swirl of drama where there was none.

That *I* wasn't ready.

"I know you don't," I said, trying to assure him with my eyes. "But how can I not try?"

That was the bottom line.

"Either I talk to this guy and I see something, or I don't," I pointed out, as the doors slid open to the fifth floor. "Either way, the question is answered. If I see something, then Kendall knows what they're dealing with and she can go to his parents or whatever."

He sighed as we stepped into the cool sweep of the exposed-brick hallway.

"And who knows," I said, downplaying it all. "Maybe whatever started at the party *will* finish tonight in a dream, and in the morning we'll have the answer."

But even as I said the words, cold whispered through me.

"Trinity Monsour," he grumbled. "Teenage psychic detective."

I couldn't stop the quick smile, even as everything inside me went on red-alert.

A few minutes later, he turned to leave as I unlocked the door and stepped inside.

Every light, every lamp, even some old lanterns I'd never seen, burned against the night. Confused, I stepped inside and onto plastic. Long, thin sheets covered everything, the antique sofa and love seat, the funky chaise, the table and chairs, the rugs and the hardwood floor.

It was like opening the door to the wrong condo, or the wrong life.

But then something moved near the biggest lump in the center of the room, and a blur of white streaked toward me.

I smiled. "Hey, kitty," I said, sweeping Delphi into my arms. After locking up behind me, I turned back to the bare walls. That morning, when I left for school, a distressed iron fleur-de-lis had hung by the big picture window overlooking the city; it was gone now, replaced by narrow blue strips running along the ceiling and baseboards.

"Trinity?"

I spun around.

Aunt Sara stood in the back corner, her dark brown hair soft and pretty around her face, her makeup glamour-magazine perfect. Her dress was little and black and totally killer. Her shoes were the stilettos we both loved.

She was standing on a ladder.

With a roller in her hand.

Paint dripped down the arm lifted to the wall and dribbled onto the plastic.

White.

"H-hey," I said, knowing I needed to say something, but not sure whether I should act like this was normal, or point out that maybe she should be wearing her ratty old Bruce Springsteen T-shirt and cutoffs. "I thought you were going to a party."

She flashed me a quick smile. "I was. I did. But I wasn't tired when I got home."

Okay. "So *you're painting?*"

She lowered the roll to the pan balanced on the ladder and shoved it around. "I'm ready for a change."

Six five-gallon cans sat on the plastic. Two looked empty. I had no idea when she'd purchased them. She hadn't mentioned a word about making a change. Just the opposite, actually. She'd always said the exposed brick was what gave the condo its character.

"White?" It screamed from the wall, bright and sterile, cold, exactly like the flash at the party and the secret second-floor room at Horizons where Julian, the owner, had taken me to access a higher dimension.

Oblivious, my aunt twirled back around and pushed up on her

toes, returning her attention to a new section of reddish-brown brick.

No, some place inside of me shouted. *No! Don't make it white.*

She rolled and globs dripped. "It's a primer."

"Oh."

"It helps the color go on smoother."

Like a bandage covering up what was already there.

More brick vanished. More white glowed. "So what color are you thinking?" I asked.

She reached over, continuing her assault. "I'm not sure yet," she said, all singsongy. "Maybe something blue-green, like the ocean."

I stilled.

"We've got to get you to Florida sometime," she whirred on. "It's so incredible."

The memory flashed: *Sugar-white beaches and turquoise water.* I could see it, the sand and the surf, exactly as Chase had described.

"Or maybe a pale yellow or gold," Aunt Sara murmured from somewhere in her own little world.

I closed my hand around the soft leather at my wrist. "Maybe you should ask Julian," I suggested. "He's all about color. He says we actually absorb—"

She whipped around. Eyes that had been doll-vacant for weeks flashed. "I told you I don't want you talking to Julian."

The edge to her voice sawed off what I'd been saying.

She had told me not to talk to Julian, true enough. But that was *before.* And while my aunt and I hadn't talked about him since he helped me figure out where she was being held (we hadn't talked about anything other than the weather or school, the shop), the vague flickers of memory from those first few days told me he'd been there. *A lot.* At the hospital. Here. At the stove, the sink. I could see him with his shirtsleeves rolled up. I had a foggy image of him by the window, with his raven-black hair loose and flowing against his shoulders. And on the sofa, holding my aunt while she cried.

I'd assumed Julian Delacroix was no longer taboo.

"I'm not talking about me," I clarified, watching her closely. "I'm talking about you, and color."

She turned back to the half-white wall. "I'm quite capable of picking by myself."

I stood there, not sure what to say, watching her jam the roller back into the tray. White splashed over the edges. A drop splattered against the black of her stiletto.

She gave no indication of noticing, or caring.

"I don't need Julian," she said, forcing another coat of white onto the brick.

Liar, some place inside me whispered, but I knew it wasn't the time to point that out. I also knew I could never tell her about the almost-vision, or that I was going to try my first cold reading, like my mom had done for a living.

My aunt didn't need anything else to worry about, especially the dark possibilities running through me.

Delphi squirmed, making me realize how tightly I'd dug my fingers into her fur.

Turning, I headed for the kitchen, where on the counter, a prescription bottle sat by an array of flickering votives. *Count how many are left,* a little voice inside me urged. There'd been nineteen that morning. But the la-la in my aunt's eyes told me she'd only taken one or two. If she'd taken more, she wouldn't be perched on a ladder. She'd be out cold.

With one last scratch to Delphi's head, I lowered her to the floor and headed for the fridge.

"Thirsty?" I asked.

"No, I'm good," Aunt Sara said, as she always did when I offered her something.

I turned, watching her go at the half-painted wall. Not that long ago, she would have asked about the parade and the party. She would have wanted to know who we saw and how many throws we got. She would have come over to inspect my beads. She'd have texted a few times, just to touch base. And I would have told her everything. About the flash of white, about Kendall and her boyfriend, *about Dylan.*

I missed the talks we used to have, the way she used to smile and hug me, give me advice and words of wisdom, make me believe everything was going to be okay.

I missed her.

She insisted she was fine. Physically she was. But emotionally a robot had taken her place. She wouldn't talk about what happened when she was missing, but I know she'd thought she was going to die. That the man we'd all trusted was going to kill her . . . and me.

That was a lot to cover up with white paint.

"You're doing this because of him, aren't you?" I'm not sure why I asked. I knew what she was going to say.

She painted faster. "You know what, maybe I am thirsty. Can you see if we have any merlot?"

We didn't. Julian had cleared out the wine one day while Aunt Sara was at the shop.

Turning, I filled a glass measuring cup with water, slid it into the nuker, then retrieved one of the herbal tea bags he'd given me. Three minutes later I carried the steaming mug across the plastic.

At the ladder, I lifted my arm. "Here."

She turned and glanced down, her shoulders rising and falling in slow rhythmic breaths. Then she went back to painting. "Just put it on the bar."

I sighed, not the happy contented kind, but like a quiet scream. "Why won't you ever talk about it?" The dull residue of devastation hollowed out her eyes, no matter how much makeup she artfully applied. "The therapist says it helps."

She dipped the roller in the thick, glommy white, then returned it to the wall, sloshing primer everywhere.

"We've already discussed this, Trinity."

It was like we were strangers, or worse, formal acquaintances.

"The past is the past," she la-la'd. "It doesn't belong in the now."

I wanted to scream, a real one with all the sound and emotion tearing around inside me. Whenever I wanted to talk, she wanted to pretend. Of course she didn't call it that. She prettied it up by referring to it as moving forward.

By smearing paint on the wall.

I watched her, watched her roll white as if her life depended on it, and realized how feverishly we worked to keep reality far away. Because when the clouds of illusion fell away, sometimes we didn't know how to live with what remained.

Setting the mug on the table, I glanced at my jeans and hoodie, then stepped toward the ladder.

"Here," I said, reaching for the roller. "Let me help."

———

It was well after two before I crawled into bed.

Delphi jumped up with me, nudging against my arm as I reached for my journal and stared at the blank page. Since I wasn't saying much in session, my therapist suggested I write stuff down instead. She said I didn't have to show anyone, I just had to let it out. She wanted me to write a letter. To Chase.

I picked up the pen and dragged the notebook into my lap, exactly as I'd done every night for the past week.

Dear Chase,

My eyes stung. I stared at the words until they blurred, then ripped out the page, wadded it up, and threw it across the room.

It barely missed my glass dragonfly. The antique nun doll wasn't as fortunate.

Dear was proper and impersonal, like my aunt. It was what you'd write in a thank-you note to an elderly relative you hardly knew.

I tried again.

Chase,

The hot, salty blur spilled over, rolling down my face to drip onto the page.

I'm so sorry.

My throat tightened, convulsed. Swallowing hard, I sank down in bed, bringing the journal with me. Delphi rubbed her pointy little face against my cheek.

I had no real awareness of drifting off, no awareness of any-thing.

Until the shadows swallowed me.

Darkness. It surrounds me, pressing from all directions, thick and pen-etrating, like a blanket thrown over the world.

Or maybe just me.

Separating me.

Holding me.

Smothering.

I shove at it, know that I have to shove at it, tear it away so I can breathe again, and see what's on the other side.

But the void swirls closer, cold and bottomless, endless, like an ava-lanche of nothingness.

I try to run from it, know I need to run from it.

But my body doesn't move. Nothing does. Nothing moves.

"No!" I scream. But there's no voice, either, no breath, only the cold seep of darkness. I try to spin, but the web surrounds me, slipping through my skin. Into my body. Oozing like cold, dark oil through every pore of my body.

I spin around, finally freeing myself.

A violent wash of white blinds, the quick, X-ray flash of the roller coaster sending me to my knees.

I came awake hard and fast, jerking up in bed and swallowing the hot spasm of a scream. Everything inside me raced, as if I'd been running, sprinting. As if I had to get away from someone, or *to* someone. I didn't know which, only that time was draining away, running out.

But there was nothing concrete, only the breath of cold from the party, the same icy awareness that had whispered through me the night I'd put my fingers to the Ouija board and the pointer slid from the D to the I to the E. DIE.

I started to shake.

The clock read 5:21, exactly like it did every time I'd awoken from a dream about Grace.

Flicking on the lamp, I squinted against the bright intrusion and fumbled for my phone, like I'd done so many other mornings before school. Sometimes Chase would text . . .

I froze, my throat going stupid tight.

Then I looked down, and saw the dark blur of letters against the soft white glow.

FOUR

I heard you've been looking for me.
I'll be in the Square tonight.

Everything inside me started to race.

Grace.

She was back.

And she was going to be in the Quarter, tonight.

Finally.

Minute dragged into minute. At work, hours stacked up, one on top of the other. I tried to concentrate on the flow of customers in and out of the shop, but my mind kept wandering to the series of unexpected little bombs that had gone off since slipping out the door for the Greenwood party: the flash of white, the dream of darkness, Grace's sudden return and—

Dylan.

I could see him still, see him standing in the shadow of the heavy, velvet curtains, watching me. Watching me the same night a vision tried to form. Coincidence, I wanted to believe, especially since he'd been AWOL at the end of the party, when all the chaos happened.

And yet there was no denying Dylan's freaky sense of timing. Just because I didn't see him didn't mean he wasn't there.

Doesn't mean anything, I told myself. *Doesn't mean* anything. *Couldn't.*

Shoving all that aside, I pasted on a smile and untangled necklaces, keeping my thoughts on the other three question marks.

Grace was right. I had been looking for her. One day she'd been in the hospital, the next she was gone. No one knew where she went, or if they did, they wouldn't tell me. I'd walked the Quarter and gone to her apartment, asked other spiritualists, merchants, anyone I could think of.

Now she was back at the exact same time I saw a flash of white. Given how tangled our lives were, I had a hard time accepting that as coincidence.

Actually, I no longer wrote anything off as coincidence.

The beads I'd been working on came free.

Around noon Deuce came in with shrimp po-boys and stayed for several hours, watching me. He knew better than to mention the night before in front of my aunt, but he wasn't above shooting me texts while only a display of T-shirts separated us.

You okay?

Yeah.

Did the vision finish in your dreams?

No.

Would you tell me if it did?

I looked up from folding T-shirts over that one, and flashed him a smile.

I could tell he knew the answer: not necessarily.

Sometimes it felt like living in a fishbowl, with everyone gathered around, watching to see what happened next. But sometimes I didn't want to be watched. Sometimes it hurt more to smile in front of everyone than to pull my knees against my chest and cry alone.

He didn't leave until Victoria slipped in, and she didn't leave until I convinced her I was going to work until closing and that she should go with her family to the Isis parade without me.

Throughout it all, I kept looking outside the window, toward Jackson Square. Kendall's text came around five.

The reading will have to wait. Will's
parents want him to stay home tonight.

By the time we closed at ten, it felt like I'd worked three days in one.

"See you at home," I told Aunt Sara, then slipped into the flood of insanity outside the door. Music blared from every shop and bar. Beads rained down from balcony parties. Singing and dancing spilled from the sidewalks into the streets.

Almost everyone wore a mask.

But none were Venetian, and none sent a dark, drugging awareness pulsing through my blood.

It took three times as long as usual, but finally the bottleneck spilled into Jackson Square, and halfway down against the iron fence, I saw the funeral-like canopy over the table draped in black, and the girl sitting in the folding chair *wearing a glittery blue butterfly mask.*

Exactly like the one I'd seen the night before at the Greenwood party.

My this-is-all-connected radar screamed a little louder.

I approached her through a long, invisible tunnel, one echoing with questions and memories and inevitability, threads of connection I was only beginning to understand. From the moment I'd arrived in New Orleans, the book of my life had been ripped open in a way I'd never imagined. The pages flew backward and forward. Sometimes it all seemed random. And yet other times, every revelation, every subsequent secret, seemed carefully plotted.

By who, I wanted to know. And why? Why did everything have to be some big mystery?

Is someone following me? I'd asked Grace the first time I saw her. Yes, or no. That's all I wanted. Was someone following me?

The answer, I knew now, was yes.

Instead, she'd looked at me through those dark, old-soul eyes of hers and given me a riddle.

Now . . . or all your life?

Four months later when she went missing and turned up in my dreams, I'd assumed it was because of the connection we made that fateful fall night.

Now I knew our lives, our destinies, had tangled long before that.

I also knew the second she saw me. I saw it in the sudden wash of stillness. She sat watching me approach with the same intensity I watched her, like the bright beam of a lighthouse guiding me in.

So many questions stood between us, not only about the picture and copy of my parents' obituary I'd found in her apartment, but the old mystic in Belle Terre and the connection that allowed us to communicate through a higher dimension in ways we'd never communicated in the flesh.

Reaching her table, I started with the obvious.

"That was you last night," I said. Maybe I should have said hi or something, but we were so far beyond small talk. "You were at the party."

Watching me through eyes the color of moss, she slid off the mask. She'd always been pretty in a haunting way, with skin like alabaster and straight white hair. Now the long, soft waves skewed more brownish amber, highlighting the color of her slightly fuller face.

"I wanted to see how you were doing," was all she said.

"Then why didn't you ask me?"

"You were with your friends," she said, as if it was obvious. "It wasn't the time."

Still talking in riddles, I almost said, but knew calling her out wouldn't get me the answers I wanted.

"No one would tell me where you were," I said, blown away by how good she looked. The last time I saw her, she'd been lying mannequin-still among trash. Through fuzzy cracks of light, Dylan and I had—

Dylan.

My chest tightened.

"I wanted to make sure you were okay," I whispered as her eyes watered. "To *apologize.*"

A single tear spilled over her lashes. "You have nothing to apologize for."

"LaSalle used you as bait to lure me into his game."

"Because of *me*," she blew me away by saying. "Because he knew I was on to him."

"What?" My voice was little more than breath.

"I ran into him one night," she said, wrapping her arms around her black tank top. "Here, while I was working. And the second our eyes met, the darkness hit me so hard I couldn't hide it. And he saw. He knew that I could see through his cop shield, to the monster inside." She closed her eyes a long heartbeat before opening them. *"That's* why he took me."

I felt my mouth open, but no words came out.

"I wanted to warn you," she said. "I tried to—"

"I saw the paper," I interjected. "Where you'd written my name."

She shook her head, sending long, amberish strands flowing over her shoulders. "That was all staged by him, to draw you into the game."

Game.

"Why didn't you tell me?" I asked, point-blank. That was the bottom line. Why did everyone think it best to keep me in the dark? "Last fall, or even later, why didn't you tell me our mothers were friends?" *Best* friends.

They'd worked together here in Jackson Square, my mother giving tarot and palm readings, while Grace's mother led Haunted New Orleans tours.

Jim Fourcade had told me that.

"Because that was the past," Grace said with a sad, reflective smile. "And my grandmother warned me not to."

I think my eyes flared first, but it was close. Mine widened in reaction to the word *grandmother*. Hers flashed in response to mine.

It was obvious she realized I'd been doing my homework.

"Madam Isobel," I supplied.

Around us, music blasted and the wind swirled, but I didn't need to hear Grace's whispered yes to know her answer.

Their eyes. They were so much alike, ancient, timeless. I could still see the way the old woman had looked at me, warning of broken illusions and hidden enemies.

"Why?" I asked. "Why did she warn you not to?"

Soft and damp, the wind swirled in from the river.

"Because the past is dangerous," Grace murmured, sounding a lot older than the nineteen I knew her to be. "If you spend too much time there, you'll always be in shadows. Your life lies ahead of you, *that's* what your mother wanted for you, to be free of the shadows."

Automatically I lifted my hand to the warm, smooth edges of the dragonfly dangling against my chest.

"Do you remember her?" I asked.

A soft light played in Grace's eyes. "No."

Not the answer I wanted, but I had so many other questions. "What did your grandmother mean by shadows? Did she say?"

I saw the change immediately, the quick flare of uncertainty as Grace looked beyond me, toward the wall of people jammed behind us. I turned, too.

Her grandmother stood with her hands folded together, her white hair long and flowing, her eyes looking at me as if through the lens of some long ago time. The same necklace hung around her neck, a collection of gemstones interspersed with old coins and a large crystal dangling in the center. But there were Mardi Gras beads, too, and instead of a lavender robe, she wore a long gold tunic over black pants—and looked pretty much like your ordinary, average grandma hanging out for Mardi Gras.

Except Grace's grandmother was neither ordinary nor average.

"Your mother was a powerful psychic," she said, her voice as rich as I remembered. "And sometimes what she saw, what she lived because of that, was ugly. Dangerous. But she believed it was her duty to try to help people, to prevent, or prepare." She hesitated, her eyes suddenly sad. "Until you were born."

Thousands of people surrounded us, but in that moment, the insanity of Carnival fell away.

Answers.

"Everything changed then," she said, stepping closer and lifting a ring-cluttered hand to slide the hair from my face. Her touch was soft, gentle, *maternal*. No one had touched me like that since . . .

An unexpected wave of emotion surged into my throat.

No one had touched me like that since the funeral. There'd been hugs, Victoria climbing into bed with me while I cried, Deuce holding me on the kitchen floor, Julian sliding his arm around me, Jim Fourcade folding me against the quiet, steady rhythm of his chest. But no one had looked into my eyes, and touched my face.

Aunt Sara didn't touch at all.

"For the first time the danger frightened her," Madam Isobel said, and it was like she knew what her touch was doing to me, because she kept her eyes on mine, her fingertips drifting against my cheek.

"She pulled back from her work with the police," she told me, her voice as hypnotic as her eyes. "To focus on being the best mother she could."

Tears spilled over. I couldn't help it. I didn't remember my mother. I'd seen only a handful of pictures. But sometimes I *felt* her, felt her so strongly it was like she was only in the next room and all I had to do was walk a few feet and she'd be there. I could even see her sometimes, in my mind, *my dreams*. I could see her turn to me and smile, the way her face would fill with warmth and she'd open her arms, and I would walk into them and she would hold me in that way mothers hold their children, and I'd hold her back, hold on *forever*, as if every moment, every breath, *every wish*, was real.

I thought about my father, too, but it was never as vivid.

"Everything was good," Madam Isobel went on, "until children started going missing."

Jim had told me some about the case, but he'd hadn't gone into tons of detail.

"And she saw them, each one: before they vanished and as they would be found."

I cringed. To see little kids frightened, murdered . . . I could only imagine what that had done to my mother.

"And she knew she couldn't pretend it wasn't happening, not when she might be able to help. So she went back."

Maybe it was the way Madam Isobel's eyes darkened, or maybe the deep, memory-carved lines that suddenly made her look years older, but from one breath to the next, I knew.

I knew what happened when my mother became involved in the case, and why Grace's grandmother looked so haunted.

"She saw *me*, didn't she?"

FIVE

Thousands of people packed Jackson Square. Music blasted from every direction, jazz and blues and rock, all fusing into a frenetic soundtrack that drowned out everything else.

Everything except the ugly kaleidoscope of truth spinning around me.

My mother had seen a vision of me. *Murdered.*

"She knew she had to send you away," Madam Isobel said as Grace slipped from behind the table and laced her fingers with mine. "The thought broke her heart, but she'd stepped into darkness, and it was coming for you."

The shadows, I realized. These were the shadows everyone had tried to keep from me.

"She made plans with your grandmother to take you from New Orleans."

My heart kicked. Gran had been in on it? Gran had known?

My mother and Gran, two women who'd never seen eye to eye, had conspired to send me into hiding?

". . . and keep you away, *safe,* until the danger passed."

Except she never brought me back.

"You were to leave early one morning, under the cover of darkness, but he got there first."

My chest tightened, and for a split second I was there again, in the darkness, the smoke . . .

"If Jimmy hadn't been there," Madam Isobel whispered.

I blinked, a new truth falling into place. "Jim Fourcade?"

"Your mother called him before she went to bed and told him she was cold, that she couldn't get warm, that she was afraid."

Cold. Like the icy breath from the night before.

"She knew," I realized. That's the way it worked. *We knew.*

"Jim arrived within minutes of the house going up in flames and made sure that monster didn't get his hands on you."

"That's what no one wanted me to know," I murmured. "That she died protecting me."

I'm not sure what I expected, but it wasn't for Madam Isobel to smile.

"Trinity," she said quietly. "Don't look so sad. Your mother had a choice, and she made it. Death didn't scare her. She was far more afraid of . . . *you."*

The wind kept whipping hair against my face, and I knew it was warm. But the cold swirled closer, faster. *"Me?"*

"Of how much she loved you. That she wouldn't be able to protect you. Death is but a transition. Rachel knew that. Love is forever, but it also makes you vulnerable. When you love someone . . ." She glanced at Grace, her chest rising with a long, slow breath. "You would go to the ends of the universe to keep them safe. You would *give* anything. *Sacrifice* anything. That's what love is."

My throat squeezed as I looked beyond the sway of the big palms, toward the glow of the old cathedral at the back of the square.

"Your mother was only three when her mother died. More than any vision, what terrified Rachel was the thought of not being here to protect you."

With the wind swirling around me, more pieces slipped quietly into place.

"That's why I didn't say anything last month," Madam Isobel said. "When you and Jimmy's boy came to my shop. At that moment, you were better off not knowing about the shadows."

The memory played through me, of her eclectic shop and the deck of tarot cards, the way Dylan had watched me, stayed with me.

"You said we'd met before," I remembered. "That I'd walked this path many times."

She took my hand again, like she'd done that February afternoon. Grace handed her a small flashlight, the bright beam illuminating the lines running through my palm.

Her eyes narrowed as she skimmed her index finger along the fleshy part beside my thumb.

"You have come far to be right where you are," she said, shifting her gaze to two horizontal lines on the side of my hand, beneath my pinkie. One was faint, the other long and deep. "You and others. Never doubt the larger tapestry being woven. You are exactly where you are supposed to be."

This, I realized. This is what I'd wanted all along. Answers. For someone to talk to me about who I was.

"The things I see," I said, thinking about the bleached-out flash from the night before. "Sometimes they *do* seem random. I dreamed about Chase lying in the grass, but not what was going to happen to my aunt. Why is that? Why do I see some things but not others?"

"Because you are not God," Madam Isobel said simply. "You have a gift," she said. "Everyone does. Some have voices like angels, or can make music that touches your soul. Others are athletically talented or good with numbers.

"You and Grace, your mother and myself, *we know things*. But not all things. Doors are open for us that are closed for most." With one of those wisdom-of-the-ages smiles, she reached out to finger my mother's necklace. "Like the dragonfly, you are of two worlds, two realms, the here and the now, while still being connected to the mysteries of the universe. You are both light and the reflection of light. You see beyond what your eyes show you."

She made it sound magical, beautiful even.

"Like the girl who painted those portraits," I murmured. *Of me.* Five had hung in the chapel-turned-gallery in Belle Terre.

I'd been unable to learn anything else about them, not what they looked like, or if they'd been found.

"The one who drowned," I said. "Faith." She'd seen things out of time and place, too. "Did you know her?"

A quick shadow crossed Madam Isobel's face. "You would have liked her," she said. "You two had much in common."

"Do you remember much about the portraits?" I could still see the four empty spaces where they'd hung, the small bronze plates, each containing a title: GLORY, ECSTASY, RAPTURE, and ETERNAL.

What had Faith seen? What had she known?

"I only saw one in the lobby," I explained.

Madam Isobel smiled. "They were beautiful," she said. "Full of love and life."

I frowned. "I was dead in the one I saw, with watery glass separating me from the world."

"That's not what I saw. I saw dreaming."

"Were the others like that, too? Just me, or were they scenes from my future?"

"That is not for me to say. Faith painted in her sleep. Sometimes the things we see are symbolic rather than concrete. Life is full of illusion. You must not let yourself get too caught up in them. What happens here, now, is only a drop in our existence."

My whole body vibrated, like a caffeine high.

"Why now?" I asked. "If you didn't want to tell me any of this before, why now?"

Grandmother and granddaughter exchanged a quick look before Grace's eyes met mine.

"Because I saw you," she said. "The darkness."

"Last night?" I asked. "At the party?"

"In a dream," she said. "Thursday night."

The night *before* the party.

"That's only happened once before," she said, lifting a hand to slide the hair from her face. "Last fall, a few nights before you ran up to my table."

For the first time I noticed a small, iridescent dragonfly tattooed against the pale flesh of her wrist.

"The things I know, they are not glimpses from the future, like you experience. They're feelings and thoughts, knowledge. But in the dream I saw you in a wooded area, and you were running and stumbling, like you couldn't see and didn't know where to go."

A vague sense of familiarity tugged at me, like a fading echo.

"It was dark," Grace said. "I could feel the evil, smell it, like a stain on the horizon, pushing closer."

The quiet words crawled over me.

"It was like I was drowning when I woke up, like I couldn't breathe, and your name kept whispering through me." Long streaks of reddish-brown hair blew into her face as she slid her grandmother a tentative, questioning look.

Madam Isobel nodded.

"Mammy felt it, too," she said, sliding the hair away. "Like a distress call."

Always before the images, the premonitions, were mine. Being on the other end felt *odd*.

"What kind of distress call?" I asked.

"That's why I came back," Grace said. "To see if I could figure out what the dream meant. That's why I went to the party."

"But why didn't you want me to see you? If you were worried, why didn't you say anything to me last night?"

"Because I wanted to see what I felt, before my presence changed anything, like watching the flow of the water before wading in."

My heart was beating faster by the second, beating in time with the loud crush of Carnival craziness around us.

Grace came back the exact night of my first glimmer of invisible lightning in weeks.

"And what did you feel?" I asked.

She kept her eyes on mine, steady, unblinking, the psychic's eyes locked on something only she could see.

"Shadows," she said. "They surround you, and they're getting closer."

Cold. Invasive.

"But it wasn't just you," she said. "It was everywhere, desperation and darkness, something waiting, gathering."

Madam Isobel shifted, sliding an arm around her granddaughter's shoulders.

And suddenly a few more pieces slipped into place. Everything
happened for a reason. "You called Dylan," I whispered.

The guilty answer flashed in Grace's eyes. "I wanted to know
if he knew what was going on with you, if you were in danger."

That's why he'd stood in the shadows, watching me. Why he
didn't care that I walked away. He'd been there because for some
suffocating reason, he thought he had to keep an eye on me.

Seeing things more clearly by the second, I filled them in on
the unease I'd felt in the shadows of the Greenwood house, the
flash of white/nonvision, and Kendall's fears about her boyfriend,
the stabbing terror in her eyes, that something bad was going to
happen to him.

"I'm going to talk to him," I concluded, "like my mom used
to do, just to check, to see if the vision finishes forming or I can
pick anything else up."

Madam Isobel let out a long, slow breath. "Trinity, I'm not
sure that's a good idea. Telling people what you see is one thing.
Chasing shadows is another."

"But it's what my mom did, isn't it?" I asked. "Isn't that the
way it works? If there's something there, don't I owe it to Will or
his family, Kendall, to let them know?"

Her expression told me she didn't like my logic. "Owe it to
them," she said all oracle-like. *"Or to yourself?"*

I pulled back, but before I landed on what to say to that, Grace
slipped closer.

"I'll go with you," she said and for a second I thought Madam Isobel was going to forcibly drag her granddaughter away. She turned on Grace, the sudden darkness in her eyes destroying the sage-like calm.

"Grace, no," she said. "It's too soon. You're still healing."

With a quiet, determined smile, Grace shook her head. "There will always be bad things," she said. "You taught me that. Hiding from them doesn't make them go away."

Her grandmother closed her eyes.

"We'll be fine," Grace promised. "As long as we all stick together."

We agreed to talk the next day, once Kendall let me know the plan.

"We'll figure it out," Grace said, and for half a second, the flicker of uncertainty in her eyes made me think she was going to hug me. Instead, with her grandmother staring toward the blur of lights from the river, Grace retrieved something from the backpack stashed under her table.

"Here," she said. "These are for you."

I took the small wooden box, like a sea trunk shrunken to fit in the palm of a hand. The top came off easily. Black velvet lined the inside.

A steady vibration tingled against my fingertips before I even touched the pouch, also in velvet but the color of sapphires. Carefully I untied the strings of gold silk.

"They were your mother's," Grace said. "We thought you should have them."

Tarot cards.

Gold stars lay scattered against a dark azure background, some big and some small, all radiant and shining, *like a window to another world.*

Long after I got back to the condo and found my aunt already asleep, I sat cross-legged on my bed amid the wavering light of seven white votives, with the amazingly well-preserved deck in my hand.

Delphi watched, a soft, monk-like chant drifted from my phone speakers, and for a heartbeat, there was no cold, not with the little waves of warmth zipping up from my fingers.

I cut the cards, shuffling them several times before fanning them against my quilt. Then, like the day in Madam Isobel's shop, I closed my eyes, stretched out my hand, and selected one.

SIX

VIII of Swords.

Against a bright blue background, a girl in robes of red stood in front of eight swords, all driven into the ground. She was bound and blindfolded. Puddles of murky water dotted the mud at her feet. Behind her, behind the swords, a castle rose on the hill.

Delphi wandered closer, rubbing her face against the unsettling image.

It was a long time before I put the card down. Needing to do something, I dragged my laptop closer and found Will's Facebook page. I hardly recognized him in the profile picture, or any of the other pictures, for that matter.

Most of them were posted by Kendall: their arms around each other along the levee and silly poses along Bourbon Street, standing with windblown hair in front of a bonfire and dressed in formal clothes for what looked like a Christmas dance.

In almost all of them, Will's eyes gleamed warm and bright, his smile wide. It was obvious how into Kendall he was and she into him. Her short, pixie hair emphasized the adoration in her eyes.

Most of the posts were from Kendall, too.

I love you.

I wished upon my lucky star, and like a gift, here you are.

I believe in you. I believe in us.
I believe in forever.
I believe in MORE.

The only entry from him was a photo album from ten days ago: a collection of black-and-white pictures of French Quarter doorways, all partially ajar, some drenched in shadows, others with light spilling from within.

He had 376 friends. His parents were teachers: his mom taught English lit at a local high school and his dad psych at Tulane. He had a younger sister, Caroline. For religion: it's complicated. He didn't list any favorites, just one quote.

The tragedy of life is not death,
But what we let die inside us while we live.
—N. Cousins

He hardly seemed like a guy on a collision course with something bad.

Hating the quick, tight constriction in my chest, I ran my

hand along Delphi's fur, then reached for my journal and opened
to the letter I'd started the night before.

Chase,
I'm so sorry.

I blinked against the burn at my eyes and brought the pen to
the page, tapping it.

This isn't the way things were supposed to be.

Again, I had no awareness of falling asleep.

At 5:21 I woke up, exactly like I did every morning. But this
time hot, salty tears squeezed from behind closed eyes. Dragging
Delphi closer, I thought about everything Madam Isobel had told
me, and waited for the sun to rise.

Kendall's text came late that afternoon, while I was at the
shop with Aunt Sara.

R U free 2nite?

The old theater sat back from the dark, tree-lined road, surrounded
by an empty sea of weed-infested concrete. The faded marquee
still stood, advertising movies playing years before, when the storm
hit—RED EYE and THE DUKES OF HAZZARD, CHARLIE AND THE CHOC-
OLATE FACTORY—as if time stood frozen, ready to resume despite
the rot and decay.

From the street, everything looked deserted. No cars sat in the
lot. No one loitered around the front doors. The windows had
been painted black so no one could see inside.

But in the back, hidden by overgrown shrubbery and old Dumpsters, a lone metal door waited, with a dark red, upside-down "A" spray-painted toward the bottom. And every time it swung open, flashes of light and music shot into the night.

Will was supposed to be here. Kendall wasn't 100 percent sure, because he'd told her he had some stuff to take care of, but he'd mentioned the party Friday, and she thought there was a good chance he'd end up here.

She didn't understand why he was pulling away.

We left her car with lots of others in a clearing several hundred yards away, surrounded by a densely wooded area. After working our way through the moonlit trees, we stood in the shadow of the Dumpsters.

Wearing an awesome black maxi dress with short, layered hair blowing against her angular face, Kendall fiddled with her phone. Grace, with her no-longer-ghost-white hair falling in soft, brownish waves, stood with her arms open and her head tilted, as if breathing in the night.

That was the only clue she was here for something other than the party, that and her grandmother's big bulky black ring on her index finger. Between her denim shorts and flowy peasant top, dark eyeliner and shimmery pink lip gloss, she looked like your average teenage girl on a spring night.

I couldn't stop staring.

"Have you ever been to one of these?" Kendall asked.

"No," I said as the door flung open and three girls in all black stumbled out. Laughing, they huddled together and skipped toward the wooded area.

"It's so beautiful!" one of them sighed. "Like the whole world is on *fire*."

"They're nuts," Kendall warned. "Basically anything goes."

I took a quick sip from my water bottle. "Hopefully Will's here." *And we'd find out if the flash of white had to do with him.*

We started toward the door but I stopped when I realized Grace wasn't coming.

I turned back to her. "Are you okay?"

She nodded, her eyes suddenly solemn. With her gaze fixed on someplace in the distance, she lifted her right hand to her forehead.

"So art thou," she murmured, "so am I connected to divine light and protection within myself."

Everything inside me stilled. She looked dead serious.

"So art thou the Kingdom on Earth," she said, drawing her hand down toward her middle, "so am I connected and rooted within my body."

Kendall edged closer, shooting me the question with a quick widening of her eyes.

I shook it off.

The door shot open, spilling a syncopated rush of dubstep and three guys. They barreled by us, hesitating long enough to undress us with their eyes, before returning to their beers and heading for the woods.

Grace, with no indication that she'd seen them, lifted her hand to her shoulder and continued the chant-like murmur, a lot like Victoria's protective prayer before the Ouija board.

"So art Thou the Power," Grace said, "so am I protected from all harm by thy Divine power." She concluded with her hands clasped over her heart. "Forever and ever."

"What was that all about?" Kendall asked.

A long reddish-brown wave blew against Grace's cheek.

"Something my grandmother made me promise to do," she said. "Just in case."

Kendall's mouth tumbled open. "Just in case *what*?"

Grace made a funny, almost embarrassed, face. It was odd, given how wise and ancient and sure of herself she usually was.

"I kinda absorb things," she said. "In crowded places, like malls or parties. It's like I feel what everybody else feels."

And she was bracing herself for whatever blast she was about to receive.

"Here," she said, pushing something into my hand.

I glanced down at the cool, glass-like stone.

"It's black obsidian," she said. "One of the best stones for psychic protection. Put it in your pocket and listen if your gut starts to tell you something."

The stone?

Kendall edged closer. "Can I have one?"

Looking less like a mystic by the second, Grace gave one to Kendall, too.

Then she pulled open the door, and vanished inside the electrified darkness.

Muted lightning assaulted the room.

Once it had been a spacious lobby, with movie posters and concession stands. Now, to the other-worldly rhythm of electronic drums, greenish lights strobed, quick, fleeting breaths of darkness interrupted by violent flashes of dancing, of faces twisted and arms lifted, bodies grinding in ecstasy.

Kendall went looking for Will, while Grace and I squeezed into the sweaty, mindless blur. Hundreds of people pressed from all directions, and from the tight look on Grace's face, I knew she felt every single one of them.

I felt something, too.

Gulping my water, I worked to the other side, scanning faces with each flash of light. But how did you find one specific raindrop, in a storm that stretched as far as you could see?

Closing my eyes, I lifted my arms as Grace had done before coming inside. But I wasn't seeking divine protection. I was opening myself to the frantic fusion of energy around me, hoping for another flash of white, and that this time it would last long enough for me to see.

I held myself there, motionless, as the party revolved around me. *Through me.* All that emotion. All that energy. It swirled through me like a riptide, pulling and pushing at the same time. Breathing hurt. Swallowing. Just being. But I made myself do all three, pulling in a deep breath and holding it until the hot rush ruptured from me, and salty tears flooded my eyes.

Music ebbed and flowed like a drug to the masses, a baseline giving way to a soft, distorted wail. I hovered there in a cocoon of clashing emotions, waiting, *feeling*. Feeling everything and nothing at all.

"Help me."

I spun around.

Grace stood wrapped in her own arms, long tangles of hair streaking across her unnaturally pale face. Her eyes were wide and dark, fixed on some point in the distance.

I turned in the direction she was staring, but saw only a sea of writhing.

It hadn't been Grace's voice.

"Grace?" So much played across her face, nothing lasting long enough to register. "What is it?" I had to shout. The music tried to steal my voice.

Alone there, alone among hundreds, she started to rock. "Desperation," she murmured, scanning the room with empty, lost-soul eyes. "Sorrow and fear."

"Is that what you felt Friday?"

She hugged herself tighter. "Everyone is screaming but no one hears."

I turned back around, watching.

"It's the perfect place to hunt."

The words froze through me, throwing me back to the afternoon Jim Fourcade had used almost those exact same words. *"Hunt?"*

Grace's eyes, still unseeing, or maybe seeing something beyond this dimension, met mine. "Someone knows you're here."

"What do you mean? Who? Why?"

"They're watching. I can feel the coldness."

I spun around, searching, but the orgy of dancing squeezed in on me, carrying me like a wave toward girls twirling in endless circles in front of the concession stand. The second I saw the shattered glass of the old popcorn machine, everything else fell away.

Jessica stood without moving, much like she had at the funeral, when she'd held a long-stem red rose in her hands, her eyes fixed on the beautiful crypt.

I could still see the way she'd dropped to her knees.

Now she wore a killer black halter dress, a lot like those worn by other girls, but she didn't dance like they did, and she didn't laugh and she didn't sing. She just stood there, watching me through a fall of dark brown hair, so much wavier now than it used to be. The lost look in her eyes carved a sharp contrast to the in-your-face cheerleader I'd met last fall.

Through the scream of the music, I would have sworn I heard it again, *"Help me."*

Jessica's mouth never moved.

Sisters, I'd thought that first day of school. We looked like we could be sisters or cousins. We were both about 5'7", we both had wavy brown hair and olive skin, we both had dark eyes. And we'd both dreamed of Chase.

But Jessica had known him since she was a little girl.

The moment circled around us, holding me against the swell of dancing, locking us forever in the nightmare that had begun last fall and twisted down a dangerous path ever since.

In my hand, my phone vibrated. I pulled it up, letting out a slow breath when I saw Victoria's name.

Where R U?

I hadn't said anything to her about tonight. She would have insisted on coming, even though she'd had plans with Trey.

With a hot, guilty flush, I gulped a quick sip of water before fingering a response.

Just needed to get out.

I hated lying.

Her response came seconds later.

Your aunt thought you were with me.

A quick flood of unease surged through me.

Oh! I didn't tell her that.

Thankfully, Victoria didn't seem too worried.

Don't worry. I covered 4u.

A few seconds later, after shooting Kendall a quick text, too, asking if she'd found Will, I glanced back to the popcorn machine. Jessica was gone.

"Did you see that girl?" I asked, turning toward Grace.

She was gone, too.

My heart kicked hard. When had that happened? And how? Where was she?

I spun around fast, straight into a tall, hard wall, a *very alive,* tall, hard wall.

"Hello, prophet," he said. "No bodyguard tonight?"

SEVEN

With dark, chin-length hair scraggling against his face, the guy from the Greenwood party stepped into me, bringing his legs against mine.

I jerked back, but the crush of bodies gave me nowhere to go. I told myself not to panic. There was no reason to. He was just a guy, and this was just a party.

"You never know when he'll turn up," I said, lifting my chin and looking him in the eye. But with the words I fingered the black obsidian in my pocket. Heat radiated from the stone in soft waves, and for a dizzy heartbeat I found myself looking beyond the guy, toward the flickering sea of dancing.

But no one stood watching. I knew that despite the darkness. I would have known that with my eyes closed. The frenzied rhythm reverberated through me. There was no stillness.

I'd made Grace promise not to involve Dylan again.

"Looks like it's just you and me now," the guy from Friday

night said, putting his hand to my hips, as his swayed with the rhythm of the music.

My skin crawled.

"Maybe later," I said, stepping back and lifting my water between us. "I'm looking for someone." The words jammed in my throat. Will and Kendall, Grace. *That's* who I was looking for. Not anyone else.

The guy's mouth curved even more. "Aren't we all?"

Gone, I realized. He was as gone as everyone else, which meant I wasn't going to casually slip away.

"Look," I said, forcibly removing his hands from my body. The second I did, mine said thank you. "I've got to go."

He looked wounded. "I didn't mean to freak you out the other night." With the "A" tattooed against his neck, for anarchy I knew, the sulkiness made a strange combination. "Let me make it up to you. Here," he said, offering me the cup in his hand. "Let's start over."

"Later," I said even more firmly. Spinning away and not looking back, I cut through the press of hot, grinding bodies. Like quick, frantic breaths, they flashed in from the darkness with each strobe of the lights then vanished with the same speed, rhythmic, repetitive.

I was halfway across the room when the horror movie–like flickers revealed Amber with her skinny arms lifted high and her head thrown back. Lucas danced behind her, his hands on her hips, their bodies bumping as one.

Eyes meeting mine, she smiled the dreamiest of smiles, and the darkness swallowed her again.

With the next flash, she was turned in Lucas's arms, their mouths locked together.

I turned away, barely catching myself as the room tilted. I

hung there trying to breathe, but the thick swirl of sweat and smoke rolled through me. Off balance I reached for my phone and shot a text to Grace and Kendall.

Where R U?

Neither responded.

Turning, I fought my way past the remains of a mini-arcade, to a long hall lined by individual theaters.

Wanting to sit for a second, I darted into one, where a huge, vacant screen played nothingness to rows of plush, rotting chairs, not all of them empty.

Here light didn't flicker, only the sounds of heavy breathing and fevered moaning, of bodies coming together.

I made my way to the next theater, smaller than the first. With no ventilation to the night, it was like walking into a life-size oven. Muggy heat swamped me, the smoke of cigarettes and weed mixing with stale alcohol and the earthiness of decay.

Everything blurred. Stumbling, I reached out, my hand slipping against something matted and sticky that felt more like a floor than a wall. Carpet, I realized. Filthy and rotting. I tried to breathe, but the putrid, saunalike warmth rushed against the back of my throat and made me gag. Dizzily I fumbled for my water and gulped greedily, but the room kept shifting, and the low vibration wouldn't stop.

A few disoriented seconds passed before I recognized the pulsing as my phone. I wedged it from my front pocket, blinking several times before the distorted letters became words.

I'm by the concession stand. Where are you?

The room kept tilting, making my fingers clumsy as I responded.

In a theater.

A few rows in front of me panting escalated, loud, urgent breaths ripping into the stillness. I stumbled toward the door, hesitating when another text buzzed against my hand.

Against the fuzz of white, I made out Kendall's name.

I found him. We're out back.
Can u come?

Another quick stab of pain against my skull made me wince as I fumbled to tap the right letters.

On my way.

I hit send and made it to the door, but then my phone pulsed again. This time it was a picture that popped up on my screen. Not thinking much about it, I enlarged the image and stared down at the girl, at the long hair falling around her pale face, her eyes unfocused, the smeared makeup and clothes clinging to a thin body.

Me, I realized with a sick feeling. Taken tonight. Here. My guess was Amber, but the sender's area code was not one I recognized.

The question came a few seconds later.

What would Chase think?

"You ready?"

Startled, I spun around, but even after I stilled, the shadows kept swirling.

Muted waves of light slipped through the open door, revealing a guy with long dark hair raining down around a tragic face, deep-set eyes and a long straight nose, lips parted, waiting. I'd never seen him before.

I tried to push past him. "Excuse me."

He smiled. "Do you know how amazing you are?"

I'm not sure how I heard him, when the music strummed so loudly, and his voice drifted so soft.

"How much more amazing you *can* be, life can be?"

Another sharp throb pulsed against the back of my head, spreading toward the front like fingers squeezing, tightening.

His smile went sad. "But you don't feel that way, do you?"

Everything blurred. Wincing, I tried to blink him back into focus.

"I have to go." I pulled away, needing to get . . .

Somewhere. I needed to get somewhere, I knew.

I couldn't remember where.

"Don't be afraid," the tragic-faced guy said, reaching for me. "It's why you're here." He had a cup in his hand, and he was lifting it between us as another vibration swept in, not from my phone, but inside me.

I stilled, trying to grab onto that, thinking I *should* grab onto that. The low hum meant . . .

Worlds fracturing, I remembered with another wobble. That's what the vibration meant. *The unseen spilling in.*

"It's why we're all here," the stranger murmured, lifting the drink to his mouth. "Because we don't want to be anywhere else. We don't *belong* anywhere else. We want to forget," he said mindlessly. "To be beautiful . . . *for bliss*."

I reached for the wall, but found only air.

He caught me, steadied me. "For forever."

A quick breath of cold moved through me.

"I can give you that," he said, more quietly this time. "If you let me."

My heart started to race. The rapid pace tripped through me, as if I was running for my life, even as I stood absolutely still.

Something was wrong, I knew. Really wrong. Pulling away, I staggered toward the door, knowing I had to get out of there, fast, back to fresh air and light, to reality and sanity, to Grace and Kendall . . .

I fumbled with my phone, trying to text.

Something wrong . . . need you.

Stumbling, I made it into the hall, where the guy from the Greenwood party, the one with the "A" on his neck, leaned against the wall, watching.

Lightning flashed, not from the dance floor, but the invisible kind. The kind that streaked like slivers of brilliant ice inside me, that only I saw.

Only I felt.

And at the end of the hall, something glowed, a single door, shimmering like a pearl lit from the inside out.

The corridor wobbled, stretched, but drawn by the radiance, I made myself move toward it. Some people staggered away. Others stopped and stared. With the light from her phone angled up from beneath her chin, Amber danced by herself.

Reaching the door, I grabbed the cool knob of sparkly cobalt and yanked as hard as I could.

EIGHT

I staggered through the darkness. *Get away.* That was all I could think. I had to get away from the theater.

Someone was following me. They crashed through the brush behind me, footsteps fast, pounding, twigs and leaves crunching. The labored rasp of breathing closed in with each rip of the wind. But I knew better than to look.

Trees surrounded me, their trunks running together in an endless, gnarled band, crowding closer. I tried to find an opening, a path, the faintest sliver of light.

Dreaming, I realized. I was dreaming. This was all some bizarre nightmare or vision. That was why I couldn't stop running.

"Trinity."

Everywhere I turned, knobby roots jutted up from the carpet of shifting . . . spiders?

I darted around them, but the vines slithered closer, reaching for me and coiling around my ankles.

"No!" I slapped at them, fighting forward to tear through the—

I stopped and stared, blinked, but the snakes writhed closer, hundreds of them, long and sinuous with eyes of unblinking red and darting tongues.

I backed away. Not snakes, I told myself. They're just sticks, dead branches. None of this was real, I reminded myself. I tried to remember how I got here, or where here was. But answers refused to come, only the strange, disjointed scene that I couldn't pull myself out of.

Stumbling, I started to run again, but above me the stars exploded, raining down and splashing up, freezing into icicles in midair. Beneath them puddles of radiant silver formed, and for a heartbeat the swirl of eternity beckoned.

"I don't understand," I whispered, going to my knees. I wanted to dip my hand into the glimmer and bring it back to me, baptizing myself in the promise of forever.

"Trinity, no! Come back!"

The voice was closer. *Too close.* But forever shimmered right in front of me, and it was beautiful.

"Where are you?"

The urgent voice echoed around me.

"Dylan," I murmured, recognizing this part of the dream. This was when he came. This was when he always came, at the exact right moment.

The wind pushed and pulled. The moon started to bounce.

Pulling back, I stood. Everything hurt. "Why can't I see you?"

"Tell me where you are!"

"Right here," I said as footsteps pounded closer, and arms caught me. And then everything settled, the stars returning to the sky as the confusion of the nightmare gave way to the familiarity of a dream.

When I was a little girl, I used to wander off to a clearing in the mountains, where pine beetles had decimated the forest, allowing wildfire to turn the brittle remnants into kindling. My grandmother called it an ugly place, barren. But that's not what I saw.

Like a church with no walls, the stumpy remains of hundreds of trees ambled across the field. I could go there and be alone, spread out the quilt my mother once wrapped me in, and lay on my back, watching the clouds parade along the front range.

It was my special place, my special time, and when I closed my eyes, I could be one with those clouds, drifting against the horizon.

Hovering there all over again, formless, aimless, the faint edges of memory played against the fringes of my mind. I could see him, more silhouette than form, could feel him running, shouting . . .

I always find you.

For a long, content heartbeat, I wrapped myself in the familiar cocoon of memory. Or was it a dream? I wasn't sure. Music drifted, the tinkling of a piano and a rich, velvety baritone from somewhere unseen, singing about wise men and rivers flowing.

Meant to be . . .

For the first time in weeks, the darkness didn't push any closer.

Take my hand . . .

Everything slowed, faded. I tried to stay there, not wanting to move, not wanting the moment to end, not even when I heard the voice.

Especially when I heard the voice.

"Just rest."

Content, I pulled the cocoon closer.

"That's it." The words were quiet, gentle, and with them warmth drifted against the side of my face. *"You're safe now."*

Dream, I realized. This was all a dream, beautiful and perfect, the silken threads of the unreal spun around the sharp, painful edges from before.

But when I opened my eyes, he was still there, sitting beside me on the edge of a bed I'd never seen, in a room with walls of woodland green and a dream catcher so big it had to be at least ten times the size of the tattoo peeking out from the sleeve of his T-shirt.

He leaned toward me, the sweep of dark hair falling like black silk against the line of his cheekbone, a stark contrast to the soft fullness of his bottom lip. He had a hand to my arm, two fingers pressed against the inside of my wrist.

His eyes were closed.

"Dylan," I whispered, and when his eyes shot open, and the burnished silver flashed against mine, something inside me exhaled. "It was you," I realized. He was the one who'd followed me in the woods, who'd called to me, helped me.

Everything crashed in on me, disorientation giving way to a breath of longing so strong there was nothing else, just us, like we'd been before, *like I'd dreamed,* and the hugeness of everything that lingered between us.

Touch him. It was all I could think. Touch him, feel his skin, the warmth and strength, the way they could penetrate. *Heal.* He'd done that before, the first time we met.

I wanted that now, I wanted that again.

I lifted my hand, not sure why it felt so heavy, and slid a finger along the line of his jaw.

He held himself so, so still, looking at me with the oddest clash in his eyes, of tenderness and violence and restraint.

Around me, the strange room kept zooming in and out of focus, glittering bright and fading fast, as if I was looking through a malfunctioning camera lens. Everything but Dylan.

"You're really here," I whispered, reaching for him, reaching without thinking, pushing up and wrapping my arms around him, holding on as tightly as I could.

Heat blasted me, radiating from his body to mine and driving away the cold I'd lived with so long I barely noticed it anymore. Touching him was like absorbing sunshine, and I pressed myself closer, needing that, the sunshine. *Him.*

The warmth of his breath feathered against my neck. His chest expanded against mine. And then with a rough breath his arms were around me, too, circling my body and holding me close, one hand along my back and the other tangled in my hair.

I closed my eyes as somewhere inside started to hurt.

But then I needed to see, not just the room around us, but him. I pulled back, leaving one hand on his shoulder as I lifted the other to his jaw. Looking up, I saw him, his eyes, burning like scorched silver diamonds.

Memory slipped against that empty place inside me, the place that wanted to feel again, feel the warmth. *Feel him.* I pushed up without thinking, lifting my mouth to his. It was slow and tentative, aching, like brushing against fragile glass, knowing that if you moved too fast or turned the wrong way, the perfection would shatter.

But nothing shattered. Nothing went away.

He held himself soldier still, like he didn't trust himself to move, didn't know what would happen if he did. His heart slammed against mine, and with each slam, more places inside of me started to fire. I hovered there in the moment, absorbing it, *needing* it.

Needing him.

He tensed, tried to pull away, but then with another rough breath between us, surrender came.

It was an odd word, surrender, like giving up or quitting, but there was neither in the way his hands found my face, strong yet gentle, sliding back the damp sticky hair and holding me there, holding me as if he thought if he let go, if he pulled back, I would be the one who vanished.

As if *he* was the one afraid.

Thoughts tried to form. Hazy fragments rushed around inside me, softly at first, sharper with each slam of my heart. But nothing made sense, not with the urgency swirling through me, consuming everything. There was only Dylan, and the dizzying sanctuary of being back in his arms.

Dream, I told myself. I wanted this to all be a dream, something without boundaries or sharp edges. Dreams played over and over, forever. They could be returned to, didn't have to end. They could linger, heal. Like aimless clouds, they weren't connected to before or after. They just *were*.

I pulled him closer—

He ripped away, pushing as far back from me as he could, hovering there with his arms like steel rods on either side of my face, his hands pressed against the pillow, his eyes on fire.

I'd never seen him look like that, not even the night he pulled me from the burning church.

I lifted a finger to my mouth, swollen now, my lips moist.

"You've never kissed me like that," I murmured, confused. "Like it hurt."

The silver of his eyes glittered. "Yeah," he said. "I have."

My eyes stung. I looked away fast, looked away because I had to. Because the sharp edges of memory came slicing back, and I realized, for a few minutes there, I'd forgotten. I'd been so caught up in the moment, I'd forgotten what happened the last time we were together. Not at the party, but *before*.

I pulled back, slowly taking in the room again, the pine chest of drawers and the matching nightstands, each with an urn-shaped ceramic lamp with a wide shade of bright white. A bundle of herbs sat next to one, with a wispy stream of smoke curling into the air. A single white votive flickered from the other.

The bed was big and tall, shaped like a sleigh, the mattress hard but the quilt thick and warm. A picture sat on the dresser, of an old man and a young boy with rugged mountains in the background.

Not a hotel, I realized with a strong throb at the back of my head. Wincing, I lifted my hand to the damp tangles of my hair, matted with mud and what felt like a twig.

It all started coming back, vague, fuzzy images, the crushing fusion of the party and the sensation of spinning, the glowing door and the realization that something was wrong, the run through the woods.

Then nothing.

Until here.

Now.

With him.

"Where are we?" I asked, trying to fill in the blanks.

Dylan eased back, his movements contained, as if holding on crazy tight, because if he didn't, if he let go for even a second, everything would spin away.

"My dad's house." He hesitated, something dark and dangerous glittering into his eyes. "He found you in the flower bed."

NINE

Everything shifted. The sudden sway rocked through me like the room had become a boat adrift on the ocean, not in a storm, but the steady onslaught of wave after wave.

"He what?" I must have misunderstood.

Dylan looked away, toward the window, for a long moment before answering. "The dogs started barking—"

Rottweilers, I remembered, big and fierce.

"Dad was checking on them when he heard the doorbell. By the time he got to the front, the car was already leaving."

I sat there, my fingers curled in a death grip against the beautiful old quilt in countless shades of rose.

"You were curled in the pansies beside my mom's Virgin Mary statue."

His voice, all scraped bare, chilled me as much as the words. My breath started coming faster, choppy-like, as I scrambled for memory to match what he said.

"You looked like you were sleeping," he said, more quietly now. "Or gone."

The room blurred. Because of my head, I realized, lifting a hand to the dull throb of pain at my forehead.

"That's when he called me," he said, and then his hand was there, too, slipping against mine with soft, gentle pressure. "Is this where it hurts?"

The calming scent of sage drifted from the bundle smoldering on the bedside table. I nodded, not feeling anything then but the warmth of Dylan's fingertips as I concentrated on breathing.

Everything inside me started to race, the holes in my memory gaping bigger by the second.

"Your heart's on fire." His hand was lower now, no longer against my face, but pressed at the base of my throat. "All your pulses are."

"*All* my pulses?"

"Something my grandfather taught me," he murmured. "That's what I was doing when you woke up. Checking your energy."

Because he could, I realized, and without thinking about it, my eyes found the dream catcher tatted against his bicep, the one I'd run my finger along before. Dylan Fourcade was only a few years older than me, but he knew things I could only imagine, as if he'd lived twice as long as the rest of us.

Because the Navajo in him was strong.

But even with his touch, even with his steadiness, everything inside me kept racing. The clock across the room read 11:13. We'd arrived at the party around 7:30. Maybe I'd spent an hour there.

That left two and a half unaccounted for.

"I don't understand," I said, barely recognizing the scrape of my own voice. "Why can't I remember anything? It's all like some bizarre *Alice in Wonderland* dream."

His mouth twitched, like a smile wanted to form but he wouldn't let it. "Seems more like Goldilocks to me," he muttered darkly, because we both knew there was nothing funny about it.

"I thought you were there," I admitted, staring at him as if answers might magically appear between us. "At the party. I thought you followed me into the woods."

His chest rose, fell. "No."

"But . . ." The horror of it all pushed in. *Someone else had been there, someone I couldn't remember.* "Who would do that? Who would bring me here, to *your dad*?"

Why?

"Who else was there?" he asked.

The room wobbled again. "Grace," I said, and then my heart kicked. "Oh, my God, Grace."

"I've talked to her," he said, sliding my phone from the other side of the lamp. "She was texting you. I told her you were here."

I sat there clenching the quilt as he told me about their conversation.

"She told me *everything*," he said quietly. All motionless he rattled off everything he knew now, about the almost-vision at the Greenwood party and Kendall and Will and why I'd gone to the second party. About the darkness we'd picked up there. "She was looking for you when she heard two guys laughing about getting rid of the prophet."

The room tilted all over again.

"And I need to know what you had to drink," he said flatly, but the darkness in his eyes burned through me. "Or what you took."

"What I took?" I pulled back, my mind racing. "I didn't take *anything*." The question hurt. "Just water."

He crowded in on me again, pulling the covers from my body. "Water didn't do this to you."

Numbly I slid my hand along the tear at the knee of my favorite jeans, to the dark, coppery smear against the stark white of his sheets, part mud, part blood. *Mine*. I shifted, seeing for the first time the deep gash curving up from the arch of my right foot—a gash that should have bled still. But didn't. Already the skin was beginning to heal, leaving only a faint warmth in place of pain.

"Trinity." His voice rasped quieter, gentler. "I need you to tell me everything you remember."

"I'm trying." I stared at the dream catcher on the wall, drawing my knees tight to my chest. "I thought a vision was forming," I said, telling him about the dizziness and how everything had spun, how I'd run, trying to get outside, away from the craziness of the party. That I'd thought a vision was coming.

"It's happened before," I told him. "Last fall Chase and I got separated in the Quarter. I was looking for him in an old courtyard, but everything flashed, and then it was like I was in some other place, seeing stuff from a long time ago." A grandfather clock and the pink velvet couch, a black mirror.

"I thought it was real, but then . . ." The memory chilled. "LaSalle showed up and we went back inside, and the room was empty." And it had been for a long time.

The silver of Dylan's eyes went crazy dark.

"I think he was toying with us even then." I had no proof, not the physical, tangible kind, but I didn't need it. "I think he was following us, that he separated me from Chase to see what would happen."

"And you thought that's what was happening tonight?" Dylan asked "A vision?"

I shook my head and sent the room tilting all over again.

"I wasn't sure," I said. "It was like when they gave me a tran-quilizer after . . ." I broke off, the way Dylan looked at me telling me he knew exactly what I meant by *after*. At the hospital. After the steady rhythm of life fell silent.

"It was like the whole world slipped away," I said, "and every-thing got dull and dreamlike."

Finally he handed me my phone. "This isn't a vision."

Dark letters blurred against the glow of white.

STAY AWAY OR NEXT TIME IT WILL BE WORSE

I stared so hard my eyes burned.

"That came about thirty minutes ago," Dylan said. "The number is a prepaid cell."

Which meant it couldn't be traced.

"Oh, my God," I whispered, trying to understand.

"Someone wanted you out of there."

I looked up through a tangle of damp, muddy hair. "That's why it's all a blur," I said, realizing where he'd been going all along. "Someone must have put something in my water."

It would have been easy, too, all those people, the strobe lighting and hundreds of hot, sweaty people pressed against each other.

Dylan looked like he wanted to put a fist through the wall. "The question is why," he said darkly, and now it was his voice that scraped. "To have a little fun?" He hesitated, a wildness I'd never seen before flickering in his gaze. "To play with you?"

While I was totally out of it.

"To get rid of you?"

"You need to be careful," Grace had said. *"Someone knows you're here."*

"To stop you?"

Because they could have, I realized. Someone could have done anything to me.

Why?

And then Dylan was looking at me, looking at me in a way I didn't understand, that burned and chilled at the same time.

"It's not like it was before," he said, his voice dead quiet. "And it never will be again. People know who you are. You can't just go to places like that anymore. People with secrets . . . they're not going to like it when you show up."

Because they'd think I knew stuff about them, their lives, their lies, even if I didn't.

"If someone hadn't brought you here," he started, but stopped when the door that had been ajar pushed open, and his dad walked in.

"I thought I heard voices," Jim said, smiling like none of this was strange. In a flannel shirt and faded jeans, with his silver hair pulled into a low ponytail and a glass in his hands, he walked over and offered me water. "Thirsty?"

Jim suggested I shower. I could have gone home despite how trashed my clothes were, but I didn't want Aunt Sara to see my matted, tangled hair, or the mascara smeared beneath my eyes. She didn't need that.

If she was even awake.

I could have stayed beneath the warm spray for hours, but it was late, and I didn't have all night.

And I was at Jim's house, in the bathroom Dylan used. The soap was his. I stared at the bar of swirled green and white a long time before picking it up and bringing it to my body, and for a second there, the strangest sensation slipped through me, almost like a touch.

I held the soap against my chest. When my eyes stung, I told myself it was only the water, but I pulled the bar away and built a lather in my hands.

After the water ran cold, I dried off and dressed, slipping on the huge sweatpants and baggy Tulane T-shirt that I knew belonged to Dylan.

Soft jazz drifted through the house when I emerged in a cloud of steam, leading me to the kitchen. Jim stood at the stove, stirring a dark liquid in a small iron pot.

"Better?"

The rich scent of chocolate drifted toward me. "Yeah."

"Good."

"Thanks."

"Clothes are in the dryer. You want to watch TV while they finish up?"

"Sure." Fingering the damp hair from my face, I wandered toward a huge sofa opposite the equally huge television. Both new, like almost everything else in the house he'd built after the storm.

I'd been here three times: the day we met, the day I came to ask him how my mother dealt with dreams she didn't understand, and the day I'd brought the picture from Grace's apartment, of my mother and hers. Each time we'd stayed outside. The first time I'd chosen not to go in, the second and third times he'd never offered.

Dark paneling covered the walls, even though I was pretty sure basically no one did that anymore. The furniture was big and sturdy, the electronics state of the art. A few framed black-and-white photos hung from the walls.

No woman lived here. That was obvious, except for the fuzzy, muted rose blanket at the far end of the sofa and the pair of leopard-rimmed reading glasses next to a book about the universe.

I smiled. Dylan's dad always seemed so lonely. I liked that he didn't spend all of his time by himself.

At the back of the room a big window gave an awesome view of the yard, all save for the security bars every two inches.

We moved away from the past, but some ghosts moved with us.

"You want to go outside?"

Jim passed the sofa with two big mugs in his hands. Steam rose from the whipped cream peeking over the tops.

I started to ask where Dylan was, but didn't. Whatever danger there'd been was over. He didn't do aftermath.

Outside, cool night air blew in from the river beyond the oak and cypress trees. And for a fleeting moment, memory played: the huge, snarling dogs running toward me, the one, quiet word freezing them in place, and Dylan, standing in the shadows.

Allez, he'd said. Stop.

But so much more had started.

Curling my hands around the mug, I turned toward the snoring dogs on the far side of the porch.

"They haven't even moved," I said.

"They know they don't need to," Jim said. "They don't sense danger."

Like they had earlier when the unknown car had come onto their property.

At the edge of the raised redwood deck, I sat on the top stair, taking a long sip of hot cocoa. Here so far removed from the lights of the city, nearby stars twinkled and faraway galaxies swirled, a lot like they had in the mountains of Colorado.

The crickets and toads did their thing, but that only added to the peacefulness. "It's so quiet," I murmured. "I've always loved being outside at night."

Jim sat beside me. "Me, too."

"When I was a little girl, I used to wander out after Gran went to bed. She always said it wasn't safe because of the animals, but I was never afraid." The memory made me smile. "It was the only time I could see the stars."

With another whipped-creamy sip of cocoa, I searched the pinpricks of light for the familiar lines of Orion.

"There was this legend," I remembered, "that they're not really stars at all, but an opening to Heaven, where the light of people who have gone before us can shine down." My eyes filled. My throat thickened. I swallowed hard, but when I spoke again, my voice was barely a whisper. *"And let us know they're okay."*

Jim moved silently, gathering me against his side and holding me there. "Sweet girl," he murmured.

Sinking into him seemed the most natural thing in the world. I'd heard so many stories about fathers and daughters, a dad being the one man a girl could count on her entire life.

This, I wondered. Was this what it felt like?

"It's Eskimo," he said. "Your mom told me that."

Everything glimmered, the twinkling of a million billion stars blurring into an endless haze.

"Yesterday is ashes, tomorrow is wood," he added quietly. "Only today the fire shines brightly. That was another of her favorites."

"I can feel her here," I told him. "When I'm with you. And it's strange, but it always makes me feel safe."

"You are safe."

I was. I knew that.

"Cricket . . ."

Something about his voice, the gentle tone, warned me we were moving away from stars and Eskimo legends.

"It wasn't your fault."

I stilled.

He eased back, letting the moonlight play along the shadows on his face, and somewhere far deeper.

"You're so like her. I can see it in your eyes, the guilt and the grief, just like I saw in hers. And maybe I shouldn't say anything. Maybe it's not my place, or tonight isn't the right time," he said gruffly. "But you're young, and your whole life is ahead of you, and I can't let that son of a bitch take that from you."

I looked back at the shifting shadows of the trees.

"People like you and your mom, it's hard for you, because you feel responsible, like you should be able to change stuff. But the things you see . . . it's like sitting in a theater and watching coming attractions. It doesn't matter whether you like it. You can't change what's already in the can."

My hands tightened around the increasingly cool mug.

"With the girl last fall and your aunt, with Grace, your role was to help, and you did."

I swallowed.

"With that son of a bitch, you stopped him. But with Chase . . ." He hesitated. "The decisions were *his,* and he made them."

A fresh wave of emotion jammed in my throat.

"It wasn't your fault," he said quietly. "You're not God."

He was the second person to say that in twenty-four hours.

"He puts us here for a reason, and he takes us for a reason. It's not up to us to decide." He reached for his own mug. "Can you imagine how crowded this place would be if we got to tell him no?"

It was one of those things that wasn't funny, not really, but made my mouth curve anyway.

"But I know how it feels." He stared straight ahead, a few long strands of silver slipping from his ponytail to slide against the shadow of his jaw. "After the fire, I held you and looked into your sweet face, so full of love and trust, with absolutely no idea how your life had just changed, and all I could think was that I failed. I did everything humanly possible to keep you safe, *all* of you. But he got to you anyway."

Damp strands of hair fell against my face, but I didn't push them back, didn't move.

"I didn't know how to live with that," Jim muttered, hunching his shoulders. "Didn't know how to live with what I let happen."

Haunted, I realized. Houses could be haunted. Places, empty old mansions and windswept fields where battles had raged and soldiers died. I'd seen shows about them, the feeling you got when you walked across the grass and felt the wind, how an essence remained, the spirits of those who had died.

But people could be haunted, too. If something dug deep enough into your soul, how could it not affect you?

Jim sat there, staring into the darkness, while the memory of all that he said played through his eyes.

"I drank myself to sleep every night and woke up every morning consumed by thoughts of finding the sick bastard who set fire to a little girl's life, and making him pay."

According to my aunt, the sociopath who preyed on children and murdered my parents simply disappeared. Some thought he moved on. Some thought he died, or that justice caught up with him outside the law.

Jim turned back toward the house, and everything about him changed, that dull glassy look in his eyes burning into something stronger.

I turned, too.

TEN

The night deepened. Dylan stood there, in the familiar shadows of the old porch, with the same quiet intensity as the night at the Greenwood party. I had no idea when he'd come outside or how much he'd heard, but the sight of him standing there, and the realization that he hadn't left, brought me slamming right back into the moment.

"My boy," Jim said, and something in his voice, the way it frayed around the edges, made me swing back around to look at him. "My boy was still here, but for a long time I couldn't see that, couldn't see anything, not until I almost lost even more."

Dylan, I realized, before Jim said anything else. Something had happened to Dylan.

Jim stared off at the trees, but I was pretty sure he saw a darkness far beyond the night. "I didn't notice he was gone at first. I woke up and drank coffee, took a shower. It was probably an hour before the quiet registered. Still, I figured he was sleeping and went back to fantasizing about revenge, until his mama started screaming."

Around us, the cool breeze swirled softer.

"I found her in his bedroom. The window was open. And all I could think was that bastard had him. That bastard had come into my house, while I was passed out on the sofa, and taken my boy."

Finally Dylan moved, stepping from the shadows to cross to his father. "Dad."

"But that's not what happened," Jim said as Dylan reached us. "My boy left by himself, to go camping down by the river, like I'd promised him we would."

My heart squeezed.

"Because I forgot," Jim said, as if trying to explain something to a cop or a judge, or an even higher power, but knowing nothing he said would ever wipe away the horror of his sin. "He was five god-damn years old and he went by himself, because his daddy forgot."

I could see him, the boy Dylan had been, with his shaggy dark hair and enthusiasm in his eyes, tromping off on his own, guided by nothing but his own internal compass.

Moving like water, like he always did, Dylan squatted by his father and put a hand to his shoulder. "I had Blackie."

Jim twisted around, the haunted glint in his eyes locking onto his son.

"I found them by a tree," he said. "My little man climbed a tree 'cause he wanted to reach for the stars, and fell."

Dylan's mouth twitched, that same ghost of a smile I'd seen so many times before. "The stars were higher than I thought."

"Broke his leg," Jim said. "Couldn't walk so he dragged himself against the biggest tree and his big old Lab laid down in front of him, and they waited.

"I lost it when I saw him," his father said. "I ran to him and dropped to my knees, and just held on, held on so goddamn tight, because I knew, I finally knew that I couldn't change what happened to your mama, and if I kept trying, all I'd end up changing was what I still had, what still lay ahead of me."

In only a few minutes, Jim had told me more about Dylan than Dylan himself ever had.

"We do what we can, darlin'," Jim said, turning to me. "We don't give up. We embrace each day that we have and live every breath we take."

He made it sound so easy.

So many people avoided talking to me about the big stuff, about Chase and LaSalle and my role in what happened. It was like sweeping dirt under the rug, or slapping paint on a wall. If people didn't talk about it, it wasn't real. Or maybe they just didn't know what to say, or didn't want to make me relive it all over again.

But here was this grizzled ex-cop, who'd tracked bad guys, and when he had to, killed them. But beneath all that lay the heart of a man, *a father.*

"Thank you," I said, but before I could finish Dylan's phone beeped, and he was pushing to his feet and turning as he stepped toward the dogs.

A few seconds passed before he turned back to us, the sweep of his hair emphasizing the sudden tension to his face. "I've got to go."

Jim and I stood at the same time. Father looked to son. Son looked back at father. Something silent and pronounced passed between them, and with a vague tilt of vertigo, I knew there was something they weren't telling me.

"What?" I crossed to him without thinking about what I was doing. I only knew that I needed to know, because it had to do with me. "What's going on?"

The phone beeped again. Dylan glanced back down, his hair hiding his eyes.

Jim moved closer.

The wind whipped around us, driving home the acute stillness to both Fourcades.

"It's about tonight, isn't it?" Grace had sensed something in the shadows, waiting. Something bad. "Did something happen? Grace said—"

Dylan looked up, his gaze slashing me to the quick. I could tell he didn't want to say anything, but I could also tell he knew he didn't have a choice. "The police are at the theater now. Someone had a knife."

My mouth opened, but no sound came out.

"A bunch of kids got hurt before some guys chased him outside and tackled him. Two girls were taken to the hospital."

"Oh, God," I whispered. "Maybe that's what I was picking up." Questions tripped through me. "Do you know who the guy was?" Will? "Who was hurt? Is Grace okay? Kendall? Are they still there?"

Dylan's phone beeped again. He looked down, immediately let out a rough breath.

I rushed forward, taking him by the arm. *"What?"*

His eyes met mine, and before he said a word, I knew.

Whatever was going on, it wasn't over yet.

"Come on," he said, reaching for my hand. "We've got to go."

And then he was running, we both were, toward his father's truck.

The night blurred around us.

With trees racing by, Dylan drove in silence, his eyes fixed straight ahead, while I sat in the passenger's seat, scrolling through the messages he and Grace had been sending for the past hour.

How's Trinity?

Resting. Tell me about the party.

It's like a bunch of zombies. There's something really dark here, something gathering. The vibrations are muted, distorted, but I can feel the panic, like someone crying out for help. It's like before Katrina, when we all knew what was coming, but knew we couldn't stop it.

Be careful and let me know if anything changes.

Trinity doesn't belong in a place like this. There's no telling what she picked up on or who picked up on her.

I was right. That was all I could think. The flash of white meant something *bad*.

Grace's last few texts, the ones she'd sent while Dylan and I had been on the patio, were about Kendall and Will.

We found Will. He was freaked, kept saying Kendall shouldn't be there. We all left at the same time, but she won't go home. We're following him now.

We tracked him to a wooded area, but we can't find him. Kendall's a mess. She won't leave without him but she's scared to call his parents. She doesn't want him to get in trouble again.

That's when Dylan texted back.

We're on our way. Where exactly are you?

City Park.

I stared at the stark words against the white background. For a second everything else fell away, leaving only memory. Of Chase. Silhouetted against a tall white column in a clearing, with the blue, blue sky behind him.

Am I ever in your dreams? he'd asked.

My heart squeezed. Everything had seemed so crazy innocent at the time. I hadn't known. I hadn't known about the premonitions, or why I had them.

Chase was the one who'd led me to those answers.

Chase was the one who'd led me to Dylan, and a dream as dangerous as it was forbidden.

And then everything went all watery, and I blinked against the sting, returning Chase to the quiet sanctuary of memory, and me to the truck with Dylan, racing toward the blur of trees hulking against the blanket of stars.

Grace met us by the fountain. Last fall water had sprayed up in a high arc to rain down around us. Now all that moved was the steady breath of the night wind through the hundred-year-old oaks.

In the moonlight, reddish-brown hair slapped at Grace's face. "We found him." Her eyes were like dark pools, reflecting the horror of all she'd seen, and all she knew. "He's in a tree."

Dylan looked beyond her, toward the line between the fall of moonlight and the shadows beyond.

"A tree?" A quick whisper of cold moved through me. "Why? Where's Kendall?"

"She climbed up after him, saying she won't come down until he does. But he says he can't. That he can't let them find him."

"Let *who* find him?" I asked, but before Grace answered Dylan took off toward the back of the clearing.

We followed, Grace shooting me a quick, worried look as we left the open space and entered the shift of shadows. "Are you sure you're okay?"

With every minute that passed, the blurry edges from whatever I'd been slipped faded, and normalcy returned.

"Yeah," I assured her, tearing through a clump of Spanish moss, that was *just* Spanish moss. The trees were just trees, the vines just vines. Everything was back to normal.

Almost.

Wordlessly we veered into the darkness, running along the carpet of decaying leaves. The night hummed around us, crickets and toads and all those other night sounds—and something else.

Chanting.

Dylan glanced back to me, his hair long and stringy against his face, but I saw the quick flash of his eyes.

We edged closer, each second playing like a slow, cautious breath as the monk-like cadence gave way to the fervor of a doomsday preacher.

"Then the kings of the earth, the very important people, the generals, the rich, the powerful, and everyone, slave and free, hid themselves in the caves and among the rocks of the mountains."

Dylan stopped, reaching back to catch me by the waist and pull me into the shadow of a double-trunked oak.

Grace slipped in beside us. "The Book of Revelation," she whispered.

Mixed with the quiet sound of Kendall begging Will to stop.

"And then they said to the mountains and to the rocks, fall on us and hide us from the face of the one who is seated on the throne and from the wrath of the Lamb, because the great day of their wrath is now at hand."

Grace frowned. "He says he's protecting her."

Dylan glanced back. "From what?"

Her eyes went really dark. *"Me."*

I went to pull my hoodie tighter, not realizing until that moment that I'd run off wearing Dylan's T-shirt and sweats. "You?"

"And you, and everyone else who's following him," Grace said.

Dylan stepped closer, the unexpected blast of heat drawing me back against him before I even realized I was moving. I started to shift away, but before I could move, his hands were there, sliding from my shoulders along my arms, warming.

"He's out of his mind," Dylan muttered.

I twisted around, our eyes meeting.

I'd been out of my mind, too.

"Maybe *that's* what I was picking up on." But even as I said the words, they rang hollow. If I flashed white for every stranger who drank too much or took things they shouldn't, my world would be an eternal North Pole.

"It's more than just him tripping," Grace said, echoing my

thoughts. "There's something else, a confusion or desperation, like he's afraid of something."

The white flash, I thought again. It meant something.

Bad.

"And then four angels stood at the four corners of the earth, holding the four winds of the earth, that no wind should blow on the earth, or on the sea, or upon any tree!"

Dylan turned me by the shoulders, leaving his hands curled there as he talked. Very little moonlight leaked through the tangle of vines, but I could tell the silver gleamed really dark.

"I need you to talk to him," he said. "Can you do that?"

I looked up at him, at the curtain of hair cutting against his cheekbone, and reminded myself to breathe. I wasn't sure why it was so hard, but it was like I'd been holding my breath *forever,* waiting for the world to start turning again.

Now it turned, but the direction was wrong.

"What are you going to do?" I asked.

"Get them down."

"You want me to distract him?"

With a quick nod, he pulled away and disappeared among the shadows.

For a crazy second I wanted to drag him back.

Knowing that was the last thing I should do, I looked back at Grace. She stared off in the darkness, her pretty white poet's shirt torn at the sleeve and smeared with blood.

"I'm sorry I dragged you into this," I said.

Tangles of hair streaked across her face, but when she glanced back at me, she smiled.

"You didn't drag me anywhere. I'm where I'm supposed to be—and so are you and—"

I'm not sure what made her stop. Maybe the quick flare of my eyes, or maybe the realization that there was no *and,* that any *and* there might have been ended the second the steady rhythm of hospital monitors fell into the scream of silence.

We could never go back to before.

"Kendall?" Slipping from the shadows, I emerged into a puddle of moonlight. "Kendall! Where are you?"

The Revelation recitation stopped. "Who's there?"

I ran toward Will's voice, searching the branches. "Kendall! Answer me!"

"Stay away," he warned.

Near the base of the tree, a shadow slipped, and I knew Dylan was close.

"Are you okay?" I called to Kendall.

My only answer was a muffled sob.

I stopped and looked up, way up, and found them, her clinging to the big trunk with her maxi dress swirling around her legs, him balanced on the thick branch like it was a pulpit, in jeans and T-shirt and the beanie from Friday, using a clump of moss like a handle to steady himself.

I wasn't sure how high they were, maybe twenty feet, but it was far enough that I couldn't make out his face, only the shadowy movement of his body, and that he had a stick in his other hand.

"Will." I did my best to keep my voice nonthreatening. "You need to let her down."

Grace rushed up and grabbed my arm. "Be careful. There's no telling what he might—"

The hum started, low at first, zipping through me like an electrical current. My thoughts scattered, but on some level I recognized the vibration from the Greenwood party. And then came the explosion of blinding white, taking away everything, everything but the quick, X-ray flash of blurred shadows against the bleached-out night. But then that faded, too, leaving only the high curve of a roller coaster.

And it all started to play, exactly like it played through the shadows of my sleep, Chase silhouetted against a bloodred sky, running . . .

Except he wasn't running this time. He stood there unnaturally still, looking down to me.

Because it wasn't Chase, I realized, trying to pull myself away from the flashback. This was Kendall's boyfriend, Will, balanced high on a tree branch, looking down at me, as if listening, waiting.

"It's her," he mumbled over the rush of the wind. "She's here. I found her."

The images blurred, *fused.* I tried to pull them apart, tried to separate before from now, memory from reality, but everything kept spilling together, and then I could see Chase again, lying on the ground trying to talk.

You're okay, I'd promised.

". . . get out."

The night stilled. Everything. Even the wind. There was no breath, no pulse.

"Get . . . LaSalle."

They were Chase's words.

Chase's exact words.

Except they didn't come from my memory.

They came from high in the tree.

ELEVEN

Chase's words, my memory.

Spoken by a complete stranger.

"Will?" Kendall's voice shook. "You're scaring me. What are you talking about?"

Help's coming, I remembered saying. *Just hang on.*

"*You have,*" he slurred, and I almost dropped to my knees all over again. "*To get out of here.*"

On some disconnected level I was aware of Grace moving, of Grace coming to stand beside me, of her reaching for my hand. But I didn't feel anything, couldn't feel anything, couldn't do anything but stare at Will as he thrust out his arm as if handing me something.

"*Take it,*" he breathed, sobbed.

Not thinking about what I was doing, I lifted my hand to do as he asked.

"LaSalle," Will narrated, quoting my mind as easily as he'd narrated the Book of Revelation.

But before I could say anything, a shadow slipped, and Dylan appeared, crouched on the branch below Will. With a hand to the trunk he twisted back to me, and though darkness stole detail, I knew he, too, realized something was beyond wrong.

He, too, was remembering.

"M-my head," Will moaned. Through the shadows he pressed his hands to the sides of his face. "Everything's so fuzzy," he muttered. "What's happening?"

Dylan started climbing again, faster.

"So beautiful," Will murmured. "Just . . . like . . . you."

Everything inside me locked up. Those were the last words Chase had said to me as he'd hovered between two worlds: me in the hospital room, and my mother beyond the stars.

Without warning Will lunged, twisting around, bracing for an attack. "No, stay away!"

I saw it in slow motion, saw him sway, his arms flail out. "No!"

Kendall grabbed him, steadying him as she used the trunk to steady herself.

The wind whipped Spanish moss into a frenzied dance. I squinted up at Will and Kendall, but saw only two shadows clinging to each other. And I knew. I knew for a second there, when Will had started to fall, Kendall's entire life had flashed before her.

But then the flash was mine again, a quick flicker of darkness arcing over a ribbon of white.

"Something's really wrong!" Kendall cried, and then it was the tree that I saw again, her crouched frantically beside Will.

"His heart's racing and he's sweating like crazy, but his skin's like *ice*."

So was mine.

"Will." I scrambled for the right thing to say, but wasn't sure that was even possible. What did you say to someone who'd just narrated your memories?

"He's terrified," Grace whispered. "Confused."

So was I. "I promise I'm not going to hurt you," I tried. "I only want to talk."

"No," he muttered. "You need to go. You don't belong here."

"Why not?" I asked, but before he could answer Dylan vaulted past Kendall, grabbing the branch above him for balance.

Will jerked back, edging closer to the thinner end of the branch.

Dylan swung back to Kendall. "Can you get down by yourself?"

She looked beyond him, toward her boyfriend. *"Please, Will."* Her voice broke on the words. "You need help. That's why I called your dad Friday. This is all because of the accident."

Accident?

"You're not well yet. But you will be, I *promise*. You have to let us help you."

He twisted without warning, dropping to swing to the branch below.

Kendall screamed. "Will, no!"

Dylan dropped down after him.

Will lunged back to the trunk, scrambling animal-like from branch to branch. I could see him coming, knew Dylan would never catch him in time. Instinctively I raced forward, grabbing Will's hand as he dropped down beside me.

The quick, violent rush of energy threw me backward.

He swung around, his eyes finding mine. They were dark, like a cornered animal, and I was the hunter.

"It's okay," I whispered. My heart pounded in my ears. "I'm not going to hurt you. I just want to talk."

Slowly, mechanically, he lifted his hand, bringing his fingers to the soft strip of leather wrapped around my wrist. His eyes, gentler now, glistening, met mine. *"You didn't take it off."*

And for that second, the world stopped. He looked at me with a quiet desperation, the beanie pulled lower making his eyes look bigger, the way they pleaded, begged.

"Everything's okay," I tried to assure him. "You don't need to be scared."

His head snapped up, alert, listening. "They're here," he muttered.

"Who?"

He jerked back, watching me a long, frozen second before twisting and vanishing into the shadows.

I took off after him.

"Trinity, wait!"

The warning in Dylan's voice registered, but I wasn't about to stop. Something had just happened. Something huge and bizarre and completely unexpected. Something that changed everything.

No one had ever looked at me like that, like they recognized me, like they knew me on a thousand different levels, but were terrified.

Except Dylan.

And *terror* wasn't the right word.

But none of that mattered then. "Will!" I shouted, tearing at the vines and moss. "Come back!" Knobby roots jutted up all over the place, tripping me. "Let me help!"

Nearby something splashed.

I spun toward the play of moonlight along the ripples of a wide creek. Not too far away, through the shroud of trees, an old stone bridge arced from one side to the other.

"Trinity!" Dylan shouted, closer. The rough edges of his voice scraped in too many raw places. *"Answer me!"*

I rushed into the reeds along the side of the creek. "Over here!"

He caught me before I could take a second step.

I fought him, twisting around. "You can't let him get away! Did you hear what he said? I need to talk to him."

Dark hair fell against Dylan's eyes, but couldn't hide the glint of silver. It was the same way he'd looked when Grace's grandmother had spoken about dreams and destiny.

"I know," was all he said, and then he was running toward the creek.

Maybe I should have stayed there and waited, but I didn't know how to do that. All I could think about was the way Will had looked at me, and what he'd said, words he should not have known, the way he'd touched the bracelet. I had no idea what that meant, but I knew it meant something.

And I knew it was huge.

"Trinity?" Grace called as I scrambled down the steep, muddy slope. "Where are you?"

"By the creek!" I waded in, searching the reeds.

Stillness slipped from all directions, a stillness at odds with the frenetic rush inside me. It was like barging into a tranquil painting, with the moonlight on the water and the serene stone bridge, the way the undergrowth looked like sleeping shadows. Nothing stirred. Nothing moved.

"Dylan?" He had to be somewhere.

Behind me, something snapped.

I spun around. "Dylan? Will?"

Kendall broke through the shadows, Grace a step behind her.

"Where are they?" Kendall cried, holding her sides. *"Where's Will?"*

"I don't know!"

She darted past me to the rocks tumbling down into the water. "Will, please!" she called, wading in. "Answer me!"

Not sure what else to do, I hurried in after her.

"He could barely stand, much less swim," she said, trudging deeper. "If he went into the water . . ."

I caught her by the arm. "If he's still here, Dylan'll find him," I promised, but the second I spoke I saw him running along the other side of the moonlit ripples, alone.

"He's gone," Kendall whispered.

After crossing the stone bridge, Dylan vanished among a cluster of trees before emerging in front of us. His hair was wet, his T-shirt and jeans clinging to his body. "He got away."

Kendall turned, hugging her arms tightly around her middle. Holding herself like that, as if holding everything together, she stared at the maze of sprawling trees and network of paths, the roads leading off to soccer fields and a dog park, a small amusement park. If someone didn't want to be found, there were about ten thousand places to hide.

"I've never seen him like that," she said into the push of the wind. Slowly, she turned back to me. "What happened back there? You had that look on your face, like Friday night, was I right? Did you get a reading from him?"

The wind kept blowing, sending hair slapping against my face. "Yes," I whispered. Darkness lurked around Will, shadows like

Madam Isobel talked about. Their residue rippled through me even now, a faint, unsettling current humming beneath the surface.

"But it was like an X-ray," I said. Black against white. Stark. Unsettling. "I couldn't make it out."

"He was terrified," she whispered. *Of you.*

I didn't need to look at Dylan to feel the burn of his eyes. "There's a lot of that going around," I muttered.

"It was all so different at the party," Kendall said. "At first he was just *Will,* like he used to be. We walked through the woods and he told me how sorry he was for how strange he's been acting." Smiling, she looked down at a simple silver ring on her right hand. "He said things were going to get better and we danced in the moonlight."

And then it was me lifting my arms and wrapping them around my body, holding on tight.

"That's when I texted you. But you didn't come, and we went back inside, and he got all edgy again, saying I had to go, to get out of there. That I shouldn't be there." She looked off again, in the direction he vanished. "And all that bad stuff happened. He got in his car and Grace and I got in mine, but he didn't go home. So we followed him and ended up here, and that's when he freaked."

Grace shot me a quick look.

Kendall's eyes filled. "The doctors said this could happen."

"Doctors?" I asked, remembering what she'd said to him before. "You said something about an accident?"

She nodded. "Earlier this year," she said. "After that is when he changed. The doctors warned us he might seem like a different person for awhile, that his behaviors might change, the things he likes. That as the brain finds new pathways his whole reality could shift."

I glanced at Dylan, he glanced at me.

"And maybe that's what's happening," Kendall kept on, before I could ask the growing list of questions firing through me. "But I think he's stepped into something dangerous, like drugs. I could smell beer on him." Her eyes filled. "Do you think that's what you're picking up?"

"Maybe," I said. There was definitely bad stuff going on at the party.

"Like calls to like," Grace whispered oddly. She stood on the other side of Dylan, looking off toward the trees. But I knew that's not what she was seeing.

"He's broadcasting," she said. "Broadcasting loud, like when you see a bunch of cars run into each other and catch fire, and you call nine-one-one, screaming." Hair blowing, she turned to me. "Like you broadcast to me," she said. "The dream I had, the woods you were in tonight." Here eyes were all dark and glowing, the psychic's eyes, seeing what only she saw. "But not everyone can hear."

I stood without moving, even as Dylan stepped closer. Vaguely I was aware of him shoving the damp hair from his eyes, leaving it to fall against both sides of his forehead.

"This accident," he said into the thickening silence. "How badly was Will hurt?"

Kendall twisted toward him, her face suddenly ashen, her eyes like an unseeing doll. "He died."

TWELVE

No.

That was my first reaction. Kendall was being dramatic, exaggerating, letting the dark current of fear carry her away.

Then I looked at her, really, really looked at her.

Fear and grief and trauma, they left a mark on people, like a weight on the soul or a scar on their heart. Sometimes it could be hidden, glossed over with a smile or perfect makeup or through a flurry of activity, a coat of paint. But then the stillness would come, that moment when pretenses fell away and you thought no one was looking and your guard lowered, your smile cracked. That's when the residue leaked through, when the shadow fell like an icy veil separating you from the world around you, the world that went on, didn't hurt, wasn't changed.

I saw it all in that one brief second before Kendall shuttered it away, exactly like I sometimes saw when I walked into the shop and found my aunt standing near a display as if she had no idea who or where she was.

"He flipped his four-wheeler," Kendall whispered. "He was thrown about twenty-five feet."

Wordlessly, I lifted my hands to my mouth.

"He hit his head on a tree." Memories drenched her eyes, dark and painful, like a movie that would never end. "They called it a traumatic brain injury, some kind of hemorrhage that wouldn't stop."

My own memories started to play, merge.

"We . . . we were all there at the hospital."

Running, falling, the sharp blast of pain. The sudden wash of white. Machines beeping.

"He coded in the ER," Kendall whispered.

Grace stepped closer, silently reaching for Kendall's hand, and I saw it, the quick transferred flood of pain that lashed through her.

"They . . . they got him back and put him in a medically in-duced coma until the swelling went down."

Everything slowed, the wind, my heart. Mechanically I stared down at the bracelet, the words burned into the leather: HONEST, IMPULSIVE, STRONG. FEARLESS.

"Because you're you," Chase had said, explaining why he made it. *"And no one else is."*

The memory hurt in ways I'd never anticipated that night, despite the shadows already slipping closer, and my inability to keep Dylan from my dreams.

Blinking, I saw Dylan lift a hand to Kendall's shoulder, touch-ing her with the same steadiness as he'd touched me earlier. But something was different. Warmth glimmered in his eyes, warmth like stars of the purest silver.

When he'd touched me, his face, his eyes, had been cloudy-night blank.

"How long?" he asked.

"Two weeks."

"No, how long was he dead?"

Kendall lifted her eyes to his, hesitating before answering. "Six minutes."

Without breath.

Without life.

Tears streaked down her cheeks. "We thought he was gone," she sobbed as Dylan slid an arm around her and tugged her closer.

Death is but a transition . . .

But not everyone completes the transition. Some people came back. Some people got a do-over.

I watched them for a disjointed second, Kendall between Grace and Dylan, each of them supporting her.

"After he came out of the coma, what did the doctors say?" Dylan asked.

She looked up at him, swiping tears. "That he might be different. But he knew who I was, who his mom and his dad were, his sister. Everything seemed totally normal until later, when we were alone." She squeezed her eyes shut, obviously remembering. "He started calling for his dog."

The night held its breath, and so did I.

"I tried to tell him that Duke wasn't there," she said, shifting to stare off beyond the trees. "But Will insisted his dog was right by the bed with a red Frisbee in his mouth."

The wind slipped around us, soft, chilly, as a new picture started to form, and a new possibility.

Was Will imagining things, or was he tapping into something beyond, like Grace and I did? Was that what I was picking up on? And if so, what was *he* picking up on?

"I didn't know how to tell him Duke died when they lived in Seattle." More tears spilled over. "That went on for a few days, but the doctors said hallucinations like that were normal with traumatic brain injuries, that there would be lots of stuff he didn't remember and needed to relearn."

Like the black holes in my own memory.

"They said it would take time for him to sort out fantasy from memory, from reality."

I'd been told the same thing.

Dylan turned to look at me over her head, and for a second it was like the Greenwood party all over again, touching without the faintest movement.

"He says it's not happening anymore," Kendall said. "But sometimes I'd swear he's living in a different moment than I am, with different people."

Because in all likelihood he *wasn't* hallucinating, something inside me whispered. He was like me.

That's why I picked up his distress call.

And, like I'd been not that long ago, he was on a collision course with something bad.

I didn't say anything to Kendall, because I didn't want to scare her, and I didn't want her to say anything to Will before I could talk to him. He was freaked out enough as it was.

Everyone dreamed and imagined stuff. Finding out that the things you saw or heard or felt were actually real and meant something, well, that took some getting used to.

Dylan knew. He didn't say anything, not to Kendall and not to me when we walked back to the car. But I knew that he knew. I could tell by the tight web of tension radiating from him, even when he moved. He didn't touch me, didn't look at me. He just walked through the woods back to his dad's truck, as if he was somewhere way far away, totally alone.

He unlocked the passenger door and I climbed in. A few seconds later he slid behind the wheel and put on his seat belt, flicked the ignition, and drove into the night.

Music played softly, something country. Neither of us moved to change the station. The clock read 1:07.

With one hand on the steering wheel, he kept his eyes straight ahead. I stared out the passenger window, trying to process all that had gone down.

"You okay?" he finally asked.

His voice, quiet, contained, totally unexpected, made me jump. I swung toward him, catching the glowing numbers of the clock out of the corner of my eye.

One eighteen. That was eleven minutes of silence. It felt like a lifetime.

Pushing out a breath, I searched for the right word. *Okay* wasn't it. *Surprised. Confused. Intrigued. Uneasy.* They came closer.

"It's always been so clear before," I said. "The things I see, even when I didn't understand, like with Jessica and Chase—"

I broke off, but Dylan's eyes flashed anyway. I saw that, saw the lines of his face tighten as he stared straight ahead.

Biting down, I breathed in like Julian said to, pulling the air as deep as I could, for as long as I could, before exhaling.

"They were like little videos," I said after a long moment. "Fifteen or thirty seconds playing in my mind. I didn't always understand what they meant, but I could see what they were. They were in color and they had detail. It was like I was right there, standing on the sidelines, watching."

"But tonight was more like an X-ray?"

"A flicker, kinda like my memo—" I'm not sure why I broke off that time. I only knew that suddenly everything inside me knotted tight, holding back the words.

"Like your memories?" he asked quietly.

My throat burned. My eyes scraped like sandpaper. "Like a horror movie," I sidestepped, "when the lights flash and all you get are these quick, fleeting images breaking through the darkness."

Dylan slid me a look. "Before it goes dark again."

Yeah. "Like that," I said, "just a real quick image, but instead of going dark, everything went white like . . ." The realization stunned me. "Like when you die."

With another look, this one longer, Dylan slid his hand from the wheel, toward me.

Before the warmth could tempt me, I pulled back.

"Is that what you think?" he asked, leaving his hand there for a second before returning it to the wheel. "That Will's going to die?"

"I don't know," I whispered, haunted by the memory of Kendall's eyes. She'd lost him once. I couldn't imagine going through that a second time. "But I feel something around him, something cold and desperate." Fear.

Gradually we slowed, finally stopping at an empty intersection.

"I–I know what that's like," I surprised myself by saying, but once the words started, I couldn't stop them. "To see things you don't understand, that frighten you. That you can't explain, *can't change.*"

Through the play of light and shadows Dylan turned toward me, and for the first time since we'd left the park I looked at him, really, really looked at him, his wide cheekbones and the sweep of dark hair, dry now and falling against his jaw. And even though he faced me, I would have sworn that whatever he was seeing, it wasn't me.

"And you do, too," I said. He'd witnessed so much, and never once had he doubted or asked for an explanation.

"You know you don't have to understand for things to be true or real," I said. That's why he wasn't saying Will was some kid whacked out on drugs, or that the quick flash meant nothing, that I should forget about all of it and walk away, leave it alone. Because from the very first moment, Dylan had never doubted. Anything. Not my visions, nor the fact that I had to see them through. He'd never tried to pull me back or stop me. He simply went with me *like the perfect bodyguard.*

"Is that because of my mom?" It made sense. Dylan had been exposed to the unexplained since he was a little kid. "Because of the work she did with your dad?"

The change was subtle, quick flares of little muscles in his arms and face I would never have noticed had I not been watching.

"No," he said with more breath than voice. "It's because of mine."

THIRTEEN

Earlier crowds and floats had filled the streets. Now, only beads dangling like thousands of glittering earrings from the trees remained.

No headlights cut in from either direction. No light at all, other than the faint glow from the dash.

"She loved music," he said, looking beyond me, toward the darkened shotgun houses. "No matter what time of day it was, my mom had the stereo on. The house was never quiet." He kept his right hand curled around the steering wheel, his arm a barrier between us. "Until she died."

My chest tightened. I hardly knew anything about his mother, other than what his grandmother had told me when she'd called *my* mother a witch. Dylan never talked about her. Actually, he never talked about himself, either.

"That's what I remember the most after she was gone," he

breathed. "The quiet, the way it poisoned the house, like this endless, silent drone."

There'd been a lot of that around the condo.

"The doctor gave my dad medicine to help me sleep, but I hated pretending like that, like everything hadn't been twisted inside out. It felt wrong. So I stopped. And one night I woke up in my room."

The room I'd woken up in a few hours before, drifting in that soft cocoon of safety and dreams.

"It was dark and I was alone, but I wasn't afraid, and there wasn't the gut punch like there usually was. Everything felt okay, normal." He looked directly at me, but I knew he no longer saw me. No longer saw the night. Not *this* night. "It took awhile for me to notice the music."

My breath caught.

"And I forgot," he said, the dull hoarseness to his voice saying how wrong he thought that was, that he'd forgotten that his mother had died. *"Everything."*

But I understood. Because sometimes it happened to me, too, in those first hazy minutes before the world crystallized around me, everything would feel all right. And for a heartbeat it was like being in the before all over again, and I'd do something like reach for my phone, or for Dylan, like I'd done earlier when I opened my eyes to find him leaning over me.

"It was like the accident never happened," he said. "Like she was there and everything was normal, *because of the music.*"

I wanted to look away. The naked emotion in his eyes hurt in ways I didn't want to feel, not anymore. I didn't want to see inside his past like that, *his soul.*

"I swung out of bed like it was Christmas morning and I was going to run in and find her sitting beside the tree."

My eyes stung.

"Except it wasn't coming from Mom's stereo," he said, quieter now. "It was my clock radio, playing her favorite song." His chest rose, fell. "And I just stood there staring, realizing my dad must have turned it on."

Already I knew that's not where this was leading.

"That went on for four weeks. I'd wake up at the exact same time, to the exact same song."

Because when we slept, our consciousness slipped from the constraints of our bodies, and limitations fell away. When we slept, forever slipped closer, and possibility took over.

"I started locking my door, but the song kept playing, even after I pushed my dresser in front of the door and a bookcase in front of the window."

And I could see him, see the little boy he'd been, with dark shaggy hair and bare feet dragging furniture across his room, to banish the music.

"That kind of music doesn't stop," I whispered.

The breath ripped out of him. "Every night Elvis sang."

Maybe a country ballad still drifted from the stereo, maybe he'd flicked if off. I didn't know, couldn't hear anything but the faint echo from a few hours before.

"Elvis?"

"She had a thing for him."

"W–what song?"

Through the sweep of hair falling against his cheekbone, his gaze burned. " 'Can't Help Falling in Love.' "

No, someplace inside me whispered. *No.* But the lyrics sang through the fringes of my memory, exactly as they had in those last moments before I opened my eyes at his father's house.

"She didn't believe in good-bye," Dylan said. "Or endings. Only transitions."

Love extends beyond any transition.

Vaguely I was aware of a car zipping around us. Only then did I realize we were still sitting at the stop sign.

"She always said if it didn't work out in this lifetime, then maybe the next."

I made myself breathe. "The next?"

His eyes met mine, darker now, not those of the grieving little boy, but the guy who dove into rivers and ran into burning buildings, who didn't fear fear, who didn't question things that couldn't be explained, but *who knew.* Who believed.

"Life doesn't begin with birth or end with death, that's what she said. Every soul has a journey, and every journey takes lifetimes to complete. The end of one is merely the beginning of another."

He didn't move. He didn't. But I felt him, felt the touch feather deep, deep inside me, in that place I would have sworn could no longer feel anything.

"Through them all, connections remain. Souls that touch, that connect, can never really separate, even if life carries them in different directions."

Around us the night deepened, and I could hear it again, the soft whir of music from the radio. And the idling of the engine. And the wind from outside, pushing against the car. But the echo of his words played through me.

Nothing prepared me for the sudden slide of his smile. "She said I was her grandfather."

I couldn't stop the quick smile. Kids coming back as parents? I knew a bunch of people who'd like to do *that.*

"Did she seem like your *granddaughter*?"

A soft light played in his eyes. "Only when she chased dragon-flies."

One after the other, the zingers kept coming. Without thinking, I lifted a hand to my chest, but before I touched the cool bronze curve of my mother's amulet, Dylan's gaze followed my hand.

"She always said they're the souls of those who have come before us," he said, and then his hand was there, slipping by mine to finger the greenish crystal in the center. "Darting by to see that we are safe, and to remind us of what is to come."

Something soft and warm whispered through me, but before I could say anything, the necklace slipped back against my chest, and Dylan turned from me, and then we were driving again, the blur of houses giving way to the sleepy mansions of the Garden District. In only a few minutes we'd reach the quirky galleries and shops of the Warehouse District, and I'd finally be home.

"W-what happened to her?" I whispered. "Your mom?" *His granddaughter.*

His hands tightened against the steering wheel. "A car accident."

"How old were you?"

"Eight."

There was so much about him I didn't know. "I'm so sorry," I said.

He slid a hand to the stereo and pressed the CD button. "It was a long time ago."

"But you still miss her." I knew he did. I could see it, feel it in the dark eddies swirling around him. That kind of loss didn't go away.

"I wonder what she'd be like," he said, "what her voice would sound like." Slowing, he eased into a right turn. "But sometimes I'd swear she's only a room away. I can feel her, see her in my dreams."

I'd never thought about Dylan dreaming.

What else do you see in your dreams? someplace inside me asked, but that question wouldn't come.

"Do you still hear the song?" I asked as we passed the World War II museum.

His shoulders rose, fell. "Not in a long time." He pulled alongside my building, stopped, and turned to look at me. "Trinity."

And I knew, I knew the second his voice tightened around my name, the conversation was turning, too, and I wasn't going to like where it was going.

"Just because Will knows things about Chase doesn't mean he is Chase, or that he's not dangerous."

I stiffened. "I know that."

"And if he calls you tomorrow? If he's ready to talk about what you're picking up from him?"

Then I would drop everything. "I'll be careful."

Dylan's eyes hardened, that was the only warning I got. "Like you were last fall when you went back to my apartment with me?"

It was a low blow. I sat there, stunned, hurting in ways I'd never expected moments before.

"When you had absolutely no idea who I was?"

I stared straight ahead, feeling it all over again, the surprise of opening my eyes, all sprawled in his lap with the warmth of his mouth lingering against mine, the shock of realizing he'd gone into the river after me.

But, "I knew who your father was," was all I let myself say.

"You knew who you *wanted* him to be. Who he told you he was. But you knew nothing for fact, and nothing about me."

That wasn't true. I had known. Without logic or explanation, I'd known Dylan wouldn't hurt me, not physically.

"That was before," I said simply. Before *a lot*. Before everything. "That Trinity doesn't exist anymore."

"And yet you went to that party tonight and have no idea how you ended up in my dad's flower bed."

Everything inside me tightened. There was no defense for that, other than the truth. "That won't happen again."

For a long moment we sat in the dim glow of the streetlamp, looking at each other. Neither of us said anything. I think we both realized there was nothing left to say.

Once it had all been so easy. All he had to do was look at me, touch me, and everything inside me slipped quietly into place. From that very first night by the river, he'd been a forbidden whisper through my thoughts, a shadowy figure I tried to forget, but couldn't. It didn't matter if my eyes were open or closed, he was never too far away.

Then I woke up in a strange hotel room and discovered that what I'd mistaken for a dream was real. That Dylan was there and had been all along.

Longer.

Later, while the world around us burned, he'd put a hand to my face and kissed me with an intensity that seared through everything I knew about right and wrong. He'd been with me in the dark corners of LaSalle's mind, and those last moments at Six Flags.

But now those memories had sharp edges, and they sliced like broken glass against my soul. And it all came back, every word, every breath, and I was there again, between Dylan and Chase, in those final moments before the illusion shattered.

And I always would be.

"Tonight—" waking up in his bed, reaching for him, kissing him, "—should never have happened." None of it even seemed real, like it had happened to someone else. How else could I explain the fact that for a few minutes there, I'd forgotten . . . *everything*?

But now I remembered, and all those hurting places inside me bled all over again.

"But I'm glad it did," I said. "Because now I know it can never happen again."

Because nothing was the same anymore, and there was no way to go back. No way to *breathe*. Sometimes you had to touch fire, *to hold your hand in the flame to feel the burn sear through you,* to know that you could never make that mistake again.

I'm not sure what I expected, what I wanted. Maybe for Dylan to say something soft and gentle and healing, like he had so many other times. Or maybe for his eyes to flash, or for him to reach for me and tell me that no, I wasn't wrong. I wasn't wrong to open my eyes and reach for him. He was my safe place, the sanctuary I could always count on.

But he didn't say anything, didn't move, just sat watching me as if I were telling him about my chemistry test.

"I can't be with you anymore," I said, reaching for the door.

"I know."

I should have stopped there. I should have stopped right there and gotten out of the car, walked away, and not looked back.

But I wasn't as good at walking away as he was.

"Is that why you stayed away?" I asked.

Finally I saw it, the slightest movement in his body, and his eyes met mine. And with one word, everything inside me stilled.

"No."

FOURTEEN

It shouldn't have mattered.

Whatever Dylan's reason for staying away, it didn't change anything. What was done was done. Days gone by could not be erased.

But I didn't know how to leave that word dangling between us and walk away. That was what he did.

"Then why?" I asked as a yellow blur whizzed by, driving home the fact we weren't moving anymore, that we were stopped, and had been for a long time.

"Trinity." Weeks had passed, but I would have sworn smoke from the fire at the gallery still roughened his voice. "Don't do this."

"Don't do what? Ask questions? Try to understand why the last time I saw you, you promised me everything would be okay, but now you're looking at me like you can't wait for me to get out of the car?"

A rough breath ripped from him. "Don't try to hold onto things that aren't there."

"I'm not."

"Then let it go."

It was hard to believe five minutes before we'd been talking about soul journeys. "Answer my question."

The way he stared straight ahead shouted that we'd reached a stalemate. The car was idling. Air whispered from the little vents. A song drifted from the radio, Arcade Fire, I think. But the tight web of stillness stamped all that out like a blanket to a campfire.

I was reaching for the door when two quiet words shot across the seat. "It's over."

I told myself not to turn back, but even as I issued the command, I knew I wasn't going to pay attention to it. It was that whole putting my hand in fire thing. I had to look, to see his eyes.

Except what I found didn't burn. It chilled.

He twisted toward me, that curtain of hair again cutting against his face. Darkness fell around us, the only light coming from the dashboard and the glow of the streetlamp. But it was enough to see the point-blank look in his eyes.

"That's why I stayed away." The words were matter-of-fact, without any emotion. "LaSalle is dead. No one's trying to hurt you."

Absorbing that, I knew he was right. I'd known it all along.

"I guess this is good-bye." Mechanically I pushed at the door and stepped into the mugginess coming off the river. "Thanks for the ride."

Maybe he said something else, maybe he didn't. I don't know.

All I could think about was crossing to the three concrete stairs leading to the door to the building, and not looking back.

Green. That was the first thing I noticed when I walked inside. While I'd been gone, Aunt Sara had painted the main room a soothing tone of green, like that of a fern. Instead of the funky, exposed brick that I'd always thought a perfect match to her personality, we now had arboretum mellow.

Sage, I remembered Victoria telling me. Julian claimed the color had mystical, cleansing properties.

Swooping up Delphi, I glanced over at the paint-splattered tarps covering every piece of furniture except the sofa. There the plastic had been pulled back, and Aunt Sara lay curled into herself, sleeping.

I walked closer, careful not to make any noise, and smiled at the green smudge against her cheek. She didn't have on any makeup. Her clothes were old and ratty, her hair soft and loose against the dark purple of the cushion.

It was the most natural and relaxed I'd seen her in four weeks.

I really missed that Aunt Sara.

Not wanting to disturb her, I tiptoed back to my room and slipped inside. The clock read 1:53, but I knew sleep was not going to happen. I'm not sure how long I stood there staring at the blown-glass dragonfly, but when the walls started pushing in, I knew I couldn't stay there, not with the enormity of all that had happened buzzing through me: someone had drugged me and dumped me in a flower bed, a guy I'd never met had narrated my memories, the white almost-vision had flashed again, and Dylan and I finally said good-bye.

No way could I sit in that room or crawl into bed and try to go to sleep, not when I could barely breathe.

After grabbing my journal, I hurried to the front door, letting myself out as quietly as possible. I knew where I needed to go, who I needed to see. The elevator brought me down to the parking garage. All I could think about was getting into my grandmother's old Buick and driving.

Halfway there, I stopped dead in my tracks, even as my heart started to slam. Because I wasn't going anywhere, I realized abruptly, not with Jim Fourcade's truck blocking my car.

Dylan hadn't gone home.

The front door pushed open, and he stepped into the yellowish lighting.

I didn't move, not at first. I just looked at him, the burn in my throat so hot I wanted to scream. But that wouldn't change anything. I could tell that by the stillness to him.

It was no accident he'd positioned himself between me and where I wanted to go.

"Come on," he said, as if we'd planned this. "I'll take you."

My throat tightened. I probably should have turned and gone back inside, but I didn't want to be upstairs any more than I wanted to be back in the truck with Dylan. All I could think about was going somewhere quiet, where no one watched and no one waited, where I could exhale, and let go. Where I could sort through all that had happened, and think.

I wasn't about to give Dylan the power to send me where I didn't want to be.

Lifting my chin, as if this was all quite ordinary, I walked past him and climbed inside. He followed and shifted the car into drive, not saying a word as we left the parking garage. Within seconds we were on Canal Street, like I'd been planning, and he kept driving, kept looking straight ahead without saying anything, exactly like I was doing. We both knew there was nothing left to say.

Once or twice I thought about telling him where I wanted him to take me. I'm not sure what held me quiet—curiosity, I think. I wanted to see where he was going.

And then we were there, where I'd intended all along, pulling off the road beside the ornate iron fence. The gate was locked, but that didn't mean anything. The fence was easy to climb.

Wordlessly I got out of the truck and made my way along the shadows of the sidewalk, toward a few big oaks. There, shielded from view, I made my way to the other side.

I didn't need to turn around to know that Dylan followed. But he didn't say anything, and he didn't try to stop me. He simply walked behind me.

It was no secret New Orleans cemeteries weren't the safest places at night.

A cool breeze swirled among the moonlit tombs. I made my way along the grassy path, past row after row until I reached a crypt surrounded by a second iron fence, this one equally ornate. There, I let myself in.

"Hey." I went down to my knees and lifted a hand to the cool, smooth marble, dragging my finger along the letters of his name.

CHASE MICHAEL BONAVENTURE

The tears didn't come as freely now, not in the big gulping sobs like they had at first, when they'd ripped up from deep inside. Now it was more of a slow swell of pressure pushing to get out.

I closed my eyes for a long moment, opening them to the shadow-draped statue of the Virgin Mary, where Jessica had kneeled long after the burial ended.

Seventeen candles sat in a series of circles with a marble vase in the middle, smooth and curved, perfect for the fresh white tulips that were always there. Nearby, amid a scatter of leaves, parade cups full of doubloons sat among water-logged envelopes with smeared ink across the front, all except the one secured in the plastic bag, with the perfect, beautiful handwriting.

"I'm sorry," I whispered for the thousandth time. *"I'm so sorry."* For everything.

The wind swirled closer.

"It's happening again," I murmured, "but maybe you know that. It's the first time since—" But he would know that, too. "You were there, weren't you?" I said, fingering the leather bracelet. It was the only way Will could have said the things he said. "I'm trying. I *want* to help." I had to. "But I can't see anything."

It was like receiving a 911 call, but having the voices too garbled to make out what was being said.

One by one, I lit the votives. "Maybe you can let Will know he doesn't need to run," I murmured. I still didn't understand how everything worked, but I got that I didn't need to understand for it to be true. "Let him know I'm okay, that I just want to—" I broke off, the quick, sudden smile catching me by surprise.

"You probably told him *to* run, didn't you?" That would be so Chase, always trying to drag me away from trouble. "But I can't pretend I don't know something bad's going to happen." Not until I figured out if I could help.

"I'll be careful," I promised, lifting my hand to drag a finger along the four words etched beneath the dates.

SHINE BRIGHT. SHINE FOREVER.

"We can do this," I said, surprised by how strong that thought made me feel.

I sat there a long while after that, letting the night whisper around me, until slowly the burn of each breath lessened.

Not ready to leave, I picked up my journal to try to capture how I was feeling. Instead I found myself opening to the letter I'd started a few nights before.

> Chase,
> I'm so sorry.
> This isn't the way things were supposed to be.

I felt closer to him here. The words flowed more easily.

> I can still see you that first day of school, when I walked into homeroom and you looked up and smiled at me. You were the first person at Enduring Grace to do that, and it was like this whole new world opened to me. It was all so normal. All I wanted was to get to know you better, be with you. I never meant

Regret stabbed at me, my gaze guiltily finding the beautiful old oak across the pathway, where Dylan stood in the shadows, guarding me still, even now, not looking at me, but totally alert. That was what he did.

When I looked back down, the words came.

to hurt you.

But I had. I'd hurt Chase by not being able to share all of me with him, not being able to let him inside. There'd been this invisible wall separating us, and I hadn't known how to tear it down.

Then I'd slipped into my dreams, and cried out for someone else. And Chase had known. He'd known someone else came to me in my dreams.

The tears fell faster as I told him how sorry I was.

I'm so sorry. I would change it all if I could.

I had no memory of falling asleep. No memory of dreaming. No awareness of anything until the chirp of birds broke the quiet, and I opened my eyes to a pale pinkish glow. Still half-asleep, like emerging from a deep coma, I lay there a few moments, not thinking about much other than how warm the blanket felt. Then I blinked a pigeon into focus, and disorientation blasted into panic.

I'd fallen asleep in the cemetery.

Jerking upright I reached for my phone and pulled up the time: 7:07.

Aunt Sara was my first thought. She had to be freaked.

No texts or voice mails waited, only my journal, open next to the remains of the votives. I reread the letter, my eyes locking onto the last two words.

I wouldnt

The handwriting was not mine.

With a hard slam of my heart, I twisted around, back toward the old oak on the other side of the path.

Dylan no longer stood there. Julian Delacroix did.

Confused, I scrambled to my feet, the blanket finally registering. It hadn't been there before.

"Hey," Julian said, coming toward me. He was dressed in all black like always, but his hair was loose and falling like dark silk against his shoulders, like I'd seen it that one night at the condo, when he'd held my aunt and chanted.

"Julian," I said, hurrying toward him. "What are *you* doing here?" Where was—

The memories rushed in before his name did, of those final minutes from the night before, when Dylan and I had sat in front of the condo, and said good-bye.

"Dylan called me," Julian said, as if that explained everything, and actually, *it did*. But then he went on. "He told me what happened."

And asked Julian to come take his place.

I hated the quick twist inside me.

Dark eyes glimmering, Julian opened the gate for me. "So about this vision trying to form," he said. "Would you like to see if we can find it?"

The astral plane. The hypnosis-like technique had worked to access my subconscious and find my aunt. Maybe it would help me find the rest of the X-ray vision.

Sitting in the front seat of Julian's car, I still wasn't sure what to make of the trippy things Will had said the night before, or what I was going to say to my aunt when I got home. But apparently Dylan's father had called her after I appeared at his house, explained that I had fallen asleep there, and that he'd bring me home in the morning.

I didn't like lying, but telling my aunt what *really* happened was even less appealing.

I was scheduled to work from ten until six, when Victoria and I were supposed to head down to the river for fireworks after sunset. Only a few minutes after eight, I had enough time to get cleaned up and slip over to Horizons before heading to Fleurish! With luck, by the time I walked through the doors, I'd have the answers I—or Will, actually—needed.

We were almost to the condo when Victoria's text zipped in.

You went to a party last night?

The dark words burned up from the little white bubble of the phone, communicating her hurt. I hadn't thought about her finding out, but of course there'd been too many mutual friends (and not-so friends) there for it to stay a secret.

Sighing, I did my best to downplay it.

Just kinda happened. I didn't stay long.

Her response flashed up the second I hit send.

You were DRINKING?

Guilt flashed, like a kid caught sneaking cookies at bedtime, but before I could say anything, another text arrived.

If you haven't seen my FB page, you better go look.

I sat there totally still, staring at the words a long moment, no special abilities needed to know I wasn't going to like what I was about to see. I'd closed all my accounts, but that didn't stop the garbage.

I pulled up the app, scrolling past a bunch of quizzes before finding my name.

For Trinity. Next time you might not be so lucky.

It wasn't the first time someone had posted a message for or about me on Victoria's page, but it *was* the first video.

My stomach churned as I put my fingers to the sideways triangle, and ninety seconds of lost time played across the screen.

I barely looked like me. My hair was wild, stringy, my eyes dark and disoriented. Outside the theater, I was running, stumbling. Twice I fell. Once I scrambled back up. The second time a guy came over and offered me his hand, the same guy who'd offered me a drink at the Greenwood party, I realized, and asked me to dance last night.

Through the grainy image I saw him help me to my feet and put his hands to my shoulders. I saw myself look at him, then twist away and run into the woods.

He ran after me.

My heart started to race. Was he the one who'd taken me to Dylan's, or the one who'd slipped something into my drink? He *had* offered me a drink at the Greenwood party . . .

And, who'd stood in the shadows, watching? *Recording?*

That wasn't really a hard question, not given the fact my BEF

(Victoria's acronym for Amber, the "E" standing for Enemy) had been there.

After stabbing DONE, I went back to the main page and stared at the poster's name: Bliss. The picture was the generic Facebook silhouette. Security controls prevented me from seeing anything else.

But none of that really mattered, I knew. Only finding a way to access the vision trying to form.

"After four minutes without oxygen, brain cells begin to die," Julian said after I told him about Will coding in the ER. I'd been at Horizons all of five minutes. My hair was still damp from my shower. Aunt Sara had been awake when I got home, but she'd just smiled that robo-smile and asked me how Jim was doing.

It was weird being relieved and sad at the same time.

Now Julian moved about his shop lit mostly by candlelight, with its mystical display of crystals and essential oils and hand-made jewelry, incense, and all kinds of metaphysical books. It was always so peaceful inside, as if simply by walking through the doors you were transported to someplace quiet and safe.

"Most people never make it back from that," he said. Hair secured in the customary ponytail now, the one that emphasized the sharp lines of his cheeks and his high forehead, he looked up, his eyes drilling into mine. "Those who do are never the same."

FIFTEEN

"Headaches," he went on, "confusion, seizures." His voice lowered as he added, *"Hallucinations."*

He totally had my attention.

"It's a lot like what you experienced after your concussion," he said. "The brain is trying to function again, but certain paths might not work anymore. Pieces of information or learning may no longer be available, so the brain compensates by trying to fill the blanks or find new ways." He smiled. "It can be quite over-whelming."

Will was definitely overwhelmed.

"But," Julian went on, "there are other changes, too, changes reported by a significant number of people who have passed through death's door, only to return. Straddling the line between this world and what lies beyond is no simple matter," he said. "Many report *gifts of spirit.*"

"Like narrating other people's memories?" I asked.

"It's like being born again," he said, "when we're pure and open to possibility, before we're limited by what's pounded into us about what's real and what's not." His eyes glimmered. "If you listen to children, it's amazing what they will tell you. Many remember where they came from, where they were before. And for many, the channels of communication stay open, until some well-meaning adult shuts them down."

Like my grandmother had done.

"Two-year-olds frequently talk about past lives," he said, turning to a shelf behind him. He scanned a row of books before selecting one and turning back to me. "The detail is astonishing," he said as I saw the title: *Past Lives*. "It's a well-documented phenomenon. They recognize places and the people with whom they are connected, *those they should avoid.*

"But it's not just children," he continued. "The only difference is they don't try to write off what they know as coincidence. The truth is, most of us know things. Most of us have the experience of thinking about a friend or family member we haven't spoken to in awhile and then suddenly they call, or getting a tight feeling in your throat long before bad news actually reaches you, or maybe it's the feeling that you're not alone, when according to your eyes, you are."

Automatically I lifted a hand to the dragonfly at my chest and closed my fingers around the smooth edges. That was all I had to do to feel her.

"Almost every time there's a plane crash you'll hear about someone who was supposed to be on board, but at the last minute changed their mind. And the stories about mothers who cry out at the exact moment their son is killed in war, or children who see grandparents beside their bed, whispering good-bye, at the exact moment that grandparent is five states away, taking their last breath."

I stood there, a quiet New Age chant drifting through the shop, something that sounded like it belonged in an ancient temple.

"You think that's what's happening with Will?" I asked after a moment. "That because of his near-death experience, he's . . ." I searched for the right word. *"More sensitive?"*

Julian laughed. "Try wide open." His eyes met mine. "Like you are. You must always remember nothing limits us more than us." Frowning, he pivoted suddenly toward the front of the shop, where a wall of windows overlooked Royal Street. "Does your aunt know you're here?"

With a quick kick of my heart I turned to see her standing across the street, unlocking the door to Fleurish! At least that's what I thought. Beneath her coat, her shoulders were stiff, her back rigid, her hair pulled into a severe ponytail. Slowly she turned, twisting to stare across the street, straight at window into Horizons.

I darted behind a tall black armoire.

"I take that as a no."

I flashed Julian a quick look.

"You didn't tell her about last night, either, did you?"

How could I? "I didn't want to upset her."

The strangest look drifted across his face. "Don't worry," he said. "She can't see you, not through the glass and the shadows."

It was an odd choice of words.

But with them he was moving away from the window, toward a large table covered by a black cloth and containing bundled herbs. "How is she? Any better?"

I sighed. "Sleeping a lot, working long hours, and painting," I told him. "The condo is now as green as a greenhouse."

His shoulders rose, fell, all fluid and smooth, like he did everything.

I picked up a pink quartz pyramid, running my finger along the cool smoothness. "I don't know how to reach her," I said quietly. "The only time she seemed alive was when you were there."

He'd taken care of everything, cooking and cleaning, sleeping on the sofa for several days, until the night Aunt Sara woke up screaming and slapped him when he tried to comfort her. She'd shouted for him to leave. She'd been crying.

He'd stood without a word and walked away.

It was almost like she hated him, *or secretly loved him,* but that somehow LaSalle was still there between them.

"You should go over and say hi," I suggested with a quick glance across the street. She no longer stood outside. "See for yourself."

Standing beside a wide table of crystals and votives, Julian looked at me as though I'd asked him to walk in front of a firing squad—or send *her* in front of one. "She doesn't want me there right now."

"That doesn't mean she doesn't need you," I blurted out.

With a quick blast of shadows in his normally all-knowing eyes, he went back to arranging crystals. Even across the room, I could feel the sudden web of tension.

"What's the deal between you two?" One of these days I was going to find out. Because there totally *was* a deal. Or at least there had been. "Why do you both get weird when I mention the other?"

He looked up, the shadows in his eyes replaced by something

dark and fathomless. "Let it go, Trinity. Not everything can be forced. Some things are simply too fragile," he said, his gaze drifting back toward Fleurish! "If you try too hard, everything shatters."

My heart squeezed, partly because of the irony of the word, *flourish,* but mostly because he was right. You couldn't see inside, not through the glass and the shadows.

"One day I'm going to kill that man for what he did to you and Sara."

Two things struck me simultaneously: one, how his voice wrapped around my aunt's name, making it sound like Laura with an "S." *Saura.* It made something inside me smile and cry at the same time.

The second was what Julian said about LaSalle. "His partner already killed him," I reminded.

The strangest smile curved his mouth. "Doesn't mean I can't do it again."

The trippy words did a quick stutter-step through me. "Like in another life?" I asked, thinking about what Dylan had said the night before. "Or the astral?" I made a funny face. "Can you kill someone there who's already dead?"

His smile widened, carving crinkles around his eyes. "I'll let you know." He glanced out the window for a long, chant-filled moment before turning back to me. "You ready?"

White surrounded me. Walls, the floor, the sofa, everything was as white as the blizzard hiding the vision trying to form.

I'd been in the upstairs room only once before, the afternoon four weeks ago when Julian had first helped me slip from one consciousness into another. With the soft, transcendent sound of harps and gurgling water drifting around us, we did everything the same: I sunk against the couch and drank chamomile tea, he kneeled beside me and fastened a cuff around my arm to monitor my vitals, *just in case.*

The first time the precaution had been hypothetical. Now I knew exactly what could go wrong when I left my body and traveled to a higher dimension.

"Do you think it'll work?" I asked. "That I'll find the vision trying to form?" *And finally see what lay beyond the white.*

Julian looked up from a laptop, white, of course. "It's possible." His mouth thinned, not a smile, but not a frown, either. "But you must remember the astral plane is not like a mall where you go shopping for memories or visions. The last time we had a target, a specific dream I was guiding you to."

I concentrated on the trail of smoke rising from a single white votive, but through the flame I could see the small dark room all over again, where my whole life had caught fire.

Sometimes I thought I'd been foreseeing the inferno at the chapel. The twist of longing and fear was the same, the intensity. Even the words.

"You're here. You're really here."

"Always."

But there'd been no fire in the shadows of the room where I'd dashed after running through the tall grass, not the kind with flames anyway.

"Don't think about last time," Julian said. "You don't want to block yourself."

If only it was that easy. "I'm trying not to." But the hard slam of my heart refused to slow.

He put two fingers to my wrist, his mouth moving in a silent count for over a minute. At least two passed before he pulled back and lifted concerned eyes to mine.

"Do you want me to call someone?" he asked. "Dylan?"

I felt my eyes flare. "No." The word came out with more force than I meant, so I softened it with a smile. "I don't need him."

Julian's brows drew together.

I settled deeper against the sofa, ready to get started.

"So if the astral is where our dreams come from," like he'd told me before, "but we don't remember dreaming, does that mean we didn't go?" Because for weeks there'd been nothing but darkness.

"Memory is not an accurate gauge of reality," Julian said quietly. "There are many reasons we forget, and many reasons we rewrite. What we think we know, what we think we remember, is barely a fraction of what there is."

The room wobbled, a faint swirl of vertigo, over the moment it happened.

His eyes narrowed, as if he could tell. "You're still focusing on your senses," he said. "That's what you've been taught. It's what's easy. But the astral is beyond that which can be seen and touched . . . remembered.

"The astral is the source," he said, more quietly now, all reverent-like. "And the source is without limits or boundaries."

A quick rush of warmth swirled through me. *The source.* "Is that how I slip between the past and a glimpse of the future, all simultaneously?"

"It's all your life, sweetheart. Past, present, and future are man-made constructs to compartmentalize time. It's tidier that way." His smile was oddly gentle. "Looking at a moment in isolation is like looking at the Mississippi River and pretending its point of origin is the past, and its destination, the Gulf of Mexico, is the future. Not true. It's all there simultaneously."

Flowing. Always flowing. Sometimes smoothly, sometimes over rapids. Sometimes in drought, sometimes in flood.

"Now allow your eyes to close," he instructed. "Let your breathing slow."

I did as he said, concentrating on the flow of oxygen moving through me while he walked me through the rest of the process. Within minutes my body grew heavy.

"You're safe," he murmured, his voice further away. "And loved. Let yourself feel it, a slow infusion of warmth through every cell of your body."

The scent of lavender surrounded me. The rhythm of my body slowed.

"You see the elevator opening before you . . ."

I did, a shimmering portal opening through the darkness, exactly like it had when Dylan and I—

I broke the thought, but not before adrenaline streaked through the calm.

"Easy," Julian said with slight pressure against my wrist. "Just breathe and step through the door."

I did.

"Now lift your hand, lift it slowly, and push a button . . ."

They all glowered, shimmery and iridescent, like the door from last night, at the party.

Everything shifted again, a stronger ripple through the stillness.

"You're going home," Julian continued, and that place inside me, that tight, locked-up place, started to open. "You're going back to where you came from . . ." *The source.*

Warmth swirled slower, deeper, insulating layer by layer, until my whole body surrendered.

"Feel the light, feel it blend with your own . . ."

His voice drifted from somewhere far away, somewhere against the horizon. And with another drugging breath I was floating, too, drifting beyond the here and now, with the stars.

"Trinity."

"I'm here," I whispered, and with my words, the doors I'd forgotten about, those to the elevator, slid open. Beyond them stretched a corridor, long and glimmering.

I hurried forward. "Show me," I called, searching.

The first door was locked. So was the second, and the third. No matter how hard I pushed or pulled, they didn't budge.

Through the silence came the drift of music, soft at first, louder with each slow breath I took. The hypnotic rhythm drew me, syncopated drums pulsing from behind a vibrant blue glow. I reached for a glass knob, cool to the touch, turned—and the door fell open.

Everything flashed, an X-ray-like explosion of shadows strewn against the bleached-out night, grotesquely twisted, frozen where they lay, as if they'd been dancing when the world ended.

But then white spilled in from all directions like thick, globby paint and the door slammed shut.

"No!" I grabbed the knob and twisted, trying to push back in. *"No."* But it was like reinforced steel between me and the other side, keeping me out.

I spun around and ran to the next door, twisting the knob and shoving inside, but stopped the second I saw the silhouette of the roller coaster against a fading red sky. *"No."* This time it was a whisper. I didn't want memory. I didn't want the past. I wanted what was yet to come.

Jerking back, I raced down the corridor, no longer shimmering but starting to fade, the doors blending together until there were no more.

"No!" I shouted, lunging.

"Trinity!"

I slammed down hard, the quick, violent impact reverberating through every cell of my body. I hung there, frozen, my breath burning from the inside out.

"Easy," came a voice from behind me.

Blinking, I found Julian crouched beside me, and the final fringes of darkness fell away.

"What happened?" I asked against the sudden sting of brightness. Everything inside me raced, like I was running still, running always, even when my body didn't move.

He reached for my arm, sliding two fingers to my wrist. "You started to run."

And now I was on the floor all the way across the room.

"Your pulse is thready," he said.

"What does that mean?"

He kept his hand on my arm, no longer taking my pulse, but not breaking the contact, either. "Stress," he said. "Anxiety, your body's reaction to what you experienced." Something dark flashed in his eyes. "Tell me what you saw."

Pulling myself into a seated position, I did. "It was so fast," I finished. "Like an X-ray, gone before I could see any details." Only the unnaturally contorted shadows.

"What about your dreams? What are you seeing at night?"

I wrapped my arms around my middle. "I'm not."

"What do you mean, you're not?"

"I'm not dreaming," I said. "Just . . ." I searched for the right words. "It's dark, like a night without stars. And sometimes I feel like I'm running. But all I ever see is the roller coaster."

His brows drew together, his lips pressing into a thin, tight line.

Suddenly I stilled. "What are you thinking?" Because he so was. The dark swirl of his thoughts gleamed in his eyes.

Slowly, they met mine. "You're blocked."

SIXTEEN

He called it psychic amnesia.

"It's like a door closing," he said. "Just as people can lose their memory or identities, trauma can impact psychic abilities, too."

I kneeled on the floor of his bright white room, trying to remember the last time I knew something before it happened. Four weeks, I realized, the morning I'd awoken from the dream about Aunt Sara, and Dylan and I realized she wasn't in Mexico, like she was supposed to be.

"It's a self-defense mechanism," Julian said, "like a scab, the brain's way of protecting you from something you're not ready to experience, grief maybe. Guilt."

"But I feel all that," I said. *All the time.*

"Then maybe you're protecting yourself from feeling it on a deeper level."

I looked away from him, toward the white sofa against the white wall, but for a second I saw the tarot card I'd pulled from my mother's deck, the woman bound and blindfolded.

"For many years I've run a Web site," Julian said as I realized I needed to investigate the VIII of Swords a little more. "With metaphysical information and quizzes, experiments, courses for strengthening abilities, that kind of thing."

His voice was so quiet it was like he'd moved away from me. I think that's why I turned to look, to make sure he was still there. He kneeled right there, only inches away, his face a harsh collection of lines and memories, broken only by a few dark strands slipping from his ponytail.

"There's a discussion forum," he said, all monotone-like, "where people talk about their experiences and share information. A lot of users post daily, comparing notes and sharing their learnings, like a public journal." He paused, his eyes locking onto mine. "Several years ago the online quiz results dropped simultaneously, and users began flooding the message boards, reporting that their sixth senses had gone silent."

Like mine.

"Within twenty-four hours, there was a surge in Web site traffic as people all over the world joined the discussion, with similar experiences, dreams, visions, telepathy, all silent. Even mine."

His?

"I'm not like you," he explained gently. "But I can sense things, feel them, like Grace does." With a rough breath he looked beyond me, toward the white blinds hiding the window to Royal Street. "Like with LaSalle. I knew he was bad news," he murmured. "And I knew he would hurt Sara." *Saura.*

My heart kicked.

"I could feel the coldness in him," he said. "But that's all it was, a feeling."

"Did you tell her?"

Julian looked away from the window, but not completely back at me. "She wasn't interested in what I had to say."

"I never liked him, either," I said.

Another rough breath ripped from him. "I know."

And just like that, a quick sharp chill cut through me. If I had psychic amnesia, how would I know the next time someone like LaSalle came along?

I gave Julian a few seconds before asking him to continue.

"We all went dark," he said slowly, woodenly. "At the exact same time. There was a disturbance in the energy field, something so strong it blotted out everything else."

He made a stark contrast kneeling in all black against a room of white. Even his eyes were spooky dark. Unseeing, I thought at first, but then realized they were seeing, seeing something *unimaginable*.

"Eight days later, two planes slammed into the Twin Towers."

Everything inside me stilled.

"One into the Pentagon, and one into a quiet Pennsylvania field."

The stillness became a rushing, sharp and cold, sweeping through me like the holocaust he described.

"Many of us felt them," he said, "*every single soul* as they transitioned, like lights going out."

"Julian," I whispered, moving without thinking to reach for him. I didn't know what to do, so I took his hands, tears stinging my eyes as my fingers closed around tight fists of rage.

"It was the same with the Indonesian tsunami and Japanese

earthquake," he said, "when tens of thousands left us. It took weeks before the residue faded enough to allow things to get back to normal."

"But that seems counterintuitive," I pointed out. "Shouldn't there have been premonitions? Dreams? Shouldn't psychics have *seen* what was coming? Isn't that what it's about?"

The light blazed back into his eyes, bright and dark at the same time. "People did," he said. "Thousands of them, for months and months leading up to nine-eleven."

Months. Not days or hours. Because dreams didn't come with timestamps or places.

"Something of that scale," he said quietly, "of that magnitude, when it happens, it's like a solar storm zapping satellites."

That's what he thought was happening to me.

"So . . ." I said, rocking back. "How do I get back to the way I was?"

Time. The trigger could be anything—*a scent or a picture, a feeling, place, person, event, even a simple word.* Or there could be no trigger at all. One day I might wake up like I'd been before, or maybe I wouldn't.

Julian's answer was not the one I wanted.

Long after I slipped into the alley behind Horizons and made my way to Fleurish!, his words lingered. Everything he said made sense, but if I was blocked, how could I warn Will? How would I figure out what the X-ray flash and grotesquely twisted shadows meant?

Customers flowed in and out all day, giving me little time to keep the cooler stocked, much less come up with ideas. *How was a blind person supposed to see what lurked in the shadows?*

Placing another round of water on the shelf, I hesitated. Blind people didn't see. They *sensed* things, exactly like I'd been doing for days.

I closed the cooler and turned back to the crowd buzzing the shop. Aunt Sara had warned me today would be nuts, but I hadn't expected *zombies*. A group of five with thick Boston accents swarmed the T-shirt table, laughing at our newest addition, a black baby-doll tee with glittery purple writing emblazoned across the front: DO IT WITH FLEURISH!

I couldn't stop the quick, silly grin or the memory of the February afternoon when Aunt Sara blurted out the phrase while cooking gumbo.

I missed the way things used to be.

"If you can't do it with fleurish, why do it at all?" one of the zombies laughed. Dancing, they twirled toward the cash register, taking their place with clumsy curtsies behind a fallen angel holding hands with a tall skinny Elvis.

The laugh just kinda happened. Despite the wild Mardi Gras stories I'd heard, no one had mentioned heavenly creatures partying with the undead. Or middle-aged ladies in cat masks and black body stockings, or drunk old men in diapers with saggy man-boobs.

Yeah.

Slipping to the back, I checked messages for the tenth time that hour, hoping to hear back from Kendall, who was waiting to hear from Will, who was at a doctor's appointment. Earlier Grace and I had compared notes, and Victoria texted about the fireworks.

Thankfully, she'd gotten past the fact I'd gone out without telling her.

Knowing I needed to get back out front, I was looking up from the phone when a name toward the bottom of the screen made me do a quick double-take at the list of recent texts: Victoria and Kendall (both from today) and three names from yesterday: Sara, Grace, and . . . Dylan.

Everything whirred around me as I slid my finger to tap his name, and the green-and-white message bubbles flashed onto the screen. Actually they were all white, from him.

> What's wrong? Where are you?
> What's happening?
> Tell me where you are. I'm in the car. I can be there.
> Send me a blank message. Do anything. Just let me know
> you're okay.
> Trinity?

I blinked, but the dark letters kept lashing at me. The texts were all from the night before, at the beginning of my missing two hours.

No, no, no, I thought. Confused, I pulled the message trail down to reveal the beginning of the exchange, the green bubble of a sent message from *my* phone.

> Sp,etjomg wrpmg///meed upi

"Oh, my God," I whispered, but barely any sound came. At some point between when the world had started to spin and I'd awoken at his father's house, I'd texted Dylan.

And never texted him back.

Looking down at the keypad, I quickly deciphered what I'd been trying to say.

Something wrong . . . need you.

With a hard kick of my heart, I switched from the texts to the phone, and found his name there, too: seventeen missed calls and four voice messages. I didn't want to listen. I wanted to simply delete them, like I wanted to delete everything that had happened after I'd opened my eyes to find him leaning over me and slipped back in time, before all the bad stuff happened.

But I couldn't delete what had happened, and I couldn't make myself delete the messages, either.

Moving deeper into the shadows of the back room, where it was quieter, I listened.

"Trinity, it's me. I got your text. Where are you? Are you okay? Call me back."

"Come on, where are you? What's going on? *Answer me.*"

By the third his voice was really quiet. "It's okay if you don't want to talk to me. Text me. Let me know you're okay."

There were no words in the fourth, only the rough sound of breathing.

My eyes flooded at the realization that I'd reached out to him, and he'd reached back. But I'd left him there, hanging, until I showed up at his father's house.

I'm not sure how long I stood there before Aunt Sara called back to me, because the bell on the door kept jangling and she needed help.

Hastily swiping my eyes, I gathered as much water as I could, hurried to the front, and restocked the cooler.

"So is this great, or what?" she laughed as the zombies blew her kisses on their way out. I think they were guys, but couldn't be sure.

Nor could I believe that beneath the coat Julian and I had seen her wearing, she'd hidden a gauzy poet's shirt and tight, laced corset, black leggings, and knee-high boots topped in gold trim. With a red bandana around her forehead and her crazy dark makeup, she looked like she belonged on the set of a pirate movie.

And she was smiling. And for a second there, when the zombies were flirting with her, something had glowed in her eyes, and I would have sworn it was the old Aunt Sara.

"Insane," I agreed, closing the cooler.

"Just wait," she said. "You haven't seen anything yet."

Everyone kept saying that.

Straightening the T-shirt table, she looked up. "Where'd you go this morning, before coming here?"

I looked away, toward a man and woman with three small kids walking in, all dressed in New Orleans Saints jerseys complete with shoulder pads. Through the open door, the Horizons sign glowed.

"Oh, you know." I didn't want to lie, but if by some chance her smile was real and not the robo-kind, I didn't want to take that from her. She'd been talking about Mardi Gras for months.

"I wanted to see what was going on," I hedged.

With a T-shirt half-folded, she smiled. "Fresh air is good."

Guilt flashed.

Across the street, a long line of people dressed in black waited outside Julian's shop. Mourners, I thought a little morbidly. That's what they looked like. But that made no sense.

"What's going on over there?" I asked.

She didn't answer.

Twisting toward her, I found her beside a wire dress form draped with gobs of gaudy beads, staring into space.

Her smile was gone.

"Aunt Sara?" I asked, crossing to her.

Not into space, I realized. She was looking out the glass panel of the door, toward Horizons.

"You okay?" She had the strangest look on her face, like regret or longing.

She blinked. "What?"

I hesitated, not sure if I should ask the question. But it was right there, right on the tip of my tongue, and I couldn't make myself bite it back like I had so many times.

"What's the deal with you and Julian?" Because there totally was one. The memory of his eyes, the dark, glassy swirl of hurt and longing, almost an exact mirror of hers, haunted me.

Her look washed so blank you would have thought I'd asked her to explain quantum physics. "What do you mean? There is no deal."

Yeah, just like there was no deal between me and—

I tried to break that thought, but the memory squeezed in anyway, of the forsaken, silver glow from the night before. I should never have let fantasy override reality.

There were a lot of should-never-haves when it came to Dylan.

For a flickering second, I would have sworn I saw all that I felt reflected in the soft brown sheen of my aunt's eyes.

"He cares about you," I said.

She looked away.

"A lot." It was so obvious. "I don't get why you keep pushing him away." It's like she had herself so focused in one direction she couldn't see any others.

"You can tell me," I said as the door jingled. "Did y'all use to date? Did he say or do something that hurt you?"

Her smile bloomed. Her eyes lit up. And the pirate-Sara swept back in. "Welcome, welcome!" Overly animated, she whirred toward a group of miniature fairy princesses.

"Please tell me you have water," begged the frazzled mom pushing in behind them.

"Of course!" Aunt Sara bustled to the cooler as the bell jingled again, and Victoria finally blew in.

"Omigod, it's crazy out there!" she said, dropping her camo-print duffle bag to the floor. "I didn't think I'd ever get here! Are the guys here yet?"

That was the only way her parents were letting her out of the house and into the madness, if Trey was with her.

"Not yet." Eyeing the bag, I asked, "What's that?"

She grinned. "Costumes."

"Costumes?"

"You know," she said, her eyes all glowy. *For tonight.*

My heart beat a little faster.

"Ohhhh," Aunt Sara gushed, hurrying over. "What do you have?"

Victoria, with Cleopatra-straight hair and little black wings sweeping from the corners of her eyes, brightened.

"*Wow,* you look amazing!" she gushed to my aunt, who dropped into a low curtsy.

"Thank you."

I blinked, my eyes darting from one to the other, and for the second time in twenty-four hours couldn't help but think I'd fallen down some bizarre rabbit hole.

"Well," Victoria was saying, "I have these amazing costumes my cousin wore a few years ago." Dropping to kneel by the T-shirt display, she tugged at the zipper. "But um . . ."

I spun around. But ums weren't good. "But um, what?"

"Well . . ." With a silky pink streak sliding against her face, she flashed a guilty smile. "They're, um, kinda voodoo queens."

I felt my eyes widen. It shouldn't have been funny. But it was.

"Oh, I can just see that," I said, laughing. Inevitably a picture of me dressed as the infamous mistress of the night, Marie Laveau, would end up splashed all over the Internet and probably the yearbook.

Victoria made one of her funny, scrunched-up faces. "I know." From her bag, she pulled out something black and silky, but before I could tell the full damage, my phone beeped.

It was from Kendall.

Everything's set. Can you meet us in front of
the cathedral before the fireworks?

"Ohhhh, the fireworks are so fantastic," Aunt Sara said from behind me, and too late I realized she stood over my shoulder, reading every word.

Thankfully there was nothing about Will or my nonvision.

"The King of Rex arrives on a Coast Guard cutter," she was explaining, "and meets up with the King of Zulu." Those were both majorly famous parades. "And the mayor is there, and he hands over the keys to the city, and there's tons of music and dancing and—"

Will. Will would be there.

That was all I needed to know. I could talk to him, warn him. Maybe something miraculous would happen.

After sending a quick text to Kendall, telling her I'd meet her, I shot Victoria a look. "So . . . where's my voodoo doll?"

SEVENTEEN

We changed in the back room, my jeans and hoodie tossed aside in favor of a long, black gown with bell-shaped sleeves longer than my arms, and a pin cushion at my wrist. Victoria wriggled into an outfit that looked more like a black corset with a short skirt in front and long train in back.

"Now your hair," she said, coming at me with a flatiron.

Twenty minutes later, my hair hung like a curtain of dark silk, white powder muted my olive skin, heavy goth-black lined my eyes, and bloodred stained my lips.

"I freakin' *love* it!" Victoria said, and for a heartbeat everything seemed so normal, so like before . . .

But the second thoughts caught up with feelings, the feeling fell away.

Hating the quick tightening of my chest, I stepped back and lowered my chin, studying my reflection in the full-length mirror for customers trying on T-shirts.

Victoria joined me, sweeping her hair to rest over one shoulder.

"Trey's gonna flip," I predicted.

"Lucas would tell me I look like a slut."

"Lucas is an ass," I shot right back.

She laughed. "Then let's do this."

Aunt Sara took pictures like it was prom or something. She had us pose all over the shop, some normal, some totally goofy with me and Victoria jabbing needles into little straw dolls while Trey and Deuce pretended to writhe in agony. Ready to get on with things, I started to protest, but in those few minutes when she had her camera to her eye, the shadows fell away, and it was just me and my aunt again, being us, being silly. And silly made something amazingly warm feather through me.

Until my hand brushed the bracelet wrapped around my wrist, and the brief time-out faded.

Wall-to-wall people crammed the French Quarter.

With the guys dance-walking a path in front of us, we made our way through the blizzard of beads and doubloons toward the square. Lights blared from every window of every building, with parties overflowing onto second-story balconies. A different song blasted from every shop and restaurant and bar.

On a normal night psychic tables would fill the plaza beyond the cathedral, with musicians and other performers. But tonight hundreds of people stood body-to-body, dancing and watching the fireworks explode over the river.

Pushing up on my toes, I looked for Kendall.

"S'okay, Primetime," Deuce said, drawing me toward the gently blowing canopy of a huge palm. "Repeat after me."

I turned toward him. He and Trey weren't the Blood Brothas tonight, they were the Blues Brothers, with black suits and fedoras, even the dark sunglasses.

"Primetime?" I asked, not needing to see his eyes to know he was about to pull a Deuce on me.

He grinned, his teeth flashing as white as his shirt. *"The Secret Life of a Teenage Psychic,"* he said, all dramatic and announcer-like. "It's the next sure hit."

I couldn't help it. I laughed. "I'm not so sure about the secret part," I pointed out. He'd seen the video of me from the night before. Everyone had.

With an arm around me, he turned me toward a blast of white exploding over the river, little glimmers falling like thousands of shooting stars against the night.

"True enough," he said, his body moving to the rhythm of the music. Nearby, Trey and Victoria danced. "That's why we've got rules."

Another volley of fireworks shot up against the sky, the boom reverberating along the riverfront.

"Rules?"

He nodded, lifting a hand to slowly slide the Ray-Bans from his eyes. The gleam there rivaled the show beyond the levee.

"No drinking," he said. *"Anything."*

He didn't have to worry about that. "No drinking anything," I repeated.

"No wandering off by yourself."

A quick little twist went through me. "No wandering off by myself," I agreed, all solemn-like.

"If you start feeling like something's wrong or you're going to have a vision—"

"You'll be the first to know," I promised as a huge ring of red blossomed over the levee beyond his shoulder.

He'd been dancing, but the rhythm stilled, the line of his jaw, where the thin stubble of his chinstrap ran, tightened. "And if you see the guy from the video last night—"

I stopped him with a quick flash of my eyes. "I know what to do," I said, playing along. Very deliberately, I pulled the voodoo doll from a hidden pocket in my costume and lifted it between us, smiling as I jabbed a needle between the straw legs.

Deuce winced. "Thatta girl."

The fireworks kept exploding, faster now, one brilliant, flickering burst after another.

"We're good," I said, with another quick scan for Kendall. It was six thirty. She should have been here. Of course, with the tight swarm of people, she could have been right behind me and—

The quick breath of cold whispered like a spider down the back of my neck. I stiffened, knowing—*knowing* someone was there. Watching.

Deuce crowded in on me. "Mile High?"

I spun around, searching hundreds of masked faces as Victoria dragged Trey over.

"He's gone," she said, saying more with her eyes than her words.

"You saw someone?" I asked.

She nodded. "Over there," she said. "I looked up and saw him staring at us." The bright red sparks showering down behind her made her darkly lined eyes look more severe. "He looked familiar, like maybe I'd seen him at a party, but he turned before I could place him."

The smoky wind tore around us, whipping at the big palms by the iron fence.

"You think maybe it was that Will guy?" she asked.

My heart kicked hard. "Maybe." That's what I *wanted* to believe, but then Kendall texted a few minutes later, and the Will theory went out the window.

> Change of plans!
> Will wanted to go to some place on Bourbon.
> I have no idea why, but we're at Club Rouge.
> Can you come?

The place was packed.

A bald, goatee'd bouncer stood at the door, allegedly checking IDs but he seemed as gone as everyone upstairs. With nothing more than a smile, the four of us squeezed past him and up the narrow staircase to the music blasting from the second floor.

Red. That was the first thing I noticed. The lights were all red, creating an amber haze against the frenzy of dancing. Black lights swirled, not rapidly like the party at the theater, but more of a dreamlike progression, pale crimson fading into shadows, shadows into darkness, hovering for a slow breath before giving way to the muted, dawn-like glow of crimson all over again, and again, like an endless roll of day into night, night into day, but with each hour lasting only seconds.

Victoria grabbed my hand, leaning in close. "Wicked," she murmured.

That was one word.

The mindless electronic rhythm hummed through me, the crowd swelling from all directions. I texted Kendall, letting her know we were there, then we split up to look for them. Victoria and Trey headed for the bar, while Deuce took my hand and soul-walked me to the dance floor. With each swirl of red into black, black into red, something inside me swirled, too, a cold aware-ness, a knowing like in the Square, making my chest tighten, as if my throat wasn't letting enough air squeeze through.

The energy was the same, broken and desperate, as the night before. The white didn't flash, but for a disjointed second I could see the twist of shadows again, collapsed against the ground, fro-zen there. *Forever.*

Half-dancing, half-walking, Deuce guided me deeper into the thrash of sweaty bodies, keeping my hand locked in his. With every step we took, every slam of the drums, the hum inside grew stronger, a low-wattage electricity zinging through my blood, telling me Will was close.

Will, or *someone.*

Stopping, I lifted my face to soft red haze, pulling in a thousand different scents, perfume and smoke and beer, sweat and some-thing else, something earthy and pungent. Something that swirled through me, quietly urging me to let go, and *just be.* For once. For that night, that moment. I'd been fighting for so long, to breathe, to understand. To forget.

Especially to forget.

Everything.

Somewhere along the line, part of me had. I'd built a quiet wall inside me, to protect, Julian said. But I didn't want protec-tion. It was like cheating—or hiding. I wanted to live, to be the me I'd been before.

Around me, hundreds morphed into a mindless entity moving

in unchoreographed synchronicity. Closing my eyes, I felt them, every one of them, all the individual strands wound together, escape and freedom, pain and agony and a desperate cry for release.

It all tightened through me, exactly like the night at the abandoned hospital where we found Jessica. Emotions lingered, echoes surviving long after bodies failed. You heard them, even when you heard nothing. You *absorbed* them, lived them, even when you felt nothing. And in that moment, I felt so much more than I had in weeks.

The numbness was fading.

Opening my eyes, I stared at the flickering contortion of bodies, knowing, *knowing* that someone stood directly behind me, waiting. But nothing prepared me for the strung-out face I found when I turned around, the sunken, raccoon-rimmed eyes and stringy hair, the diamond stud in the left nostril, and the wobbly way she reached for me, as if we were BFFs, rather than BEFs.

"Trin-Trin!" Amber slurred, holding onto my arm. "I almost didn't recognize you!"

I'd noticed the differences before, that she was paler if possible, skinnier. And I knew she'd bombed a few tests, that her grades were slipping. And of course the ickiness with her and Lucas.

But seeing her like this three out of four nights sent a bad feeling sinking through me.

"Isn't it *a*mazing?" she sang-said, wobbling into me.

I caught her, holding her up so she didn't fall.

Deuce and I exchanged a quick look. His was total WTF.

Amber gazed up at me, her eyes somewhere between lost and gone. "I should have known you'd be here when I saw your hot friend . . ."

The quick tightening was automatic. "Deuce and I—"

"No," she said, all dreamy-like, and yeah, I was still holding her. All I had to do was let go, and she'd drop like a rock. "Not the Blood Brotha."

I wasn't following her. "Who? Where?" How could she know about Will?

"Your bodyguard guy," she muttered.

My heart kicked, and the current inside me revved into a dark rush. A rush I recognized.

A rush I didn't want.

Spinning around, I searched the shadows.

Amber pulled back, looking at me through a tangle of sweaty hair stuck against her mouth. "He was with some girl."

I stilled.

It didn't matter.

It so didn't matter.

He could. Dylan could totally have a girlfriend.

How could he not?

"He can be with whoever he wants," I whispered over the forceful rush of blood through my ears and into the even louder techno rhythm. The two merged, fusing, pounding.

"Really?" Amber breathed, gazing up at me as she swayed. Or was she dancing? I didn't know, wasn't even sure there was a difference. "That's what I was hoping you would say."

Disconnecting myself—from her, the moment, from the iciness seeping through me—I pushed up on my toes and looked beyond the wall of Deuce and the girls swarming him, searching for Kendall or Victoria or—

I stopped before another name could form.

It didn't matter, though, even if his name *had* formed. I

couldn't see anyone. The trancelike pulse of the dance floor stole faces and identities, leaving only amorphous anonymity.

"Wasn't last night amazing?" Amber sighed, hanging onto me again.

I turned to look at her.

Lost, I thought again. She was so totally, completely lost.

"I saw you with that guy," she murmured, smiling.

And I knew. She so took that video.

"Do you want some more?"

We bobbed along with the crowd, the strangest sense of vertigo and this-isn't-really-happening carrying me. Me with Amber. In a Bourbon Street bar. Kind of . . . dancing together.

"More what?" I asked.

The dreamiest look blanked her gaze. *"Bliss."*

The bad feeling from a few minutes before got a whole lot worse.

"Here," she slurred, pressing something into my hand. "It helps, doesn't it? Makes the bad go away, the pain, and leaves only the *bliss.*"

I looked down. Three little yellow pills rested against my palm.

"You wanna go to the bridge with me?" she ask-slurred. *"It'll be like old times."*

Everything inside me tightened. With a steadying breath, I reached out and touched her, running my hand along her bony arm.

The rush of heat shocked me, the rapid-fire flutter of the pulse at her wrist. And her eyes, I realized, they were wide and dark, completely unfocused.

"Amber," I said, as my phone vibrated against my thigh. "I don't think you should be here."

Closing her eyes, she kept right on swaying. It was like talking to air.

Sighing, I reached for my phone and pulled up the text, eager to get on with talking to Will.

People who play with fire get burned.
Go home now, while you can.

Then I was the one swaying. I spun around, searching: Amber danced by herself, Deuce looked up from over his harem, crimson faded into black, and Victoria broke through a group of guys.

"Trinity!" she shouted over the music. "He's here! You have to come, hurry!"

"Where?"

With pink highlights falling against her Cleopatra eyes, she twisted back around and wedged her way through the hot, sweaty kaleidoscope, to the back of the club.

Holding her hand, I shoved Amber's pills into my front pocket with the other and hurried after my friend.

Beyond the dance floor the insanity thinned, but the music still pulsed, and the lights flickered, red then black, black then red.

Five or six girls stood staring wide-eyed toward the narrow hall to the bathrooms. Hands pressed to their mouths, they watched in horror.

Then I got closer, and recognized the dark gleam for what it really was.

Fascination.

Heart slamming, I ran past them, and saw Will crammed against the back wall and Kendall crying.

"Trinity!" she shouted as the guy shoved up against Will went statue still. "Make him stop!"

But I was the one who stopped, the one who froze, staring at the guy with his back to me, the way he stood in a fighter's stance with his feet shoulder-width apart, the sinewy strength, the jeans hugging his legs and the black T-shirt stretching across his wide shoulders, the dark, silky hair cutting in a line beneath his ear, and the intricate lines of the dream catcher inked against his arm.

EIGHTEEN

"This isn't a game," he seethed. "This is real, and if she gets hurt—"

So much hit me at once, dull, little pebbles of anger and frustration and confusion, all rolling through me, giving way to the soft swirl of inevitability.

Dylan.

I should have realized there was no way he was going to let me get out of his car and walk away, not after the bizarre encounter with Will, and not after I mysteriously appeared in his dad's flower bed with no memory of how I got there. Not after Will narrated my memories. Not after everything Dylan and I had been through.

Not when he knew exactly what I was going to do next.

Which he always did.

Whether I wanted him there or not, he always was, at the exact moment I needed him most.

Part of me wanted to be mad or annoyed, to shout at him that I meant what I said in the car, that I couldn't be around him anymore. But life didn't grant time-outs like that, not with Kendall crying and Will staring over Dylan's shoulder, directly into my eyes, like he knew I was the only one who could cage the animal.

Disconnecting myself from the unwanted rush, I squeezed toward them.

"It's okay," I said, sliding in next to Dylan. He stiffened as I reached for him, but I took him by the arm anyway, not thinking about what I was doing until a different rush went through me, this one hot and dangerous. "Don't hurt him."

Moving fast, I caught a glimpse of Victoria and Deuce out of the corner of my eye as I spun toward the wood door of the bathroom and pushed it open.

A group of girls stood bunched around the cup-lined counter, sliding lipstick over their mouths and redoing their eyes, not looking up until Dylan escorted Will to the graffiti-filled wall near the air blowers.

"Hey you fuck-head!" a skinny blonde protested. "What the—"

All Zen-like, Dylan looked at her. That's all he did. Looked at her.

Her eyes, one artfully remade and the other still smeared, widened before glazing over, and without another word, she motioned to her friends. They ran out as a toilet flushed and an older woman hurried from a stall.

Then we were alone.

I shot Dylan a quick look.

Silently he backed off, relocating to stand beside the door so no one could come in, or get out.

Question after question tripped through me, but I had *no idea* where to start. At the Greenwood party, when I'd agreed to follow up with Will, I'd known it was the right thing to do. Because of the flash of white. Now, three days and a whole lot of bizarre later, I realized there was way more at stake than I'd first realized.

It was that whole coincidence thing. *They didn't exist.*

But where did you start? By telling him about the vision trying to form? That I thought he was in the path of something bad? That I thought someone might be following me, too? That his near-death experience had changed him?

The way he stood looking at me, with the breath ripping in and out of him, courtesy of Dylan, told me he wasn't exactly going to be receptive to anything.

But then Kendall looked at me, and gave me the opening I needed.

"I told him what happened at the party Friday," she said. "When y'all were looking at each other." She hesitated, shooting him a tentative look before continuing. "I told him that I asked you to do a reading."

He hardly looked like the guy from the park. The clothes were the same, the jeans and T-shirt and beanie, but there was a quiet control to him tonight, like someone standing guard rather than spinning away from reality.

Through narrowed eyes he looked at me, as if Kendall had requested I perform some bizarre ritual rather—

That's when I remembered I *was* dressed like a voodoo queen. The mirror above the sinks showed dark hair streaking against a pale face, the heavy eyeliner and the faded red of my lips, the little doll hanging from the pocket of my dress.

Wonderful. Not exactly the best start, given there were entire blogs dedicated to the bad things that happened to people after being around me.

The dull throb of music pulsed through the walls and the door, muted, indiscernible, a world away. There was just Will and Kendall and me, and Dylan.

Trying to put him at ease, I offered my best voodoo-queen-next-door smile.

"Kendall's right," I said. "There's nothing to be afraid of. I only want to talk to you."

It would have been way easier without feeling the hot burn of his stare meld with the heat from the exposed bulb overhead. Already little streams of sweat ran down my chest.

"I read about you," he finally said, confirming what I already saw in his eyes. Last night they'd looked dark, but tonight the bright light revealed the color of emeralds, swirling with doubt and apprehension, a determination that hadn't been there before.

"None of that stuff's even real," he said.

I smiled, realizing *exactly* where to start.

"When I was a little girl I had a dog," I told him. "A golden retriever, Sunshine. One day we were playing and she ran into a thicket, and I started to scream. I didn't know why, it was like there was something inside me, something squeezing so tight I couldn't breathe. And then everything started to flash and I saw her, saw Sunshine, lying dead in the grass."

Kendall's eyes filled. Will, never ripping his gaze from mine, simply tucked her closer, and waited.

"But then she was there, running up to me and licking all over me," I said, and for a second I was that little girl again, so crazy relieved to see her dog, and that whatever freaky thing had just happened was only that. A freaky thing.

"Two days later I found her dead on the other side of the thicket," I whispered, and out of the corner of my eye saw Dylan shift.

She'd been alive when he'd come to visit that summer. He'd taught her to fetch.

"Exactly like I saw in the vision."

Kendall paled.

Will took a quick step back against a scrawl of graffiti.

"It was *real*," I told him. "And so was what you said to me last night." I stepped forward, saw him try to step back again. But the wall left nowhere to go.

Lifting my arm, I turned my hand up, allowing him to see the leather coiled around my wrist. "Do you remember what you said about this?"

Unblinking, he stared down at the small dangling charms. "That you didn't take it off," he murmured, for the first time sounding confused.

More pounding at the door. Louder.

"That was a promise I made," I told him. "The day someone special to me died."

Slowly Will's eyes met mine.

"I've known things before they happen since I was a little girl," I said. "And Kendall's right, something happened Friday at the party. I feel something around you, something bad. I can't see it yet, but I feel danger. And . . ." I hesitated, deciding to just throw it out there. "I don't think you're hallucinating. I think you're like me. I think your near-death experience changed you, like it does lots of other people, and that whatever it is you're experiencing, it's real. And that's why I was drawn to you."

Like calls to like.

"Because your energy matches mine," I pressed on, concentrating on him and not the music and shouting from the other side of the door, and not the way Dylan stood there, making sure the moment didn't break. "I think I'm supposed to help you. I *want* to help you. But you're going to have to trust me. You can't keep running."

Kendall pulled back, gazing up at him.

Will looked from me to her, holding her gaze a long moment before looking back at me.

"If you're not seeing anything, how can you help me?"

With a quick glance back at Dylan, I stepped forward. "I'd like to touch you. Sometimes that helps."

You would have thought I'd asked to drive a knife through his heart. Fear, I realized as the blood drained from his face. Will was afraid. But the way he turned to Kendall, the quick streak of regret in his eyes, told me that the fear wasn't for himself.

It was for her.

So much played in her eyes, the memories she'd told me about the night before, of when he'd died, and the desperation from Friday, when she'd asked if I could help, but happiness, too. And love. Hope.

"Please," she whispered. "For me."

He squeezed his eyes shut.

I felt like a voyeur watching them.

Finally he looked at her again, a rough breath shredding from him as he turned back to me and offered his hand.

Not sure what to expect, I stepped closer and pressed my palm to his.

The quick jolt knocked the breath from my lungs.

I made myself hold still, bracing against the current revving between us, stronger than the night before.

The green of his eyes went dead dark. *"He wasn't afraid,"* he said, looking beyond me, beyond *everything.* "Your mom was there."

Everything tilted. *"What?"* I whispered, but before he could say anything, white exploded against black, and the shadows returned, sprawled against the ground with their arms and legs twisted, frozen where they lay.

I sagged, and then Dylan was there, crowding up against me and sliding an arm around me, murmuring for me to breathe.

I did, but each quick pull scraped more than the one before.

"What is it?" Kendall asked while Will continued to stand there, as frozen as the bodies strewn against the darkness of the X-ray flash.

Bodies?

"It's like they all just collapsed," I whispered. In one instant. One heartbeat.

"Who?" Kendall gasped. *"Will?"*

His eyes flashed, and then he was shooting me a don't-say-anything look as he wrapped her up in his arms.

"I don't know," I answered as the door swung open, because Dylan was holding me instead of blocking the entrance. "I couldn't see faces."

Girls rushed in, laughing, ranting. "Omigod, are you idiots crazy?" a Lady Gaga–wannabe shrieked, darting into a stall.

"It's going to be okay," Will murmured to Kendall, staring at me over her head. "I promise nothing bad's going to happen."

But the way he looked at me told a way different story.

A few more girls rushed in. "Come on," Dylan said. "We can wait in the hall."

I looked at Will, the way he'd turned to Kendall and was

holding her, and knew Dylan was right. For now, with the flood of girls to the stalls and the mirrors, we'd have to go somewhere else to finish talking.

Drained, dazed, *disappointed,* I walked to the door and stepped back into the slow roll of amber into black.

Dylan moved so fast I had no chance to prepare, dragging me past the blur of my friends to the back of the hall and bracketing me there, against the wall in the same spot he'd caged in Will.

"What are you doing?" I breathed, but the second I saw the burnished gleam of his eyes, everything inside me jumbled.

"Don't fight me," he muttered, bracketing me so tightly I could feel every vibrating line of his body.

"Dylan—"

He leaned down, brushing his mouth along my ear. "Put your arms around me." There was nowhere to go, no way to escape, no way to miss the hard slam of his heart reverberating through me. "Pretend you like it."

My mouth went dry.

"Now!" he commanded with an odd softness.

Finally the urgency in his voice registered, the same urgency I'd heard when he'd kicked down the door to my aunt's bathroom to prevent me from finding a way to make myself go to sleep. More than a little dizzy, I lifted my arms around his middle and held on—

It was already too late.

NINETEEN

"Trinity."

The voice cut through the pulsing music, low, quiet, so totally, horribly familiar. I looked up, the moment snapping into focus as I realized what Dylan had been trying to do: hide me.

In the shadows of the narrow hall, Detective DeMarcus Jackson stood with his eyes blazing like hot, glowing coal, exactly like they had a month before from the bottom of the stairs leading to Grace's apartment.

It was the first time I'd seen LaSalle's former partner since the funeral.

"Detective Jackson." I kept my voice strong. I wasn't doing anything wrong.

The artsy dreadlocks and big diamond earring made him look like a musician. His silky black shirt made him look successful in a dangerous kind of way. But he was a cop. And he was trained to hide what he thought. Blending in kept him alive. He could be anyone, I remembered thinking once. Like a chameleon, he could shift in the blink of an eye.

But in that moment, I knew exactly what he thought. It glittered in the way he looked at me, the surprise and the disappointment, the accusation.

"Don't make a scene," he growled, and when his eyes slanted over to Dylan, an unspoken conversation flashed between them.

Very unlike Dylan, he eased away from me, giving me a quick glimpse of Victoria and Deuce and Trey.

Jackson took me by the elbow, turned, and stiff-armed the thin wood door behind him. It flew open, and a guy jumped back from a urinal, grabbing himself.

"You need to be done," Detective Jackson said.

It was a good thing the guy had just finished or he totally would have peed himself. He was huge, bigger than Jackson, but whatever he saw in the detective's eyes made him bolt faster than my heart could pound.

Wonderful, I thought as Jackson dragged me in. Another bathroom.

Stale urine hung in the air, the faint residue of fresh pot. Pulling back, I twisted toward Dylan.

Three obviously underage girls stood beyond the door, watching. I couldn't tell if they were fascinated, terrified, or jealous: with his glistening ebony skin and ultratoned body, Detective Jackson looked like he'd stepped straight out of an action flick.

He slammed the door, and locked it.

"What are you doing here?" Something hot and a little wild flashed in his eyes, like that of a father catching his daughter in her boyfriend's bedroom.

It didn't matter if I lied or told the truth. He wasn't going to like either.

I went with truth. "Looking for someone."

"With the Fourcade boy? Did he bring you here?"

I chewed on the inside of my lip, shaking my head.

"You know what this place is, don't you?"

I tried to retrieve my arm from his hand, but his hold tightened. "I'm not doing anything wrong," I pointed out.

He was a big guy. I'd always known that. But he dominated the small, boxy bathroom like a street cat prowling a dollhouse. "You're sixteen years old."

Okay, there was that. Club Rouge *was* a bar.

I told myself not to be afraid. This was Detective Jackson, after all.

But LaSalle had been a detective, too, *his partner.* And we were alone in a small locked room. And his eyes were really wild, not the least bit controlled or cop-like, as they usually were.

"It's Mardi Gras," I pointed out, blinking against the burn of ammonia. "Half the people here are underage. No one's checking IDs."

Everyone knew the cops had bigger things to worry about with thousands of people packed into the Quarter.

"And I'm not drinking," I said.

He came at me without words, wedging me against the disgusting wall and taking my wrist in his hands, pressing two fingers to the pulse point there.

I knew that it raced. How could it not?

"What are you *doing*?" The first claws of panic worked up the back of my throat and thinned my voice. "This is me, Trinity."

Releasing my wrist, he lifted his other arm and shone a pen-light in my eyes. "And this is the third place like this you've been in four nights."

Whoa.

Someone pounded on the door.

"You think I'm on something," I realized. "That's why we're in here." Where Jackson could be a cop and his cover wouldn't be blown. Where he could test me for signs of illegal substances.

Concentration carved a deep line in his normally flawless forehead. His pupils were small, focused, his breath amazingly rhythmic.

I swallowed hard. "I promise I'm not. I was looking for some-one. That's all."

He lowered his arms and stepped back, and right before my eyes, the cop/drug dealer persona morphed into just a man, the one who'd stood steely-eyed with his gun in his hand, his partner in a pool of blood at his feet.

It was one of the few things I remembered from that afternoon.

"I don't ever want to see you in a place like this again," he said in a voice so dangerously quiet I barely heard him. "No matter how bad things get."

Scared, I realized. Detective DeMarcus Jackson actually looked scared. For me.

"You said you were looking for someone. Who?"

I thought about hedging, but didn't see the point. I wasn't doing anything wrong, other than the underage thing.

"A friend's boyfriend." I slid my phone from my pocket as the pounding at the door started again.

"Hey! Open the eff'in door!"

"His name is Will," I started, distractedly.

"Ingram," Jackson finished for me, and with the name the bathroom shrunk around us, creating a nauseating little box.

"How'd you know *that*?" I asked.

Water dripped from the faucet, one drop after another, leaving rust in place of enamel.

"The better question is," Jackson said, "why are *you* looking for him?"

"I told you. He's a friend's boyfriend."

"Kendall," he supplied.

"Yes."

"And how do you know her?"

I told him. With the assault on the door over, I told him about the Greenwood party and the vision that was trying to form, my concern that Will was in the path of something bad.

"How do *you* know them?" I asked.

He let out a slow breath, much like the first time we met, when he and LaSalle had come to talk about Jessica's disappearance. He was so stalling.

"Please," I said. "If there's something—" My mind raced with possibilities. Jackson was a cop. He knew about Will. I had a vision trying to form.

There had to be a connection.

"If there's something I need to know, if something's going on, you need to tell me."

His frown told me he knew I was right. I could also tell he hated that.

"Not here," he said with a quick glance at the two urinals I'd been trying not to look at. "We've drawn enough attention."

I pressed my lips together. If there was one thing a cop who tried not to stand out didn't like, it was drawing attention. "Y'think?"

After explaining to Deuce and Victoria what was going on, we left the bar, Dylan first, me second, Jackson last. He escorted me to my car and followed me home. Dylan, thankfully, rode with him.

Inside the condo, everything looked as it had that morning, with paint-splattered tarps covering the furniture and the ladder still propped against the sage green of the wall. Not yet nine, Aunt Sara was still at the shop and would be for at least another hour.

"Redecorating?" Jackson asked.

Acutely aware of Dylan standing by the window, I reached down and snagged Delphi. I kept forgetting to eat, but she didn't. I was pretty sure my once-emaciated cat had put on another pound.

"Aunt Sara wanted a change," I said, focusing on Jackson.

He ran a finger along the newly sage surface. "That's understandable."

"I like the brick better," I murmured.

"How's she doing?" He turned back to me, his eyes suddenly haunted. "I keep meaning to give her another call."

But what did you say? They'd both been deceived at a fundamental level. I could only imagine what it was like for Jackson, a cop—*a detective*—to realize how completely he'd been played.

"She's trying." It was that whole illusion thing Gran had

perfected. If you pretended the world was a bright, shiny place, if you pretended you were a rock-solid person, then maybe, like slathering paint over bricks, that was the world you were creating.

"She's trying to make everything okay," I said.

A flicker of rage crossed Jackson's face. His dreads gave him the musician look, but in that moment, he was all murderous, betrayed cop.

"So . . . about Will," I initiated as Delphi wriggled from my arms and trotted over to rub against Dylan.

If Jackson wouldn't get to the point, I would.

"What's going on? How do you know Will?"

His eyes met mine, and from one breath to the next, cool, calm slid over the rage.

The prelude was over.

"Six months ago a kid named Jeremy Albright hung himself from the family basketball hoop. He was nineteen, a premed major at Tulane. He was the first."

I cringed, lifting my arms to hug myself. Suicide was one of those things I didn't get.

"All-state basketball player in high school," Jackson said. "Straight-A student."

"What happened?" Dylan asked from across the room.

Girlfriend? Parents? Pressure?

Jackson's mouth formed a flat, straight line. "Two weeks later, a seventeen-year-old in Baton Rouge loaded her three little sisters into the car and drove into one of the LSU lakes."

I cringed.

"There were witnesses," Jackson went on, as if that was what he was, a witness giving testimony. "Some guys riding bikes."

How had I not heard about this?

"That's the only reason the little girls lived."

"And the seventeen-year-old?" Dylan asked.

Jackson shook his head, bringing a few messy dreads against his eyes. "She made it, if you want to call it that. She's alive, but has no memory of what she did. No memory of anything."

It was a lot to take in.

"No idea how she got pregnant."

I braced my hand against the plastic-covered table, only peripherally aware of Dylan scooping Delphi into his arms.

"Her parents said she was always a quiet girl," Jackson said, "never dated, never talked about boys. Until three weeks before the lake stunt."

Dylan, sounding very much like a cop's son, wandered closer. "What happened then?"

"She came to New Orleans for a choir concert and met Jeremy Albright at a club in the Quarter." He did that cop, pause-for-emphasis thing. "Club Rouge."

My eyes widened.

"That's when she changed."

Dylan's gaze, all steady and sharp, met mine. "You think he gave her something?" The question was for Jackson, but it threw me back to the night before, when trees had chased me from the club, and the moon had bounced like a yo-yo.

Jackson kept surveying the condo, lingering for a moment on the counter, where Aunt Sara's la-la pills sat next to the votives.

"We started investigating," he finally said. "Aaron . . ." His breath sawed off. His eyes were tortured. Shoving all that away, he pushed on. "There were others, a few suicides, a couple of runaways, but nothing that linked them together. No pattern. Nothing widespread."

In my head I did the math. Six months before placed us back in the fall. "That's around when Jessica went missing," I realized.

"We thought her disappearance might be related, yes," Jackson said. "LaSalle pushed that theory."

I bet he did.

"And he might have gotten away with it, *with her*," Jackson said quietly. "If not for you."

Eyes stinging, I looked down at the soft band of leather around my wrist.

"There was another incident last night," Jackson said, "at the old multiplex in N'awlins East."

That had me snapping back to attention.

"Not as severe," he said as the memory of Grace's texts came back to me. "But a sixteen-year-old thought it would be funny to run through a party with a switchblade."

At the same party where Grace had sensed desperation, I'd been drugged, and Will had frantically fled.

"So what are you thinking?" Dylan asked. When had he ended up right beside me? "Bath salts or something?"

Jackson nodded, his eyes darker than the night beyond the window. "They call it bliss."

Bliss.

"*It's why we're all here,*" the guy at the party had murmured. "*To be beautiful, for bliss.*"

"It's a potent hallucinogen," Jackson was saying, but I barely heard, not with the memories tripping through me, of Amber's glassy, doll-like eyes, and her offer of bliss. "Small doses make for short trips; larger doses combined with alcohol send you so far out of your mind some people never get back."

"It helps, doesn't it? Makes the bad go away, the pain, and leaves only the bliss?"

"It showed up in Europe first. We're only beginning to see it on the street here," he said as I slid my hand into my front pocket. "We know it's highly addictive. But because effects are either short-term or fatal, without a cluster or a pattern, by the time we isolate a user, it's too late."

My fingers closed around the little pills Amber had given me. "What do you mean too late?"

TWENTY

"Their brain is fried."

A new picture started to form, *a bad picture,* a lot bigger than I'd thought at the beginning of the night.

"You think Will's a user," I realized, but even before Jackson pulled his phone and crossed to the sofa, the answer glinted in his eyes.

Yes. He thought Will was a user.

He stopped beside me, angling the screen so that I could see it. "These are the known victims."

Victims. Not users or addicts.

Too fast he scrolled through the pictures of a bunch of kids, guys and girls, flicking from one to the next before I could make out much besides empty stares. They all had that.

Just like Amber.

Finally he stopped, giving me plenty of time to take in the image of Will curled in a fetal position in front of an altar. Naked.

"That was ten days ago," he said. "At the cathedral."

My stomach rolled. *What?* "He doesn't even look alive." His skin looked like the pale marble beside him.

"Father McSweeny found him. He was unconscious."

"What happened to him?" Dylan asked.

Detective Jackson took the phone from my hands. "He ran. Before any of us could get there, he shot up and started spouting off from the Bible, and bolted out a back door.

"By the time he showed up at his house the next day and his parents got him to a hospital, blood tests didn't show anything."

The coldness swept in, worse than before. The shadow-bodies on the ground, the vibration from Will . . . totally not a coincidence.

"He was in an accident," I started, trying to knit the pieces together.

"Yes, I know," Jackson said. "And he's hallucinating as it is. Combined with bliss, that puts him doubly at risk."

But they're not hallucinations! part of me wanted to explain, but I saw the look in Jackson's eyes and knew now wasn't the time. He'd come to accept the things I could do, but without further evidence, there was no point saying anything about Will. The best thing to do was to get Will to Julian and see if he could help us find the rest of the vision. Maybe together it would work.

"He's going to get the help he needs," Jackson added. "And you need to stay away from him, away from that whole scene." He hesitated, his gaze gentling. "The people behind bliss . . . the last thing they want to see is someone like you walking among them. Let us take care of this."

A blast of cold shot through me, while a blast of heat shot from Dylan. Someone like me. *Someone who knew stuff.*

"She's not going to any more parties," Dylan said.

Before I even looked at him, before I met the dark intensity of his eyes, I knew what he was thinking: the people behind bliss had already tried to get rid of me once before.

"What kind of person *does* that?" I whispered, shaken. "What kind of person puts a drug like that on the street?"

Jackson's smile was the sad, point-blank kind.

"Monsters walk among us," he said simply. "It could be a husband, a father, a teacher." Suddenly the cool undercover vibe hardened into the bleakness of a cop who'd seen too much. "I was at Aaron's house hundreds of times. I ate there. I slept there. Watched the Super Bowl." He looked beyond me, through the big window to the darkness outside.

"Even when I went back, I still didn't see anything out of the ordinary," he said. Rage twisted his face. "Except in the attic. He'd refinished it into a big media room. That's where we found . . ."

I knew the second he realized he'd said more than he meant to. "Found what?"

He let out one of those rough, frustrated breaths, obviously debating what to say. "That's why I called your aunt."

Dylan moved closer.

"Tell me." I didn't need to be unblocked to know it was bad. "It's about me, isn't it?"

He stood there all contained, every muscle tight, vibrating. "The portraits," he said, and it all glittered there in the dark coal of his eyes, the truth and the agony, the disgust. "He had the portraits from Belle Terre."

At first I thought I must have misunderstood him. But the way he looked at me, the way Dylan closed the rest of the distance between us and came right up to my side, standing so close the heat from his body warmed mine, told me there was no misunderstanding.

The portraits still existed, the images of GLORY and ECSTASY, RAPTURE and ETERNAL. Of me. My life.

My future.

Or was it my past?

Increasingly I didn't know that there was a difference.

"That's why I called your aunt," he said. "To see what she wanted me to do with them."

He'd seen them. He knew what they contained, what a complete stranger had seen, and painted.

"Where are they now?" I asked, more desperately than I meant. "I want to see them."

He glanced at Dylan, as if asking if that would be okay.

"They're of *me*," I reminded, annoyed. "I have a right to see them." I *needed* to.

Frowning, Jackson reached for his phone. "They're at headquarters."

"When can I—"

"But I have pictures," he said, stopping my question. Within seconds the cool, heaviness of his iPhone pressed down against my hand.

I stared down at the image of my face against a sea of shooting stars, with soft waves of brown falling against bare shoulders. My gaze was open, seeking, my lips parted.

After weeks of worrying about what the portraits might show, a quick breath of relief rushed out of me.

Until I thumbed to the next one and saw the tree-shrouded altar glimmering in the moonlight. I lay on top with my arm falling limply over the edge and my face turned to the side, exposing eyes wide and unseeing, exactly like I'd seen in my dreams, so many times before.

But I had no idea if the scene was only that, a freaky, recurring dream, *or my future.*

At the bottom, silvery letters swirled into one word: GLORY.

Mechanically I flicked to the next picture, the slam of my heart slowing when the tarot card appeared, the one I'd drawn two nights before, of the girl draped in robes of red and standing in front of gleaming swords, with a puddle at her feet and a castle in the distance behind her.

Me. My hair blowing in the wind. My cheekbones. *My* drag-onfly with the glowing greenish crystal dangling from a chain of bronze.

Bound and blindfolded.

"It's the Eight of Swords," Detective Jackson said.

I swung toward him, he was so not a fortune cards kind of guy.

"I looked it up," he said, pushing a thick gnarled dread from his face, reminding me for a minute of a kid caught sneaking cookies and trying to explain it away. "Something about facing the truth and emotional release."

Needing to move on, I dragged my finger against the cool glass, pulling up the fourth image, and realizing too late that sometimes what came next was only more of the same.

Flames stained the darkness in violent red streaks, consuming the old white chapel while, amid the sanctuary of ancient trees, I kneeled. My head was tilted, long dark hair flowing in the wind, my eyes closed.

But I wasn't alone.

Dylan was there, too, kneeling in the moonlight, with his hands tangled in my hair and his shoved back from his face to reveal the wide slant of his cheekbones, and the burn in his eyes.

"Blew me way," Detective Jackson said, but I barely heard. It was one thing to live a moment, to take pictures so you could look at them later and remember. But this . . .

It was like having one of the most forbidden moments of your life tattooed in plain view, a moment you'd give anything to erase, or completely rewrite.

"Why?" I asked, trying to understand. "Why did LaSalle take these?" The thought of him having the portraits, the random illustrations of my life, made me want to throw up.

"Because they were important to you," Dylan said, sounding a lot like his father. "Having them gave him power."

"I'd kill him every day for the rest of my life, if I could," Jackson vowed darkly. "And it would still be too good for him." His eyes met mine, and hardened. "If not for you, he'd still be preying on young girls."

I gave Jackson the pills, but didn't tell him where they came from, only that someone had given them to me at Club Rouge. Amber didn't need the cops breathing down her throat.

She needed bliss to go away.

It took awhile to get Jackson to leave. Finally I closed the door behind him, but it was a long moment before I turned around. *Everything had changed.*

Dylan stood against the sea of paint-smeared plastic with Delphi in his arms. Her eyes were closed, her body fluid, but her motor-boat purr rumbled between us.

He didn't belong there. That was all I could think. I needed to be alone, to figure out what I was supposed to do now.

Needing to do something, *anything,* I headed to the kitchen for a glass of water.

"You want some help cleaning this up?"

"No, thanks," I said, turning back around to the crinkled tarps. Helping me meant he would stay longer. "I'm not sure Aunt Sara is done."

His eyes met mine. "Neither are you."

I froze mid-sip.

"You're not going to stop," he said, watching me with the quiet burn of understanding in his eyes. "You're going to try to talk to Will again."

I set down the water more forcefully than I intended. "I have to." The reality of bliss was the missing piece, the one that made a picture start to form. Whatever danger I was picking up around Will, whatever secret someone wanted to make sure I didn't un-cover . . . bliss resided at the heart of it.

"It's like I'm following this trail of bread crumbs—"

Dylan's mouth curved, a faint, ghost of a smile that jumbled up my thoughts.

"What?" I said. "Why are you looking at me like that?"

The smile turned lopsided. "Now you're Gretel? No more Alice? No more Goldilocks?"

This time it was my turn to stare, my turn to stand in the re-cessed lighting of the kitchen and watch *him* as my mouth curved. "It's probably best if I quit waking up in strange places, don't you think?"

His hair fell against his face, sliding in along his cheekbones and making his eyes look deeper set.

"Probably," he agreed, but just as quickly the moment passed, and his smile returned to the shadows.

"You need to be careful, Trinity. There's a real chance the people behind bliss know who you are, that they're the ones who got rid of you last night. You don't want them to think you know who *they* are."

I looked away, staring at a glass-like rock toward the back of the counter, nearly identical to the one Grace had given me the night before. Black obsidian.

"I know," I said, picking up a half-burned bundle of herbs that had not been there that morning.

"Smudge sticks," Dylan said.

Sage, I realized, recognizing the pungent scent from his father's house the night before—and Horizons.

"For cleansing," he said.

I dragged them closer, inhaling deeper. "It didn't seem like that big of a deal Friday night," I whispered. "I thought I'd see if I could do a reading of Will, and that would be that." I drew in another deep breath, let it out slowly. "Three days later, I realize a lot more is at stake."

"You need to let the cops deal with the bad guys, Trinity."

Before they dealt with me. "I'm not going to any more parties," I said. "But I do need to talk to Will again. In the bathroom, it was like we were having two conversations, one with words, the other with our eyes. If he's picking up stuff from me, if he's going to those parties and experimenting with bliss—"

"Then maybe he's picking up stuff there, too," Dylan finished for me.

Not too far from the obsidian, the little prescription bottle sat near a partially burned votive, Aunt Sara's pills, her own personal primer to cover up what she didn't want to feel.

"Maybe that's why he's taking it," I said. "Because everything's different after his accident and he doesn't know how to handle it." He wanted to dull the edges, like Amber said. "But instead he's put himself in the path of something even worse."

The quick white flash, the distorted shadows . . . "Maybe if we can get Will to Julian. We can try to access my—"

We. The word lodged like a rock in my throat.

When had it become we?

"Why?" I asked before I could talk myself out of the question, or remind myself that the answer didn't matter. "Why are you always there when things get crazy?" Even when I asked him to stay away. "Because of your dad?"

He stood there all crazy-still, watching me across the bar. Silence screamed between us.

"No," he finally said, lowering Delphi to the back of the sofa. "Because of you."

TWENTY-ONE

Slowly he crossed the plastic between us.

"Because I saw you last night after my dad found you," he said, "and I know how much worse it could have been."

I told myself to look away, but couldn't.

"Because I don't want you to get hurt again." His voice roughened around the words, ripping against the quiet of the condo, and me. "Because I'd change it all if I could," he said, coming up next to me and taking the bundle of herbs from my fingers. Lifting them, he dragged the sotty ends along my forehead. "But I can't."

This, I thought a little frantically. This was why I couldn't be alone with Dylan, exactly the kind of conversation we couldn't have, that I didn't know how to have—that I didn't *want* to have. Because when he looked at me like that, with quiet understanding in his eyes, little fissures started springing up inside of me, and it was all I could do to breathe. Being with him hurt in ways

I'd never imagined when I first saw him standing in the shadows of his father's porch last fall.

Except, that was the problem. Last fall was not the first. I'd seen him, *known him,* long before that.

Once, knowing he had my back made me feel crazy strong. Now I couldn't help but think about my glass dragonfly, and how fragile perfection could be.

"Because I can't let you fly blind," he added, and then he was touching me, turning my hand up to drag the bundle along the inside of my wrists.

I stared down at the smear of white ashes against pale flesh. "You talked to Julian," I realized.

"He's worried about you." *And so am I.* But Dylan didn't say that. "Tomorrow's Mardi Gras," he said instead. "With the crowds we'll want to get an early start."

The quiet words drifted through me. I knew there was no point telling him no, that there was no *we.* Because until the whole bliss/Will thing was over, there *was* a we. No matter how much I didn't want him around, I couldn't deny we made a good team. I'd have to be reckless to not want Dylan to have my back.

Done smudging, he released my arm and stepped back, returning the herbs to the counter.

"You better get to bed," he said. "Eight's going to come pretty early."

I couldn't sleep.

Every time I closed my eyes, my mind raced. I could see Will holding Kendall while she cried and Detective Jackson checking my pulses, Dylan holding my cat, and *the portraits:* me starring as the VIII of Swords and draped across a stone altar, kneeling in the moonlight with Dylan while the world around us burned.

Everything kept swirling. I tried a long hot shower, a cup of warm milk, deep breathing, meditating, even counting sheep, but nothing worked.

At eleven thirty Aunt Sara got home. We talked about the shop and the parades, but nothing big or important. At twelve thirty she went to bed and I excavated the sofa and curled up with my journal to sort through all the questions, but instead found myself returning to the letter.

> Will said you weren't afraid. You didn't seem afraid.
> I remember when I thought I was drowning, and the fire.
> It was like a door opening, a door to somewhere else, and I

I closed my eyes, letting out a long, slow breath before continuing.

> I wanted to see what was on the other side.

Delphi chose that moment to leap up beside me. "Hey, girl," I said, dragging her to me.

Cold, I realized sometime later. Shivering, I curled into myself and reached for my blanket.

Abruptly I opened my eyes to early morning sunlight slipping through the gauzy sheers, and Delphi's wide, unblinking stare. With her ears perked, she sat crouched on the arm of the sofa, her round eyes focused beyond me, toward the door.

I swung around.

All the chains and dead bolts were secure, and the steady red light of the security system glowed. Nobody could get through that.

At least not physically.

I shifted into a sitting position, and the pen fell from my hand. And with that the haze lifted and reality slipped in: somehow I'd fallen asleep. It was morning.

The clock said 7:21. That gave me half an hour before Dylan showed up.

With a caffeine-rush of adrenaline, I swung to the floor and saw the journal, no longer open to the letter, but a new page, blank except for the two lines scrawled in a dark bold print.

Watching you.
Time running out

I had no memory of writing the words.

I had no memory of thinking them, of what they meant. What if Julian was wrong, I wondered as I stepped into the hot spray of the shower. What if I *was* dreaming? What if the problem was remembering? What if opening my eyes whitewashed the images from my mind? What if that's why I'd written in my journal, to remember?

The possibilities opened a whole new series of doors.

I stood there thinking longer than I should have. By the time I dressed and reached for my phone, the clock showed a few minutes after eight, and texts waiting from Victoria, Deuce, Kendall, and an unknown number.

I went for that one first.

It's Will. I need to talk to you.

My heart slammed hard. My hands started to shake as I fumbled along the keys.

Where? When? Are you OK?

I hit send and waited. And waited.

No response came. Dylan did. The buzz at the door blasted into the silence, followed by voices. After a quick check in the mirror of the awesome little black dress Victoria had insisted I wear to the parades, I hurried from my room to the kitchen. The second I saw him sitting on a funky bar stool, I stopped, almost tripping on Delphi.

Smiling. That was the first thing I noticed. Dylan was smiling. It was full and sharp with a flash of white, the killer kind that hit you with the force of a searchlight.

Aunt Sara was smiling, too. On the kitchen side of the bar with her hair piled high on her head, she plucked something from a small plate and popped it in her mouth.

Delphi meowed.

My aunt looked up. Her eyes widened. "Wow!" she said, coming around the counter. "Look at you."

Dylan did. I could feel the burn of his eyes, even though I refused to glance his way.

"Look what Dylan brought," she said, sliding a second plate to the edge of the bar, where a tall paper cup sat next to something I hadn't noticed in those few seconds when his smile had overshadowed everything else.

"King cake and mochas," my aunt gushed, but I couldn't stop staring at the plush puppy on the counter, with its light-gold fur and wide, love-me eyes, and the little, heart-shaped tag dangling like an earring by his face.

Of all the things I'd prepped myself for, a stuffed animal had never entered the picture. And not just any stuffed animal, but a golden retriever.

From Dylan.

Knowing I couldn't stand there all day (even if I wanted to), I crossed to the kitchen and lifted a hand to the soft, fuzzy fur. My throat got stupid tight, and the backs of my eyes burned.

I didn't want that, didn't want to feel the wad of emotion wedging into my throat, the alternating flashes of warmth and confusion, the smile that hovered inside of me, and the hurt and guilt that kept clawing over everything else. I didn't want any of that. I didn't want Dylan to slowly lift his eyes to mine and touch me in that invisible way of his, without even lifting a hand.

But it was all there, and until the Will/bliss thing was over, that wasn't going to change.

Needing to do something, I picked up the puppy and ran my thumb along its nose.

"Isn't it sweet?" Aunt Sara smiled. "He said he saw it and thought you might like it."

I knew better than to do it, but I glanced at Dylan anyway, sitting there in his long-sleeve charcoal T-shirt and faded jeans, with his wide-palmed hands wrapped around a tall paper cup, and would have sworn he looked as awkward as I felt.

"It was in the grocery store," he said with a no-big-deal shrug.

I'd never seen Dylan Fourcade do anything no-big-deal, or look awkward.

"He looks like Sunshine," I whispered with a quick memory of the bathroom at Club Rouge, where I'd told Will about my first premonition of death.

Dylan's eyes, more guarded now, lifted to mine. "That's what I thought, too."

My chest tightened. Making myself return the dog to the counter, I reached for the mocha. "Thanks."

He shrugged. "It was no big deal."

Yeah. He actually said it.

Lifting the hot chocolate to my mouth, I had no idea what to say next.

Aunt Sara hovered, chattering about the parades and how much fun we were going to have, seemingly oblivious to the tension winding tighter by the second.

Dylan sat all still and contained, nursing his mocha.

I did the same. Picking at the amazingly cream-cheesy king cake, I knew better than to look. I knew what I would see, feel. I already had enough memories of him here, in the condo. I didn't need another.

I looked anyway.

Dylan's eyes met mine, held.

I looked away, but even staring at a blob of pastry, I could feel him still, feel the awareness winding tighter and tighter, something strong and invisible and *waiting*.

It took a few seconds to realize Aunt Sara had stopped talking. She looked from me to Dylan, back to me, then muttered something about needing to make a phone call and vanished down the hall.

Finally we were alone.

TWENTY-TWO

I had my journal in my hands within seconds. "I need to show you something," I said, flipping to the most recent page. "I found this when I woke up this morning."

Dylan looked down for a long moment. "Who wrote it?"

"I think *I* did."

He shot me a look. "You *think*?"

I made a face. "I don't know, it's like with the way I normally receive messages being blocked, they're finding other ways, like when a river hits a dam."

Slowly, he dragged his index finger from letter to letter. "Who's watching you, the people behind bliss?"

Something quick and cold went through me. "Maybe," I said, then, "Will texted me."

Dylan looked up so fast our faces came within inches of each other, and that threadbare place inside me unraveled a little more. "When?"

I pulled back. "Half an hour ago. He wants to talk to me."

"About what?"

"I haven't heard back from him." Pushing out a breath, I guided the conversation back to an idea I'd come up with in the shower.

"Can you help me set up a camera?" I asked. "One of those nanny cameras that monitors an entire room?" I hesitated, trying to read his eyes. That, of course, was impossible. "I want to see what happens when I start writing," I went on. "If my eyes are open or closed." I didn't know why it mattered, or even what exactly I thought I might discover, but the need to fill in the blanks drove me. "Can we do that?"

That curtain of dark hair slipped against his cheek. "Yeah."

For the second time that morning I smiled and said thank you.

"You ready?" he asked.

After a quick check of my phone to see if Kendall or Will had texted back, I scooped up the journal and the puppy and took them to my room, redid my lip gloss, and hurried back to the front and straight into Aunt Sara. With *her* phone.

"I can't let you out of here without pictures!" she announced, all cheerful-like. "You two look awesome!"

I froze.

Eyes sparkling, she breezed around the condo, ultimately settling by the bar, where she dragged a few candles into an artful arrangement. "How about here?"

She had the wrong idea, was all I could think. She thought Dylan and I were together because we wanted to be, not because we had to be. But there was no way to explain that, not without telling her things that would make her worry, or call Detective Jackson.

That was worse than a picture.

Woodenly, I let her pose me, turning me just so and putting my hand on my hip. "Now smile," she instructed.

I faked it as best as I could, until she twisted toward Dylan and crooked her finger. "You, too."

Everything inside just kinda stopped. No, I thought frantically—*no*. I didn't want a picture with *him*. That's not what this was about.

But apparently I didn't have a choice.

He came toward me, sliding a Zorro-like mask over his eyes.

My breath turned to more of a stab.

His smile was slow, razor sharp, the small, dark slits emphasizing the glow of burnished silver.

"Wonderful!" Smiling, Aunt Sara nudged us so that we turned in to each other. Maybe she lifted Dylan's arm—maybe he did that by himself. All I knew was his hand slid against my waist as she stepped back, lifting her camera. The moment held, locked us there pressed into each other with the heat of his body blasting into mine, exactly like the night he'd carried me from the fire.

And my throat closed up all over again.

Except this time I couldn't slip out of his car like I'd done Sunday night. And I couldn't tell him good-bye, not when every road I took kept leading me straight back to him. This time I had to find a way to ignore the wrongness of being with him, and go to a parade.

It was like stepping into another world, some alternate universe where five different kinds of music blasted from five different directions and people danced in the streets, where the sky rained beads and doubloons, jesters ruled, women who looked like they belonged in some suburban home lifted their tight-fitting shirts for anyone who asked, and Dylan wouldn't let go of my hand.

I didn't try to pull it back, either, not with thousands of people swarming around us. If I let go, *if he let go,* the crowd would spill between us, and even with our phones, we might not be able to find each other and—

I didn't know. I didn't know what would happen if he wasn't there. *That* was the problem. No matter how many wounds being with him tore open, as long as I was trying to help Will, I was better off *with* Dylan, than without him.

Safer.

We worked our way uptown, where Victoria, Trey, and Deuce waited by the Robert E. Lee statue. An assembly line of robots marched single file in front of us. Beside us a group of older women in red hats bobbed fringed parasols to Lady Gaga.

All thousand of us stopped at one of the few corners where cars still inched along the street, and Dylan tugged me closer. "What do you think?"

I stared at a grown man in a diaper. "I . . . Wow." There really were no words to describe the euphoria. "It's *wild.*"

He laughed. "Just wait."

The crowd thickened as we neared the parade route, with ladders jutting up next to the grandstands along the curb and more than one person perched in the oaks, waiting.

Everyone was waiting.

So was I.

Heart racing, I fumbled with the zipper of my wristlet and retrieved my phone for the hundredth time, knowing I would never feel it vibrate.

No messages waited.

By the time we pushed our way toward the statue, the parade was about to start. Waving, Victoria shoved her way forward, sliding a quick, questioning glance from me to a still-masked Dylan. This was the third time in five days she'd found us together.

Shaking my head, I flashed her a look and mouthed, "Later."

I could tell she didn't like that, but she took my hand anyway and dragged me to the curb, where Trey and Deuce waited between ladders crammed with little kids.

"Mile High!" Soul-dancing to a blast of music from across the street, Deuce shot a quick look at Dylan and twirled me under his arm. "Get ready!"

His eager, little-boy grin made me smile.

With horns and drums announcing the start of the parade, I fumbled for my phone.

Dylan's hand slipped against mine, stopping me.

The press of people boxed us in so tightly there was no room to step back.

"You just checked," he said, and somehow I heard him even though he barely raised his voice. "Three minutes isn't going to change anything."

Technically, I knew he was right. "But I feel like I should be *doing* something," I said, going up on my toes so that he could hear me. "Something other than standing around, waiting."

Up the street, sirens wailed.

"You are," he said as the crowd swelled around the barriers and into the street.

Uniformed police pushed everyone.

"Now it's up to Will," Dylan said, anchoring me against him. "You can't help him if he doesn't want you to."

That was the problem.

"It's his choice, and only he can make it. You can't force him to do what *you* think is best."

I'm not sure why I looked away, maybe because the music was pounding faster, the tempo increasingly frenzied, or maybe because the truth reached inside of me, and scraped.

Choices.

Chase should not have been at Six Flags. We'd broken up. He'd walked away. And, crushed by his inability to trust me, I'd chosen not to go after him. I'd chosen to let the air clear and see what tomorrow brought. I'd chosen *not* to tell him my aunt was missing or that I'd finally figured out what I'd been seeing in my dreams.

I'd chosen all that, never imagining that instead of calling me or confronting me, *he* would choose to follow me.

Such simple, seemingly benign choices, but for the rest of my life I'd wonder what would have happened if I'd chosen differently. If I'd called him after learning my aunt was missing. If I'd let him know about Six Flags.

Would he have stayed away, stayed safe?

Or would he have made the exact same choice? Would he have gone anyway, wanting to be there . . .

"There he is!" shrieked the little girls in front of me as a masked horseman emerged along the parade route. Concealed from head to toe, with elegant gold robes and a feathery plume jutting up from his military-style helmet, he slowly surveyed the masses.

"Sometimes you have to let go and tr̶

can't yank the sun from the sky just becau̶

The words whispered through me, eve̶

drowned out everything else. I turned, th̶

ing us so close I had to look up to see hi̶

He answered before I could ask the q̶

"My grandfather," he said, steadying me with a hand to my back. "He has a saying for everything."

For a second I could see them, a young Dylan with his wise, Navajo grandfather. It explained a lot, the things he said that I couldn't imagine any other eighteen-year-old saying, and his freaky sixth sense, not necessarily psychic, but more like he existed in his own harmony with the world around him.

Three more masked riders appeared, one in a uniform of purple, one green, one gold. Matching feather plumes swayed from their helmets.

"Is he still alive?" I asked.

"In New Mexico."

"Do you see him often?"

"Summers."

I could tell that wasn't often enough. "So does it work?" I asked. "Letting go, trusting?"

Against me, his body stiffened. "I trust."

He didn't say anything about letting go.

Around us the crowd bulged, a group of guys mouthing off, shoving their way directly in front.

"Hey!" Victoria shouted, but Trey was already going down on a knee so she could climb onto his shoulders. "Here comes the king!" she called.

I squeezed in front of Dylan, watching the first float, a huge, ornate cake, roll by. The King of Carnival waved from an elaborate throne. Children in glittery gold robes with massive white feathers stood along the sides, tossing beads of purple and gold and green.

Victoria waved her arms, snagging a handful still banded to-

caught a second strand, and draped them around my

neck. His body was alert, ready, but when his eyes met mine, warmth glimmered in the silver.

I smiled back before I realized what I was doing.

One float after another rounded the corner, a giant cow surrounded by masked chefs, a huge beehive surrounded by flowers, a castle swarming with pink and purple fairies, all throwing beads and coins and cups as fast as they could.

Children scrambled into the street. Feet stomped down on hands. Perched on ladders, women (beautiful and not so beautiful) did their own version of cage dancing in exchange for throws.

It was easy to lose track of time.

With a military-style marching band rounding the corner, Dylan was draping another strand of beads around my neck when I noticed Victoria stop shoulder-dancing. She stopped everything, actually. Stopped cheering, smiling. Stopped moving.

I turned in the direction of her stare, and saw Lucas.

Dressed in street clothes, he stood not twenty feet away, blasting her with his eyes.

Edging closer, I whispered in Trey's ear. "Lucas is here."

He tensed, glancing not at Lucas but at Victoria. I didn't hear what he said, but I saw her shake her head. Then the most amazing thing happened: she lifted her chin and turned back to the parade, completely blowing her ex off.

Proud of her, I glanced at my phone, not paying attention to the crowd swelling against me. Until I heard the voice.

"Trinity."

I saw her eyes first, once all sparkly and mocking, full of confidence and challenge and hate. Now they were stripped down and bare, exactly like they'd been when we'd both said good-bye to Chase.

"Jessica." My mouth got really dry. She was the last person I'd expected to see.

"I thought that was you," she said with a tight smile. "When I saw Victoria's check-in, I was hoping you'd be here."

Vaguely I was aware of Dylan turning to look, and Victoria scrambling down from Trey's shoulders.

"Why?" I asked.

"Because I wanted to make sure you're okay."

Everything kinda wobbled.

"I–I saw that stuff on Victoria's Facebook," she said as a group of her cheerleader friends, minus Amber, danced over.

Twirling a black and gold parasol, one of them, Teri, hooked her arm with Jessica's. "Quit wandering off!" she sang-shouted. "It's Quarter time!"

Jessica's eyes, so much more alive than only a few minutes before, met mine. "I gotta go," she said. "But . . . be careful, okay?" And then she was gone, disappearing with her friends among a sea of jesters.

Not sure what to make of that, I glanced at my phone and saw the text that had not been there three minutes before. From Will.

I'm in the Quarter.
Come alone.
Text me and I'll tell you where.

I looked up at the swirl of color and motion and found Dylan standing in that unnaturally still way of his, watching. And without a word I knew he'd read the message and had no intention of letting me go anywhere by myself.

TWENTY-THREE

I grabbed him by the hand and pressed close, so he could hear me. "You have to let me do this. It's the only way."

Through the slits of his Zorro mask, his eyes burned darker than before, and without a word, I knew he was seeing the video clip all over again, of me stumbling through the darkness.

"I'll be careful," I promised, using my eyes to emphasize the words. "I won't take any chances."

He dragged me back from the sidewalk, toward the center of the circle where the crowd didn't press so hard. "Ask him where."

I did.

Will's response came seconds later.

Not yet.
Not until you're closer.

"Dylan," I said quietly. "Don't make this harder than it has to be. Don't back me into a corner. You have to trust that I'll be careful."

"It's not about trust."

I kept my eyes on his. "No," I said. "It's about letting go."

His eyes flashed.

"And that's what I need you to do." I made myself step back. It shouldn't have been hard. I had to do this alone. I knew that. It was what Will wanted, and Will was the one in trouble. "Let go and trust."

The warmth of Dylan's body fell away, leaving the breeze to swirl between us.

"Where's your phone?" I asked.

Watching me, he slid it from his pocket.

With another step back, I tapped out his number. "Two minutes," I mouthed.

His phone started to ring.

"Then you can follow."

Never looking away, he pushed the answer button.

"You can hear everything," I said over the hard slam of my heart. "It'll be like you're right there with me."

He lifted the phone to his face. "No, it won't."

Through the phone, the words, so raw and threadbare, scraped in ways I didn't want to feel. "If anything happens . . ."

"I'll be there."

It was all I could do to breathe. Because I knew he would. Dylan would be there.

He always was.

Not trusting myself to stand there one second longer, I turned and darted into the crowd.

One minute, two, it didn't matter, not with the swell of people cramming from all directions. Seconds, a heartbeat. That's all I needed to lose myself.

All it took to change everything.

"Talk to me," Dylan said.

My heart kicked, hard. "About what?"

"Anything. Just let me hear your voice."

Seven words. That's all they were. Words through a phone. But with them the racing inside me quieted, and I had something to hold onto. "Tell me more about your grandfather."

"What do you want to know?"

Up ahead, the parade continued along St. Charles, toward Canal Street. I darted right, away from the noise and the congestion. "Anything. What's he like?"

"My dad calls him the old tree," he said, and I couldn't help the quick smile that flashed through me. "But to me he's more like a mountain."

An intersection waited up ahead, fairly quiet given the chaos behind me, but in my mind I saw the starkly beautiful peaks of the Rockies, jutting against the vivid blue of a Colorado sky. "Why?"

"Because he's always there."

Always. "When was the last time you saw him?"

"Four weeks ago."

And for a second there, it was all I could do to breathe. Four weeks ago was two days . . . *after.*

"Did you go see him?" I made myself ask.

"No, he came to me."

I walked faster.

"That's when he told me I couldn't pull the sun from the sky."

Just because it burned.

I started to run. I didn't know why. I only knew that walking was too slow, and Will was waiting, and I had to talk to him, about bliss and the things he knew and the disturbing X-ray shadows, and the words from my journal: *Time running out.*

I sprinted onto an eerily quiet Magazine Street, shoving at the hair blowing into my face. "Where are you?" I asked breathlessly.

"Not far."

I twisted around, scanning the broken sidewalk behind me. "It's so quiet," I said. "Like everyone in the world is at the parade."

"Not everyone," he said, and with that I swung back toward the jumble of shops crammed along the famous shopping district.

"Trinity."

Cars lined the streets. Shadows slipped from alleys. "Yeah?"

"You don't have to run," he said and with the quiet words, I would have sworn he was beside me again. With me. "Slow down and take a deep breath."

Somehow I did.

"But don't stop talking," he added, steady, always so steady.

I scrambled for another question. "What do you do . . . when you're not helping me?"

We'd never talked about that, because he never stuck around after danger fell into normalcy.

"I work construction, and I'm taking some online college courses."

Last month, he'd told me he'd had to drop out. "In what?"

"Criminal justice."

My smile just kinda happened. That explained a lot.

"Did you . . ." I hesitated, not sure if I should ask. Then I took a leap of faith, or recklessness, and did. "Did you ever tell me not to put a dragonfly in a jar?"

He laughed. "Yeah."

"You were only eight," I said against the play of memory. "Was that another of those Native American things?" Why he always seemed so in tune with the world around him.

"No." His voice roughened. "There's no age requirement for knowing what happens when something can't breathe."

And then the hitch was mine.

He'd been eight when his mother died, had that already happened when he came to see me that summer? Had he and Jim held all that inside? Was that why he knew what happened when you couldn't breathe?

"What was the best thing that ever happened to you?" I detoured.

I think he laughed. It was a soft sound, something garbled from his throat, and for a heartbeat I could see the silver glow of his eyes.

"Hasn't happened yet," he murmured.

His voice was all smoky, as if even though it hadn't happened, he knew *exactly* what the best would be.

I didn't let myself think about that. Instead I fished for another question.

"What about the worst?" I rolled along, not thinking, not thinking about all the things that littered his past, until the question already lay between us.

The edge of his breath roughened the quiet, dragging seconds into eternity. Maybe more. I didn't think he was going to answer.

Then he did.

"When I had to leave you beside the roller coaster," he said woodenly, "then answered my phone a few minutes later and heard you screaming my name."

The words sliced through me like shards of glass, slicing away little bits and pieces of me everywhere they touched.

"*And hearing him,* LaSalle, threatening you, and knowing how far away I was."

Everything inside me tightened.

"And running," he said, and with the word I could hear his breath coming faster, harder, as if he was living it all over again.

Running.

Shouting.

"Hearing you scream, hearing *him,* what was happening—and knowing I should never have left you alone."

Oh, God.

Oh, God.

"And that I might not get there in time."

And then I was running, too, not through memory but across Canal Street to the edge of the French Quarter.

"*That's* why I was there the other night," he added roughly, and I felt it, the words and his voice, shred all the way through me. "Why I can't let you try to help Will by yourself. Because I'm not going to turn my back on you again."

I kept running. "I'm sorry," I said for some reason. "So sorry. I didn't mean to drag you into this."

"You didn't."

Around me the crowd again thickened, forcing me to slow. I worked my way through them, knowing I had to—

Will.

I'd forgotten.

With a quick surge of adrenaline I darted into the recessed doorway of an old hotel and forced myself to focus on a quick text.

I'm close. Where are you?

His response flashed up less than twenty seconds later.

Go to the cathedral.

I'd been running and running, for so long. Far longer than the last ten minutes.

But in that moment I stood absolutely still, staring at the black letters against the glow of white, and without warning, Grace's words came back to me, about the shadows slipping closer.

What if that wasn't Will?

On a hard slam of my heart I crammed the phone back to my face. "I'll call you right back," I said to Dylan.

"Trinity, what—" But I disconnected before he could finish and jabbed out Will's number, holding my breath with each ring.

After three he answered. "Are you close?"

It was him, *it was him*. "I'm on my way."

Then the line went dead and I was running again, just as Dylan was running across the street.

"No!" Frantically I glanced around. "You can't let anyone see us together!"

He sprinted toward me anyway.

And with a quick twist, I realized what I'd done, that by hanging up the phone, I'd sent him straight back into the worst moment of his life. Before I could so much as move he was there, backing me against the cold brick of the old hotel. "Goddamn it, you can't do that!"

"Oh, God, I'm so sorry!" I said, trying to breathe. "I had to call Will, to make sure it was him."

Dylan went absolutely still.

"To be *safe*," I emphasized, more quietly this time.

Through the slits of his mask, the silver of his eyes burned through me.

"And it *is* safe," I assured him. Without thinking, I lifted my hands to his arms, as if to push him away or pull him closer.

I did neither.

"But you can't go with me," I whispered, swallowing hard. "You can't let Will see you."

From the street behind us, sirens sounded. "Don't hang up on me again."

I lifted my phone, and pushed his number. "I won't."

Never looking away, he answered.

So much twisted through me at once, a quick swell of gratitude and relief, trust and regret. Regret for things I'd said and hadn't said, for things I could never say. For the before that had come and gone way too fast, and the after that could never be.

"Count to one hundred this time," I said, and then I was running again, worming my way into the swarm of revelers and not letting myself look back, knowing I *couldn't,* because Will could be anywhere and . . .

And.

It was always the *ands* that got me. *Ands* could take you anywhere, or nowhere at all.

Not letting myself go anywhere past the moment I was in, I worked through the crowd to the beautiful old church, stopping by the fountain for my next instruction.

From there, the instructions came one at a time, thirty to forty-five seconds apart, each arriving at precisely the right moment, as if I was being monitored.

Go to the street behind the church. Walk one block. Turn left. Walk another block. Turn right. Look for a peach building. Walk between it and the green one.

I did exactly as he said. With each turn the crowds thinned, until finally they dispersed, and the old peach shotgun house came into view. I looked up, to the building on the other side, the pale green one and everything flashed.

TWENTY-FOUR

Life unfolds moment to moment.

Most of the time we roll from one breath to the next without thinking a lot about it. But sometimes everything explodes into sharp, excruciating focus, each sensation so acute it's like a knife to flesh. The softest sound blasts, and the gentlest touch stings.

I stood staring at the narrow concrete path winding between two buildings, the same path I'd taken six months before, two days after Jessica went missing. *With Chase.*

It was one of the first times I'd seen beyond the here and now, to some other time, when a tiered fountain sprayed against the sky and clay pots overflowed with colorful flowers, and an old woman spoke in riddles.

At the time, I'd thought something was seriously wrong with me.

Now I knew I'd been picking up psychic residue.

"Talk to me, Trinity. What's going on?"

I was too close to risk speaking. Lifting my phone, I shot Dylan a text.

Everything's OK

Then I sent one to Will.

I'm here

There was only one way he could have brought me here, one person who could have guided him. The voices he heard were so not a drug-induced trip, like Detective Jackson claimed, or hallucinations from his NDE, as his parents believed.

Julian was right. I was right. The things Will heard were real.

"I'm here," I whispered, hurrying down the path to the rusted gate. The old hinges creaked as the courtyard that once belonged to my mother's cousin came into view, the fountain dry and forgotten, the clay pots cracked and overtaken by weeds, the table and chairs rusted.

I stepped in as Will's next text arrived.

Go inside door B. I'm upstairs.

Door B. *Like last time.*

I made my way through the shadows, toward the door that had transported me into a twilight zone of desperation and desecration, of death, of misery and sacrifice and love, of memory or prophecy. But that door didn't exist anymore. LaSalle had kicked it into a pile of splinters. This was a new door.

I stood there in the late-morning breeze, wondering which world I'd find this time: the now, or that other time?

"Where are you?" Dylan asked, breaking the momentary trance. "What's happening?"

Only then did I realize I'd slipped between the buildings without telling him what I was doing. Texting him, I told him about the green and peach houses, and that I was going inside.

"I don't like it," he said seconds after I hit send.

I texted him back.

I'm OK. This place is

I hesitated, replacing the last three words.

I've been here before.

With a slow, steadying breath, I stepped through the door and into the room with the rose walls and grandfather clock, the curved velvet sofa and the black mirror, through which I'd seen my mother running toward a pale, still body draped atop an altar of stone, exactly like Faith had painted.

But none of that was there anymore. Only my memory populated the emptiness.

"I'm outside the gate," Dylan said. "One word I don't like, and I'm coming in."

Lowering my phone, I glanced at the unnatural white of my fingers curled around the edges. Making them relax, I assured Dylan I knew what I was doing.

His response was little more than breath. "So do I."

I turned to the back of the room. Outside the sun shone, but here, inside with no electricity, the meager light leaking through dirty windows mixed with the darkness rather than chasing it away, creating a filtered, twilight effect.

Using my phone to guide me, I worked my way to and up a narrow staircase. A soft glow spilled from a doorway halfway down. I turned to go in, but stopped the second I saw the wall.

Dragonflies swarmed against faded peach, big and small, in red and black, hundreds of them, as perfect as they were out of place. Not real, but painted. *Spray* painted.

For a disjointed moment I couldn't move, think, couldn't do anything but stare at the hauntingly beautiful dragonflies, flying not up but down, all of them, angled toward the corner.

"Hi," someone said, and I snapped back to life, twisting to find Will standing among the shadows with a bottle of water in his hands.

Only a faint haze made it through the grime-smeared window, but it was enough to make out the graffiti scrawled over all the walls.

"Hey," I said, trying to make him feel comfortable.

He stepped toward me. "Thanks for coming."

He was different. That was my first thought. His clothes were similar to the night before, faded jeans that looked a few sizes too big and a Metallica T-shirt, the beanie pulled low to his eyes. It still made him look stylish and vulnerable at the same time. But he was different, more *here,* almost . . . excited.

Jerkily he gestured to the wall behind him, more like a whiteboard now, with three labeled columns: RANDOM WORDS, FEELINGS, and WARNINGS.

And I knew. Before Will said another word, I knew what I was looking at.

"I couldn't stop thinking about everything you said," he blurted as I moved closer to the list of words. "But the stuff I hear seems so random. So . . ." He hesitated, like a kid turning in homework late. "I just started writing it all down."

I stared at the insanely organized brain-dump, all categorized and labeled, like a glimpse into somebody else's mind. The words and pictures filled up all four walls, and I couldn't help but think with all this whispering at him, no wonder he thought he might be crazy.

"Where's Kendall?" I asked.

"I didn't tell her."

I turned back to him.

He frowned, shaking his head. Something hot and dark and protective flashed in his eyes. "She's already freaked enough."

"That's why you were so quiet yesterday," I said.

He nodded. "At first I didn't want her to think I'm crazy. Now . . ." He pushed out a frustrated breath. "I don't want to scare her if I'm not."

He so wasn't.

"Why here?" I asked before I could talk myself out of it. I knew Dylan was listening. I knew he would want to know everything.

"It's like that sometimes," Will said from behind me. "Like someone's telling me to go somewhere."

Chase.

I scanned the light of my phone around the wadded-up fast-food wrappers scattered among dirty blankets and dried flowers, the little piles of corn and ash, and for a second it was like walking into the house on Prytania all over again.

"Something happened here, didn't it?" Will murmured. "Something important?"

I stared at the words on the wall, the passage from Revelation he'd recited Sunday night, about four angels standing at the corners of the earth.

"A long time ago," I said.

"When you . . ." He hesitated, like he wasn't sure about something. ". . . lived here?"

"No," I said quietly. "I never lived here."

"Are you sure?"

Yes, I started to say, but before I could, the soft tinkling of a piano rushed through the silence of my mind, and I could see two little girls with long dark hair dancing in white dresses by the grandfather clock.

I had no time slot for the quick memory.

"I don't know," I said instead, but that fraction of an instant was all it took for the blank look to come back into Will's eyes, as if he wasn't there anymore.

"Are you picking something up now?" I asked.

He blinked, and the Will from a few minutes before came back.

"All the time," he admitted, staring at the swarm of dragonflies. "Especially in public, like school or parties. It's like whispers from another room, like a door got left open." He hesitated, looking more like a fascinated little boy all the time. "A door that's supposed to be *shut*."

My heart kicked, hard. "A door to where you were?" I asked, already knowing the answer. "After the accident?"

He looked beyond me, toward the hall, but I knew that wasn't what he was seeing.

"It was so cool there." The memory, like that of an awesome vacation, flickered through his eyes. "I was like a bird, floating and watching everything happen around me, but not feeling anything. I could see the doctors and nurses around the table." The happy part ended, and his eyes darkened. "The blood."

I angled my phone back against the three columns on the wall behind him, and with one scrawled word, everything inside me locked up: FOREVER.

It was the last of the Random Words list, right below DESTINY and STOP.

"It was like some trippy cool *movie*," Will kept on, "like I was watching it happen to someone else. The ceiling was all glowy, and it started to expand, like a window opening to a whole other world."

Like when I'd almost drowned. "Somewhere you wanted to see?"

He nodded quick, still like a little boy, but now guiltily at the confession. *"Like being inside some super-bright star,"* he described, and the light of that, the wonder of it, glimmered in his gaze. "I felt all free, like when you go skinny-dipping."

I couldn't help it. I smiled.

"And there was barking, and then *my dog* was there, running like he used to, toward me . . ."

I shifted my light, this time to his list of warnings and found the two darkly scrawled lines in a different handwriting.

Watching u.
Time running out

"I hugged him and he was licking me," Will said as a quick blast of cold went through me. The warning was the same, the handwriting the same, the exact same as in my journal.

"But then I heard Kendy screaming and I turned to see her

running toward the ER, where I was. Except I wasn't there any-more. And then there were all these voices, whispering, coming at me from all directions: *Will, please! Will, come back. I love you. Don't go. You can't stay. Please don't go. It's not time. You have to wake up!*"

"But you didn't want to," I whispered, turning back to him.

He lifted his hands behind his neck and squeezed. "Not until I saw Kendy beside the bed, crying."

My eyes stung.

"That's when everything got tight again," he said, "like I was putting my clothes back on, and I could feel her kissing my face and I woke up. Everyone was there, Kendall and my mom and dad and sister, some nurses and a doctor. And Duke," he murmured, hesitat-ing a few seconds before adding, "but no one else heard him."

So everyone decided Will was crazy. "Are you still hearing him?"

"And the whispers," he said, looking around the room at the endless sea of words and pictures as if just tuning back in. "At first, I didn't pay a whole lot of attention. It was like when I was in the coma, except I was awake. Then I noticed the more people I was around, like at school, the more stuff I heard."

"That's where the energy is," I told him.

"It was kinda wild, so I started playing around with it, going to the mall or movies, to see what kinds of things I heard. That's how I ended up at the Greenwood party." He hesitated, frown-ing. "But it was different there, more intense, like I'd walked into a nightmare instead of a dream."

My breath caught. "How?"

He shook his head. "Just bad," he said. "Like, all these warn-ings about something dangerous." He sighed. "I got kinda scared and Kendall noticed—"

"And called your parents," I filled in.

He nodded. "I didn't know how to tell her what was going on. I mean I wasn't sure *what* was going on," he added as the soft glow of my phone slipped across an intricate series of curves above the baseboard.

Mechanically I crossed to the wall and dropped to my knees, dragging a finger along the highest slope of the hand-drawn roller coaster.

Will was definitely picking up Chase.

"I tried to tell my mom when I got home," Will was saying behind me, "but she got upset and started crying, saying none of it was real, and showing me all these Web sites about traumatic brain injuries and hallucinations." He frowned. "Yesterday she took me back to the doctor and got something to make them stop again."

Two things hit me simultaneously: the fact he'd been given medicine to make the voices stop, which would explain his zombie-like state the night before, and the last word he said.

"What do you mean *again*?" I asked, looking back toward him.

He shrugged as if it was no big deal. "I used to talk to people who weren't there when I was a kid," he said as a garbled sound broke from my phone.

My heart kicked hard. Dylan.

"In preschool," Will was explaining. "That's how my mom met my stepdad. He's the psychiatrist she took me to. He knows how to make them stop."

Dylan was *not* going to barge in, I told myself. There was no reason to.

"That's what happened Sunday. I went to the theater party to prove to myself it wasn't real, but it started happening again, and some guy was there, offering me something to *make it all better,*" Will murmured, all distracted, as if he was spinning through thoughts. "I shouldn't have taken it." His eyes flashed dark, like they had when he'd swung down from the tree. "But it was like this crazy, freaky dream. Everything got louder, the whispers shouting that it needed to end, to be over."

Not sure how much more time we had, I ran through his lists of words, skimming along the column I hadn't paid much attention to before: FEELINGS. Close to the bottom, written in a beautifully swirled handwriting, one word stood out: BLISS.

And everything started to crystallize. So. Not. Random.

"Will," I said, gesturing for him to join me. "This isn't a feeling," I said. "It's a drug."

He froze. His eyes darkened.

"A *bad* drug," I emphasized. "People are dying." Wanting to make sure he understood, I turned to look him in the eye. "Teenagers. I think it's what you took Sunday night. I . . ." What *I'd* been given. "I think this is what's connecting us, the parties and the bliss. I think it's what my vision is about."

For a moment he just stood there, paler than before, staring.

"You have to stop going," I said.

Turning, he crossed to the wall behind us, the only one I hadn't looked at yet, where two more columns waited: PLACES and PEOPLE.

It was darker back there, the shadows deeper. Angling my phone, I moved closer and scanned through the places, shopping malls, and schools (including Enduring Grace and Tulane); the abandoned multiplex from Sunday night and a few other movie theaters, all still open; the Greenwood house and Club Rouge, City Park, and railroad tracks, *Six Flags.*

"These are all places you went to?" I asked.

He shook his head distractedly. "It was just a game."

A game that put him straight in the path of something bad.

"One place leading me to another," he muttered, shifting his attention from PLACES to NAMES.

Jeremy Albrite

D.D. Wilson

Sean Mitchell

Brandy Lane

Mark Jacks

Trinity

Chase Dylan

It was all I could do to breathe.

"Oh, my God," I murmured, suddenly so, so cold, like ice overtaking everything inside me. My hand shook as I lifted it to streak a finger along the first name.

"He died," I managed, "From Bliss. And . . ." None of the other names meant anything to me, except . . .

Brandy Lane.

A strangled sound broke from my throat. I didn't know a Brandy Lane, but I did know *Amber* Lane.

And then there was my name. Maybe Will wrote it down because he saw me, but Chase and Dylan . . .

My mind raced. There were other reasons Will could know them. Chase's name was linked to mine all over the Internet, and Dylan had been there last night. But had I called him by name?

I didn't remember.

"This all means something," I said. "We need to show this

to—" I broke off, realizing I shouldn't refer to Detective Jackson by name. Will didn't trust the cops.

But Jackson needed to see this.

"I have a friend," I said, remembering my plan from the night before. Julian. "He helps me figure things out. We can go talk to him." Maybe I could try to project to the astral plane again, this time with Will. Maybe . . .

I stilled, hearing the faint groan of the floorboard too late.

Will jerked back.

Dylan, I thought, starting to turn, but before I could something hit me from behind, a vicious jolt of energy, zapping every nerve ending in my body. I tried to rip away, but it was like I was holding a live wire or a live wire was holding me. The current screamed through me, locking me there. Vaguely I was aware of shouting, and then as quickly as it began, everything stopped, and the floor fell away.

TWENTY-FIVE

Everything blurred. I tried to move, couldn't. My whole body shook. I couldn't key onto anything, anything but the panic, and the pain. My whole body screamed.

Oh, God, I thought somewhere inside. What had just happened?

It took a few more seconds for the quiet to register. Forcing a blink, I rolled to my side, searching the shadows, knowing—

I was supposed to know something. I knew that. But everything was blank, like *before,* when LaSalle tackled me and I hit my head. Everything was jerky, disjointed. Nothing made sense.

Minutes passed. I had no idea how many. I made myself count, concentrating on each number.

Someone would come. I knew that. Someone would—

Dylan.

My heart slammed hard, sending a strong, forceful rush through me. My phone. Where was my phone? Where was *Dylan*?

Thoughts began to string together. He'd been in the court-yard. He'd been listening. He'd promised—

I barely recognized the sound that ripped from my throat. Everything inside me rushed harder. Frantically I tried to move, this time making it to my hands and my knees.

My phone. I saw it on the floor. Dragging myself, I fumbled for it and dragged it to my face. *"Dylan."*

Nothing.

"Please," I said, my voice stronger by the second. *"Where are you?"*

Nothing.

My blood raced so hard I could feel it, each hard thrum through my body. Knowing I couldn't stay there, knowing I had to get out, I crawled to the wall, realizing belatedly that it was easier now. That my body was responding.

I concentrated on breathing and pulled myself up. Steadying myself, I tried a step. It was wobbly, but my legs worked. The next step was stronger. And the next.

I was halfway to the door when the sound of running broke the silence. "Trinity!"

I froze as a haze of light swept into the room.

"Trinity!" the girl shouted, swinging toward me. "Oh, my God!" she gasped as our eyes met, and then she was rushing to-ward me, and I was wobbling toward her, even as none of it made any sense.

Jessica took me by the arms—or maybe I took her. I didn't know. It all happened too fast. All I knew was that I was holding onto her, and she was holding onto me, and we were both shaking.

Through streaks of tangled hair, her eyes met mine. "What happened?" she asked. "Are you okay?"

"Yeah," I whispered. "I think."

"Then come on," she said before I could say anything else. "Your friend's not moving."

Everything blurred, the past and the present, memory and premonition, light and darkness and that hazy, desperate place somewhere between. It was all there, swirling with the quick rush of adrenaline.

My body more mine by the second, Jessica helped me down the rotting stairs and through the shadows, toward the glow of light beyond. Together we burst into the courtyard—and for a heartbeat, everything stopped.

A second. That's all it was. I knew that. I didn't really stop. I didn't really stare. I didn't even scream. But sometimes time could stretch, and sometimes time could deceive. Sometimes a single breath could feel like a lifetime, and a lifetime could masquerade as a fraction of a second.

And in that one second when I saw him, when I saw Dylan sprawled in the fall of shadows near the old fountain, with his legs at an angle and his arms reaching out, the sweep of dark hair against his face and the blood on the ground, dark and red and oozing along a crack in the concrete, time rolled backward and forward, creating the illusion of standing still.

But just as quickly I was across the cobblestone and dropping down beside him, reaching for him, touching him.

"*Dylan.*" My voice shook. My hands trembled.

This was *his* role, some rapidly spinning place inside me screamed. *He* was the one who found *me*. He was the one who dragged me to safety. He was the one who put his hands to my neck and checked for the soft flutter. He was the one who held my hand and urged me back.

He was the one who promised.

"Dylan." Crouching over him, I slid the hair from his eyes, leaving my hand along the line of his cheekbone. "It's me. Trinity. *I'm here.*"

Against the inside of my wrist, the warmth of his breath feathered.

"Oh, God, thank you," I cried, running my hands along his side.

The warm stickiness stopped me. With another quick kick of my heart I carefully slid his T-shirt up along his body, and found the gash at his side. Not huge, not deep, but bleeding.

He groaned.

"Hey," I whispered, leaning over him. "Everything's okay."

His eyelids fluttered.

"Oh, thank God," Jessica said, dropping down beside me. "I was so scared when I found him."

On some level the bizarreness of that registered, but my questions didn't matter, not in that moment.

"I'm right here," I murmured, leaning closer.

Dylan coughed, softly at first, progressively more forceful, as if expelling something. And then it was like a switch flipped and he went from barely there to fully there, surging up and reaching for me, taking me by the arms.

"Easy," I said, as he'd said to me so many times before. "Everything's okay."

His eyes went a little wild, that fire within him flaring again, consuming. "I tried to stop him—"

"It's okay," I whispered, vaguely aware of shouting beyond the courtyard. But Dylan had his arms around me, and he was *okay,* stronger by the second.

Don't cry, I told myself as Deuce and Detective Jackson ran through the gate. *Don't cry.*

"Holy God," one of them shouted, and then they were both there, with Jessica, crowded around us as my tears spilled over, and Dylan gathered me against the warmth of his body.

"You're safe," he whispered. "I promise you're safe."

And so was he. For that moment, despite the questions racing through me, he was safe. That was all that mattered.

The paramedics showed up. Three more cops ran in. Dylan and I were pronounced okay, although they wanted us to go home and rest. He'd hit his head. I'd been on the receiving end of a stun gun.

Jackson and his team, including his new partner, KiKi, a tiny woman who barely looked out of college, were *very* interested in the room upstairs.

One by one questions got answered.

"I had a bad feeling," Deuce said, explaining why he followed me and Dylan from the parade. "I didn't want you running off doing that Primetime thing without backup."

"That's the way it was for me, too," Jessica said, hugging her arms around herself. "The way you tore off kinda . . ." Shadows crossed her face. "I don't know. I wanted to make sure you were okay."

They ended up together, but when they turned onto the street with the shotgun houses, Dylan had already slipped back to the courtyard.

"We were looking all over the place when we heard shouting and saw two guys running from back here," Deuce said.

"He said one of them was Will," Jessica said. "The other one had on a jester mask."

Deuce sprinted after them, while Jessica ran to the courtyard and found Dylan by the fountain, then me. Somewhere along the line she called Detective Jackson, who'd kept in touch with her since last fall.

Dylan stared off toward the door with the "B". "He came up from behind me." The paramedics wanted him to sit, but he refused, standing all Dylan-still instead, with his bloodstained shirt in a heap on the ground, a big white bandage at his side, and against his left breastbone, a small tattoo I'd never seen before.

A green dragonfly.

I slipped toward him, stopping when I saw the way he stiffened.

"I should have stopped him."

I'd never heard his voice stretched that thin. I could tell he blamed himself for what happened. But that's not what I saw. "You did," I said. "If you hadn't been here, he would have come back for me."

His eyes darkened, but he said nothing, just stood staring at something only he could see.

By the time a patrol unit drove us back to the condo several hours later, the only questions remaining were ones we couldn't answer.

Where was Will? Who followed us there? And how much had they overheard?

————

A cardboard box sat outside the door, and thankfully, Aunt Sara wasn't home.

Red. That was the first thing I saw when we stepped inside the condo. The disturbing color screamed from the walls, uneven streaks and swirls and drips that had dried inches before reaching the tarps scrunched against the floor. Bold and dark and angry, it was like bucketfuls of blood had been thrown at the soothing sage walls.

Three open paint cans sat by the ladder.

"Mile High?" Deuce asked, looking at me as Dylan set the box on the table. "Red?"

It looked more like a crime scene than a room in midrenovation. "Yeah," I said. "She keeps changing it."

I made myself look away. "Anyone hungry?" I asked lamely.

No one said yes.

"Dad sent over a camera," Dylan said, and with the words, I saw the quick wince, the way he automatically lifted a hand to the bandage at his side.

It wasn't white anymore.

"You're bleeding," I whispered. Everything was.

He glanced down, frowning. "It's not bad."

He was so lying. I'd seen him by the fountain. I'd seen the gash torn into his side. I knew what could have happened. "Maybe you should go home and get some of that salve you used for me." The one that reduced deep gouges to faint welts in only hours.

Only a few feet separated us, but it might as well have been miles. He stood by the plastic-covered sofa, watching me carefully, as if I was the one who'd been knifed. His chest expanded with each rhythmic breath, sending the dragonfly tat into a slow-motion flight. "I'm not leaving."

My breath caught.

"And," he said, and finally the stone of his expression cracked, freeing the faintest twitch at his mouth, "I don't need the salve."

I couldn't stop staring. "Then—"

"Just a bathroom."

Delphi wandered over to say hello, smears of red paint dotting the white of her fur.

"Trinity."

I looked up.

His eyes gleamed. "I'm okay."

My throat knotted.

"And I'm going to stay that way," he said more quietly. "And so are you."

I swallowed, knowing I needed to say something, but not sure what. "There are clean towels."

And then he was gone, turning to limp down the hall and vanish into the bathroom. I stood watching him, not sure why each beat of my heart felt more like a rip.

"What about clothes?"

It took a second for Jessica's words to register. "What?" I asked, blinking her and Deuce back into the condo.

She was holding Delphi, running a thumb along her little pink nose. "For Dylan," she said. "He can't put the bloody ones back on."

I hadn't thought about that. Grateful to have something to focus on, I hurried to my room, hesitating before turning in. We'd done this before. We'd lived this moment, but the other way around. That very first night Dylan had taken me to his apartment, to get cleaned up after I fell into the river. After my shower, he'd given me a T-shirt that hung to my knees and gym shorts.

My T-shirts and shorts were never going to work.

Swinging back to Aunt Sara's room, I let myself in and wandered to her closet, thinking she might have a pair of sweats that, while not necessarily fitting Dylan, might make it over his thighs. And she loved big T-shirts. She was bound to have something.

Clothes hung neatly on both sides of her closet, dresses and pantsuits to the left, shirts and blouses and slacks to the right. It was a ridiculous time to grin, but the image flashed as I ran my hand along silk, of Dylan in a ruffled blouse and—

Shaking it off, I dropped to my knees and slid plastic tubs from beneath the clothes. The first held swimsuits. The second held purses. The third—

Everything started to rush, an invisible vacuum sucking all the air as I hung there, staring at the two stacks of neatly folded men's clothes. My stomach turned. Bile backed up. My chest hurt.

Why in the world would she keep LaSalle's clothes?

But the second the thought formed, memory rushed forward. He'd spent a lot of time here. They'd cooked and hung out, worked on projects for the shop and watched movies.

Had he spent the night? I scrolled through their months together, but couldn't find any morning that I'd awoken to find him here. I'd always felt bad that my presence was cramping her love life. He'd never spent the night. I was sure of that.

Intrigued, I leaned forward, running my hand along a black T-shirt.

Black.

That's when it hit me. They were all black, the shirts, the sweatpants, even the flannel pajama bottoms, which turned two shades of black into a plaid.

Black.

Julian, I realized, smiling softly. My aunt had some of Julian's clothes.

After selecting pajama bottoms and one of the five identical shirts, I carefully replaced the tubs and left the room, hesitating outside the bathroom.

"There are clothes by the door," I said, setting them down.

Over the rush of the water, I heard Dylan's voice, but not his words.

Needing to do something, I headed for the box on the table, but stilled when I noticed Deuce watching Jessica dragging her finger along the wall.

"It was green this morning," I said as if that mattered.

She shifted, and the random lines and circles became tall, skeletal trees with moss dripping from branches. "It's what she feels inside."

Aunt Sara.

Jessica was right. My aunt was an artist. She expressed herself through her work. When she was happy, her art was sweet and simple. When she was stressed, even her jewelry got darker, lots of twisted metal and asymmetrical designs.

The room, the room she'd painted three times in the past three days, was a reflection of what Aaron LaSalle had done to her.

Hugging myself, I watched Jessica trace the the stick-like scene my aunt had painted, the birds in the trees with featherlight clouds and a sun sinking against the crimson horizon.

"Sometimes it helps," she murmured. "You don't even know what you're painting until you step back and it's there."

I couldn't stop staring. "I didn't know you painted." Didn't know a lot about her, actually.

She glanced back through a tangle of wavy hair, flashing a

smile that erased six full months and threw me back to the first day of school, when I'd seen her across the courtyard with Chase. Her hair had been long and wavy, and she'd been smiling.

Even in the conservative white shirt and blue skirt of the Enduring Grace uniform, she'd been beautiful.

I saw it all over again, for the briefest sliver of a moment, before the shadows crowded back into her eyes, and the months returned.

She stepped back, inspecting what was more of an etching than a painting. "Up until a few months ago, I couldn't." Her sleeve slipped, revealing the bracelet Chase had bought for her. "Or at least I never tried. My parents aren't crayons and finger paint kind of people."

I stared at the soft strip of leather, identical to my own, except with different words: FAITH, BELIEVE, TOGETHER.

"Now I love it," she said. "My dad got me an easel and I'll go in the backyard and paint for hours."

To let out what she felt inside. Because of what LaSalle did to her. To us all.

"Sometimes Chase would sit with me," she whispered. "Sometimes I'd swear he still is." Hesitating, she glanced at Deuce, who flashed her one of his Deuce-smiles before she turned back to me. "I think that's how I knew to follow you today."

I felt myself get really still.

"You need to stay away from that guy Will and those parties," she said. "They're bad news."

Several things hit me at once, how bizarre it was to have Jessica in my condo with red smeared along her fingertips, warning me, and the fact that she knew about Will.

"I know things are bad right now," she said, stepping toward me. "But taking chances isn't the answer. You're playing with fire—"

I don't know which happened first, if she stopped, or my eyes widened as another piece of the puzzle drifted into place.

"You sent that text," I realized, the one at Club Rouge:

> People who play with fire get burned.
> Go home now, while you can.

Dark hair slipped against her face. She made no move to push it back. "Yeah," she said quietly. "I did."

Of all the possibilities I'd considered, she'd never crossed my mind. "But why?"

"Because I could see how much you were hurting. And I know what that feels like, to have a huge hole inside, a hole that won't go away, that keeps getting bigger and bigger. Because I saw you at that party Sunday, I saw you run outside, and that guy follow you." She pressed her lips together, hesitating. "I wanted to make sure you were okay."

I just stared at her.

"I found you in the woods."

She found me in the woods?

"You were on the ground and you weren't moving, and at first I thought . . ."

Her words trailed off, telling me exactly what she thought, the same thing Jim had thought. "That I was gone."

Her eyes filled. "But then I heard you, and I asked you if you were okay, and you kept saying 'Dylan.'"

Delphi rubbed against my leg. I couldn't move.

"So I took you to him."

"*You* took me to him?" It was hard to process what she was saying. "But why didn't you say anything? Why didn't you tell us what happened?"

"Because I knew I was the last person you'd listen to or trust." Hugging her arms around herself, she started to rock. "And I couldn't risk Jim Fourcade telling my parents where I'd been. They'd keep me home and . . . well, I knew bad stuff was happening, and I knew I had to try to warn you."

The moment locked around us, drowning out everything else.

"I was so horrible to you," she whispered with tears streaming down her face. "I was horrible to Chase, too. I loved him, but I didn't know how to be the girlfriend he wanted. He was always trying to fix *me*."

I'd never thought about it like that.

"I think because he couldn't fix what was broken inside him," Jessica whispered.

"Because of the adoption," I knew. That's why Chase had helped me learn about my parents, because he'd never been able to learn about his.

Tears streamed down Jessica's face. "And I resented him for that, for not loving me the way I was. So I punished him. I lied. I cheated. All to make him feel the way I felt, like I wasn't good enough.

"Then you came along," she said, smiling through her tears. "And you were everything I wasn't, and I knew it. He knew it, too." She looked down a long second before continuing. "I *hated* you," she said. "All I could think about was punishing you, too."

My eyes burned.

Lifting her hands as if she had no idea what to do with them, she pressed them together. "And because of that, because of *me,* he died."

TWENTY-SIX

The bright afternoon sun made the big window glow, leaving shadows to fall around Jessica. She held her hands prayer-like against her mouth, her long sleeves slipping against her pale, bony wrists. The bracelet wrapped around one. Faded red slashes streaked the other.

"Jessica," I whispered. Maybe I should have stayed where I was. But that was impossible. Stepping toward her, I reached for her wrist, skimming my finger against the crisscross of scars that had not been there the night we'd found her at Big Charity.

Cutting.

Sometime between last fall and now she'd started cutting herself, but the scars were from Aaron LaSalle all the same.

"No," I said. "It's not your fault."

"Yes, it is." Tangled hair fell from the center part, framing eyes that had once been defiant, but were now devastated. "A few days before that night at the old house, Chase and I had a big fight.

He told me it was over. I told him it was just beginning, that if he thought he could go off and fix *you,* then I'd give him something to fix."

I winced.

"That's what the truth or dare was about, hurting you. And him. It was all so stupid." Tears fell. Her words were garbled. "If I hadn't been so consumed with punishing you . . ."

Yanking her hand back, she wrapped her arms around herself again, holding on tight.

Not knowing what else to do, I put my hand to her back. "It wasn't your fault."

"Yes, it was," she sobbed. "If we'd never been in that house, you would never have had that premonition, and that sick cop would never have known you existed."

And if he'd never known I existed, he would never have decided to play with me. Aunt Sara would never have fallen for him, Grace would never have been kidnapped, and Chase would never have . . .

The hugeness of the crashing dominoes blew me away. Without thinking I felt myself reaching for Jessica. She was living with that, the awful scenario she'd painted in her mind.

"You can't know that," I said, hugging her. "There's no way to know how things would have played out."

She pulled back. "Me. I was the one that psycho wanted. It was only supposed to be *me.*"

"Was it?" It was easy to think like that, but I was coming to realize no one thread made a tapestry fall apart. "How do you know I wouldn't have had a premonition anyway?"

She stilled. I could tell she'd never thought about that.

"I play the what-if game, too," I said quietly. It was always there, in the back of my mind, all the hindsight-enhanced choices and decisions, the consequences. "What if I'd warned you about what I saw? What if I'd gone back to the house the second I learned you were missing, instead of turning to the police?" Maybe I could have picked something up or caught another glimpse of what was to come.

"But I didn't understand what I was seeing, or *why* I was seeing it." Like now, with Will. "If I'd just been more like my mom."

"You *are* like her," she countered. "You *found* me." Eyes glowing, she twisted a long strand of hair around her finger. "There was no reason you should have helped me, but you did. You found me when no one else could. *You.*"

She smiled the old Jessica smile, but with a glimmer of warmth that had never been there before.

"*That's* why I took you to Dylan's and tried to warn you," she said as the bathroom door opened. "That's why I followed you today, to make sure you were okay. Because it's what you would have done."

Long after Jessica and Deuce left, the hugeness of all she'd told me lingered.

"Are you hungry?" I asked Dylan, after telling him everything. "I can get you a sandwich or something."

"Trinity."

Just my name, that was all he said, but even though he stood on the other side of the bar, I would have sworn he reached out and feathered a hand along my neck. Because of his voice, I knew, the way it could pitch both rough and soft at the same time.

I made myself keep walking. I made myself ignore the picture on the door of the fridge, the one Aunt Sara had taken that morning, of me and Dylan, and reach inside for some turkey and cheese.

"You don't have to do that," he said.

I pulled down the bread.

"I can take care of myself."

I stilled, closing my eyes. And then he was there, coming up behind me, and I could feel him, feel him long before the fresh, clean scent of soap drifted around me.

"Let me take care of *you*," he said, taking the sandwich stuff from my hands.

I didn't turn, knew I couldn't turn, not with how raw I felt after everything that had happened, and not when I knew how close he stood, that if I did I'd find myself staring straight at his chest and shoulders. "I'm okay."

He smiled. I didn't see it because I still faced the fridge. But I heard it in the hoarseness to his voice, like his vocal chords had turned to sandpaper. "You don't have to pretend, Trinity. Not with me. It's okay to be scared."

I swallowed, furious at how badly it hurt. If I couldn't manage simple things like swallowing and breathing, how was I going to get through what came next—what always came next with Dylan.

Another good-bye.

"I was," he said, his voice quieter. "Today, when you were with Will."

My eyes burned, but I didn't look, not at him, anyway. But with a hard blink the picture my aunt had printed on plain computer paper came into focus, and my heart squeezed. Dylan stood with an arm around me, anchoring me to his side. Silver gleamed from behind the black Zorro mask. His jaw was set, his mouth hard.

I was . . . looking at him. Aunt Sara hadn't snapped a pic of us both facing the camera, but of me facing Dylan, with my hair falling into my face and the oddest look in my eyes, surprise and caution, but something else, recognition, almost.

Longing.

Regret.

"But you didn't try to stop me," I whispered.

Behind me, he stiffened. "Why don't you go get cleaned up?"

And I knew this conversation was over.

I started to protest anyway, but before I could Dylan put his hand to my arm, his fingers streaking first against the dark smear of blood on my shirt, then lower.

I stood without moving, staring at his thumb skimming my wrist, then on to my fingers, leaving swirls of warmth where he touched and pools of cold where he didn't.

Slowly, methodically, his index finger slipped along mine, down to the broken nail, and the dried blood against my cuticle. "You need to wash this off."

My chest tightened. He made it sound so easy. Wash it off, make it go away.

"It's your turn," he said with a quiet that played against the fringes of memory. "Let me make the sandwiches."

It was the right thing to do. A shower, wash it all away . . .

"Okay," I said, glancing up without thinking, without remembering everything I'd just told myself about not looking at him.

Damp hair slipped against his face, emphasizing his cheekbones and the hot silver of his eyes, the way he looked at me, the way he watched me, as if he didn't trust himself to look away, but knew that he had to. But not yet.

Later. That's when he'd look away, when he no longer needed
to watch my back.

And he knew it.

We both did.

Turning, I walked to the bathroom.

Will's text arrived as I was stepping into the shower.

> I'm OK. Somewhere safe. Can't go home.
> The bliss people know we're on to them. Be careful.

By the time hot water ran cold and I slipped into my favorite pajamas, the silly flannel ones Aunt Sara gave me for Christmas
with big wide-eyed owls against a turquoise background, quiet
filled the condo.

Following it, I slipped into the main room. On the table, a
plate with a turkey and swiss sandwich sat next to the open cardboard box. On the bar, votives flickered, and sage smoldered. On
the sofa, Delphi lay sprawled on Dylan's chest. They both slept.

Quietly I crossed to the bundle of herbs and dragged my
thumb and forefinger through the ashes before slipping to the
sofa. There, I kneeled in the shadows.

Looking at him hurt, because looking at him reminded me of
all the things I'd tried to forget. Looking at him lying there
erased the past four weeks and threw me back to the hotel room
in Belle Terre, when he'd been the one kneeling beside me, when
I'd opened my eyes to the clash of tenderness and violence in his.

That was the moment. That was the moment everything turned.

But there were no rewrites. I knew that now. Maybe in my
dreams, but not in reality. We didn't get to go back, only forward.
Mistakes could not be erased. Choices could not be changed. You

couldn't pretend before still existed, not when you'd felt the jagged shards slice down around you.

The world got watery. I blinked, and the silent tears spilled over.

"I'm sorry," I whispered, lifting a hand to slide the hair from Dylan's forehead. There my finger lingered, leaving a smudge of sage. "It's my turn to protect."

Then I rocked back, and cried.

I awoke in the predawn darkness with Delphi pressed against my chest, in my room. I yawned and stretched, trying to remember when Dylan left and I slipped into bed.

Then I noticed the pen in my hand, and the journal at the foot of my bed.

Heart slamming, I scrambled from the covers and crawled toward open pages. Delphi followed, positioning herself directly on top of the bold, dark scrawls.

I dragged her toward me and saw the words.

2 LATE WALK AWAY U HAVE 2
STOP HIM OR HE'LL STOP u

Beneath them, like a signature, was a hand-drawn picture of a roller coaster.

My eyes burned. It was too late to walk away, or I *had* to walk away? I didn't know! All I knew was I was supposed to do *something*. But . . .

I looked up, staring at the small red light shining from the camera Dylan had placed on the chest while I showered. Just as quickly I was on my feet and crossing the room, picking up the device and looking for . . . what? Dylan had set the equipment up. I had no idea how to retrieve the video, or if it had even worked.

I fiddled with it, turning the cube over in my hands and looking for a port or some other way to connect it to my computer and finding the memory card.

From there I rushed to fire up my laptop, climbed back onto my bed, and slid the card into the slot.

I was waiting for the image to load when a soft knock sounded against my door.

Startled and not wanting Aunt Sara to see what I was doing, I shifted the computer.

"Trinity?"

It wasn't Aunt Sara.

TWENTY-SEVEN

Dylan.

It was 5:26 in the morning.

I slipped across the room and opened the door. With sleep-messy hair falling against his face, he stood in the shadows of the hall, still wearing the black T-shirt and plaid pajama bottoms.

Barefoot.

Beyond him shadows slipped, stillness stretched, and Arcade Fire no longer played. My aunt's door was closed.

"Dylan," I whispered, realizing that just like last month, when I'd dreamed of Aunt Sara and he realized she was in trouble, he'd never gone home.

His eyes were dark, drenched with an intensity that made my heart beat faster. "I thought I heard you."

"It happened." Quickly, I took him by the arm and tugged him into my room, closing the door behind us. "I wrote something."

With two steps he was beside the bed with the journal in his hands and Delphi rubbing his arm. On my laptop, the video played.

The image was grainy, but clear enough to show the transformation from sleeping cat to crouching cat. Her eyes went round and dark. Her ears perked up.

"*Dylan,* look," I murmured.

He shifted toward me, coming up beside me to watch as, on the monitor, light flooded my room and I came into view. I moved slowly, more like flowing than walking, eyes fixed on some point in front of me. But I didn't look scared. I looked at peace.

Standing there watching, I hugged myself, running my hands along the flannel of my pajamas to generate some warmth. From the corner of my eye I saw Dylan's arm lift and thought he meant to touch me, but he only leaned over and braced his hands against the heap of my covers.

I kept watching myself on the monitor, the way I reached for the journal and the pen, the way I eased onto the mattress and looked up, staring in the same direction as Delphi. In my hand, I cradled the little stuffed puppy Dylan had given me.

In real time he went down on one knee beside me, watching.

The surveillance footage ran on, chronicling second after second of me sitting on my bed, staring at something unseen while fingering the soft leather bracelet. Minutes passed, long, excruciating minutes, before I looked down at the blank page of the journal, closed my eyes, and started to write.

With my left hand. Just. Like. Chase.

"Oh, my God." It was barely more than a breath. I watched myself, watched the way my hand moved in jerky movements, the way Delphi stayed crouched beside me, her eyes still unblinking.

"It's like I'm in a trance," I murmured. "Either that or some-one else is guiding my hand."

"Both," Dylan said.

The hair on my arms lifted.

"Dad said your mom did the same thing, filmed herself paint-ing, because she wanted to see."

I looked up. "*What?* My mom painted?"

Finally Dylan moved, angling toward me so that I could see his face, and the wash of something I didn't understand in his eyes. "Sometimes."

Shock tripped through me. "Did she paint me or the fire?" Slowly, achingly, my fingers stroked the dragonfly at my chest— *my heart*—and curved around the smooth edges. "Is that how she knew I was next?"

A quick chill ran through me.

"I wish I remembered her," I said as my own eyes filled. "And him, my dad." On the monitor, I stopped writing and stared into space. "I wish I had more than dreams."

Dylan moved slowly, but it seemed fast, a blur of movement before his hand found the side of my face, sliding the hair from my eyes, and lingering.

"Memories fade," he murmured. "But dreams are always there."

A single tear spilled over. Then another.

With a slide of his thumb, he wiped both away.

And it hurt, it hurt all over again. Blinking, I looked away. The image of me in the surveillance footage looked away, too, smiling softly and slipping against the mattress, pulling the covers high and snuggling the little golden puppy close.

"It's over," Dylan said as Delphi's ears relaxed and she shifted down on her side, curling as her eyes slid shut.

"Almost." I stared at the open journal against the old quilt, the words I'd written that belonged to someone else. "But not yet."

Aunt Sara didn't say anything about Dylan spending the night, other than that we'd both been sleeping in the main room when she got home, so she'd left us there. She grabbed a quick cup of coffee and flashed a perfect robo-smile, then she was out the door for Ash Wednesday mass at the cathedral.

Minutes dragged into an hour. Dylan scrambled eggs and fried bacon. I tried to eat. I got dressed, I paced, I texted.

Kendall responded within seconds.

> OMG. I'm at Will's house. The police are here. No one
> knows where he is. He says he's OK but won't say
> where. He says it's too dangerous. His parents
> want them to do one of those Amber Alerts, but
> the cops say they only do that for abductions.
> I'm so scared. Have you seen anything else? Do you think
> this is what you've been picking up?

Across the room, the grandfather clock ticked. One second. Two. Three. Four. Each louder than the one before.

"I feel like I should be doing something," I said, after promising Kendall I'd let her know if I came up with anything. "Hanging out feels wrong."

Dylan looked up from the sink. "You have done something. You've done a lot. You've done everything you can to follow up on a vision that won't form, and you led the police to everything Will's been picking up at parties."

Jackson and his new partner Kiki were following up on every name and location Will had written on the wall, but so far they hadn't found anything they didn't already know.

I could feel Dylan watching me, even though I'd looked down. "You've risked your life," he said, more quietly this time. "And you've gotten hurt. You can't keep putting it all on your shoulders."

Beyond the big picture window, the sun slipped higher against a pale blue sky, making the red walls of the condo glow. There was a stillness to the city, as if even the office buildings and Super Dome needed to rest after the party the day before.

Rest was the last thing I wanted.

Restless, I stalked over to the bar and found matches in a drawer, then lit the bundle of herbs. The flame flared between me and Dylan.

He leaned in to blow them out.

"What happens if we let it keep burning?" I asked.

His eyes met mine. "You really want to find out?"

A quick little streak went through me. "Probably not the safest idea," I said, then puffed out a breath, dropped the herbs back to the decorative ceramic plate, and reached for my journal. Maybe if I wrote, I thought, flipping to a blank page—

There were none.

Crude drawings stared up at me from every page, those in the back and even those in the front, where I'd been writing for the past few weeks: roller coasters. Some small, some big, some perfect, some *broken*.

Hundreds of them.

"Trinity?" Vaguely I was aware of Dylan coming around the bar and crowding in behind me, of his hands on my shoulders, but it was all so very far away, disconnected somehow, disconnected from everything. Or maybe that was *me*. Maybe I was the one who'd left the moment and the room, who'd slipped somewhere else.

But then I was moving, lifting my hand to the page to drag a finger along a high curve, where a small, perfectly drawn dragonfly fluttered.

Dylan's hand joined mine. "This took longer than just last night."

"It's what I've been seeing in my sleep," I whispered. "And in the astral, when I tried to pull the vision into focus and . . . Will drew it, too." My eyes stung. My throat burned. "I thought it was a memory."

The warmth of Dylan's breath feathered against the side of my face. I twisted toward him, searching his eyes with mine. "What if it's more than that?"

There was only one way to find out.

A beat-up white El Camino sat alone in the parking lot.

"Come on," I said, stepping into the warm, late-morning breeze. Jackson and Kiki were already inside the abandoned amusement park, along with several other plainclothes officers. I didn't know what they might find, but I knew I had to follow the bread crumbs. They meant something. They always did.

I also knew Deuce was right about the so-called adventures of a psychic teen. Backup was a good idea. I could follow clues, but I wasn't a cop.

"They've done a sweep," Dylan said, coming around the other side of the car. I tried not to stare at the faint bloodstains on his jeans, still there despite the fact that Aunt Sara had washed them sometime during the night. His shoulders strained against Julian's black button-down. A few steps behind him, Grace stood staring at the sign that still read CLOSED FOR STORM. She'd insisted on coming with us. "No sign of anything so far."

Which meant maybe what waited beyond the welcome center was something only I could see, or Grace could feel. It was that whole places had memories thing. Maybe, like the house on Prytania or the old hospital, the shadows had a story to tell. Abandoned places were the perfect hiding and rendezvous spots for people who didn't want to be seen.

Please, I thought. *If there was something I needed to see, let me see it.*

At first I walked. Then I ran. "I'm here," I murmured, racing through the cluttered welcome center. *"Show me why."*

It was all the same, the exact same, the faded pastel French Quarter–styled buildings along the main drag, with their dark, broken-out windows and scrawls of graffiti. Halfway down, a man in a cowboy hat and tight-fitting jeans lifted a camera toward a woman in a white tank top and denim shorts posing by a huge broken urn.

Pretending to be tourists, Detective Jackson and Kiki looked nothing like cops.

They barely glanced at me as I hurried past them, but I knew they were 100 percent dialed in.

About to round the corner, I glanced back to find Grace staring at the building where we'd found her lying like a discarded mannequin.

I hurried back. *"Grace,"* I said, taking her arm in my hands. The sun shone bright and hot, but her skin was like ice. "You don't have to do this."

Long, reddish-brown hair whipped against her face. "I'm not afraid of this place," she said, blinking. "Running from what happened doesn't make it go away."

I let out a slow breath, and with it a low, steady current echoed through my blood.

"Trinity."

I spun around, searching. Swarms of black birds dipped and soared. Hundreds flocked to overgrown bushes, resting before lifting back toward the pale blue sky. The past and the future, the now, they merged, fusing into something so seamless it was impossible to know where one ended and the other began.

"I'm here because you are."

I turned the corner and started to run again, and then Dylan was there, beside me in the twirling kaleidoscope of buildings and rides and memories. Sharp gusts of wind pushed us past the ghostly metal swings and the collapsing carousel, toward the ice cream shop with the vanilla swirl rising up from the roof.

"You have to get out of here!"

Around the corner the Mardi Gras Madness ride waited, with its long-abandoned cars waiting in an eternal line. Beads still lay scattered against the cracked concrete. The jester, so like the one from the Rex parade, still hung upside down.

Everything inside me raced, faster now, faster with each step I took deeper into the park. "It's all the same," I murmured.

Dylan stopped, scanning the restrooms and restaurants of the concourse, where together we'd searched for my aunt.

Nothing had changed.

And I didn't understand, didn't understand how time could stand still like that, how everything could be *exactly* the same, untouched, despite the fact that life barreled on.

I felt it then, the vibration inside me, faint at first, stronger as I twisted toward the weed-infested path winding beneath the JESTER sign. Without hesitation, I ran toward the rusted gate.

"Trinity."

I kept going. *We* were the ones who needed to compartmentalize life into beginnings and endings. *We* were the ones that needed limits, boundaries. But nothing ended. Not really. Not even death and devastation had that power. It was only *to be continued*.

Changes. Transitions. They were everywhere, from season to season, dormancy giving way to rebirth. It was all so clear as I followed the path that Chase had, through the overgrown shrubbery crowding the sidewalk and the birds swarming the roller coaster, one purpose giving way to another.

"Trinity!" Dylan shouted, and this time I turned. He sprinted up behind me, his eyes dark, tortured.

"I have to do this," I whispered. To fill in the blanks and understand what it had been like for Chase in those final moments, to pull the random images into a coherent picture. "Don't try to stop me."

With the wind slapping against him, he stood without moving, watching me in that way of his, touching me, holding me, despite the distance between us. It was like he was etched into the moment, etched with something sharp and permanent and *painful*.

"Come with me," I said, holding out my hand.

He didn't take it, but he did come up beside me. Together, we made our way through the empty station, exactly like Chase had done four weeks before. Heart slamming, I worked my way onto the track and toward the high curve, the incline so gradual I had no idea how high I moved, until I looked down.

I swayed, throwing out my arms to catch myself at the same moment Dylan reached for me.

With the park swirling around us, we stood like that a long moment, my arms thrown out for balance and his hands at my waist. I wasn't good at distances, but guessed we stood three stories from the ground.

"You can see everything." The rides, the buildings, the paths. The sprawl of trees and interstate beyond, farther away, toward the east, the hazy city skyline.

A few steps brought me to the curve where the tracks fell away, and the ground gaped below.

"I think about him sometimes," I said. "Up here, alone." My eyes filled. "When he told me to go with you, he was so calm and sure, as if he knew exactly what he was doing."

For the first time, I didn't yank myself back from the memory. "And I wonder if he had any idea of the danger."

The angles of Dylan's face tightened. "Sometimes it's not about the danger," he said. "It's about what's on the other side."

I looked down, toward the broken tracks.

"That's why you're here, too," he said, "why you never pull your hand back from the fire, no matter how hot it burns. Because you need to know what's on the other side."

"I have to," I whispered. "I can't pretend I don't know the things I know. I can't pretend something bad isn't happening, not when there's something locked inside me that might be able to help."

The wind picked up, sending that long curtain of dark hair into Dylan's face. "I know."

"My grandmother was so afraid something bad was going to happen to me," I blurted, shifting to take in the expanse of the park. "I know *why* now, because of what happened when I was little and my mother saw me dead. But I couldn't live like Gran wanted me to, alone in the cabin all the time, like that dragonfly in the glass jar. I loved being outside. It made me feel alive, connected to something bigger. It's like I've always known something was waiting for me."

On a deep breath, I turned back to Dylan. "And so do you," I said. "You know, too. You're always there when I need . . ." *You.*

But the word wouldn't come.

"It's like you have this freaky fear-radar," I said instead, "that goes off whenever I do something dangerous."

The corner of his mouth lifted. "It's not radar."

"Then what is it?" I asked before I could talk myself out of it.

The sun, so high and bright against the sky, caught on the silver of his eyes, making them burn hotter than I'd ever seen them. "It's you."

TWENTY-EIGHT

"Because you're *not* afraid even when you should be."

He made it sound so simple. And yet *that* was the lie. That had always been the lie. From the moment I'd seen Dylan standing on his father's porch, something inside me had stirred, *called*.

Recognized.

That's why I kissed him that first night, after he pulled me from the river, because it felt like I'd been waiting forever.

There was so much more to knowing someone than flesh and blood.

That's why it hurt every time he walked away.

Except now it hurt when he walked back. When he looked at me.

"So you keep racing in after me and dragging me out of rivers and fires," I whispered over the wind. None of that scared him. But I did. I scared him. "Because you don't want me to get hurt."

But the water kept filling my lungs and the flames circled closer, because every time he looked at me, touched me, time rolled backward and the darkness fell all over again, and with it the hurt slipped back into my soul.

Now the wind whipped at him, at us both, slinging long hair against my face but pushing his back and exposing his eyes. And in them the truth glittered.

"That's why you're always there." And how the fantasy, the illusion, started. It was what little girls dreamed of, the fairy tale, the hero, the protector, the mysterious figure emerging from the darkness in the nick of time, and making everything better.

But that's where most fairy tales stopped, with that great big swelling moment, like a pretty package with a ribbon and a bow, where everything is tied up and happy.

"And why you walk away," I whispered. "When the danger's passed."

Except real life didn't stop like that. Real life went on, into the after.

"Sometimes I feel like we're actors on a stage, and we've stepped into roles that were already there, with me playing my mom and you playing your dad, and each of us trying to play the part better. To get a different ending."

Where no one died, and good always won.

"But we can't, Dylan," I said, hurting all over again. "I'm not her and you're not him, and no matter how many dreams I have or new fires we walk through, we can't change the one that took them away from us."

Stone. That's what he looked like. Absolutely, unmovable, un-yielding stone.

"I need you to quit rushing in every time you think I'm in

trouble." Because *I* couldn't keep stepping in and out of illusions, *fantasies.* "I *want* you to stop."

Because there was so much more to life than the big dramatic moments. The spaces between, the quiet, were even more important, because that's where *real* life happened.

Those didn't exist for Dylan and me.

His shoulders rose with a deep breath, slowly dropped. "It's almost over," he said, as if that was a good thing.

My throat was so dry I could barely swallow. "I know."

I didn't even realize he still had his hands at my waist until he pulled them away and stepped back. "And you can say good-bye again."

Once, when I'd mistaken fantasy for reality, the thought of never seeing him again had ripped me up inside. Now it was all I wanted, to be in that moment, in the after when he was gone again, and I could breathe.

"And you can walk away," I said over the soundtrack of wind and birds and memory.

Until I dreamed again, a little place inside of me tried to say, but I wouldn't let the words out. Because they were wrong. Maybe I would dream again. Maybe my visions would come back. But I'd make sure Dylan Fourcade never knew. It was time for fantasy to end, and reality to begin. I couldn't let him keep slipping into and out of my life.

I turned away, scanning the concourse for Grace or Detective Jackson and Kiki, the other cops, *anything.*

"I don't see anyone," I said. The park was quiet and still. Needing to do something, I reached for my phone to check in with Grace, and saw the text.

Get down. You shouldn't be up there.

My heart kicked hard. "Will," I said, running my fingers along the keys as Dylan stepped closer.

You're here? Where?

His response came seconds later.

Somewhere safe.

Taking my hand, Dylan did what he always did, leading me down the steep incline back to the platform.

"He doesn't know they're cops," I realized, skidding to a stop at the gate. I texted Will back, telling him everything was okay.

His response came as we passed the Jester ride.

The ice cream shop.

I stared at the dark letters of his name, WILL, but with a hard rush inside me, I realized the words were not from him.

I ran, ran as Dylan caught up with me and took my hand as we rounded the corner toward the remains of the kiddie play area.

She stood in front of the tubular slide, staring at the violently flapping flags of red and blue. "Grace!" I called, running toward her—but for a ghost of a moment it was Aaron Lasalle I saw, La-Salle with his face twisted up in rage, holding the gun on me.

Everything slowed. I felt myself moving, felt myself *running,* but the wind pushed and pulled all in one motion, whirring into a vacuum around me.

I blinked, and it was Grace again.

I sagged.

Dylan caught me. "Trinity!"

I shook him off as another text beeped in.

That's where it happened, isn't it?

I stared at the blur of black words.

"Come on," Dylan said, still holding onto me. "This is the last place you need to be."

I shook him off, shook the past off, and focused on why we were here. "Will's here," I told Grace. "Do you know where Jackson is?"

She shook her head.

Another text came in.

Don't be sad.

Beyond the twisted slide, the kiddie swings dangled from rusted chains, exactly like before.

"Time's up."

Around me the breeze swirled. Vaguely I was aware of looking down at my phone, at the new smear of letters against the white.

She was here, too. She still is.

Everything blurred, the rides and the shops, light and shadow, the scream of the quiet and the cry of the birds, the past, the present, swirling so fast that it was impossible to tell where one began and another ended.

I started moving toward the swings, not realizing Dylan was holding my hand until the contact broke.

"Talk to me, Trinity," he said, but each word was quieter than the last. Further away. "Tell me what's happening."

But then it wasn't his voice anymore.

"Game's over, sweetheart, and I win."

Pain splintered against the back of my head. I winced, lifting my hands to press, but the voices wouldn't stop. They stabbed through me, fast, frenetic, drowning out the slam of my heart and rush of my breath until—

"Trinity!"

I heard that, my name. But I had no idea where or when it came from, or who. Dylan or LaSalle? Because for the first time since I'd woken up in the hospital, with my head throbbing and my memory blurred, I could see him, see him so clearly, standing in front of me smiling, with a gun in his hands.

I staggered.

"Trinity!" That was Dylan. This time I knew. I tried to twist toward him, but the moment exploded into a thousand pinpricks of light, whitewashing *everything*.

TWENTY-NINE

"*Trinity no!*"

Dylan, I know. He's close. "By the swings!" I shout as LaSalle's eyes go dead dark and blood blooms against his shirt. He staggers forward, taking me with him. I slam down hard, crying out at the pain. I try to crawl away, but his hands circle my throat, crushing and squeezing as everything starts to fade.

"Trinity!" someone shouts, and that place inside of me responds, giving me the strength to fumble for the switchblade and jab it into LaSalle's side.

He jerks back. His hands go slack. But the fading accelerates, the edges blurring, color washing white until nothing remains.

"Sweet, baby girl . . ."

The voice is whisper soft, gentle.

"Trinity!" The shout is farther away, somewhere else. Desperate, terrified. "Is she breathing?"

Hands feather gently through my hair. "It's going to be okay," someone promises. "I've got you."

Open my eyes. I know I have to. It's all I can think.

She's beautiful. That's my first thought, singing through me with the force of summer thunder. She's beautiful and she's here, with her long dark hair flowing around her, leaning over me, running her fingers along my face.

My heart stutters. "M-mom."

Her eyes flood. Tears spill over. "Sweet, baby girl," she whispers. "I'm so sorry."

I blink, trying to understand how I'm floating but can still feel arms around me, holding me. "W-what's happening?"

"She's so pale!" rips in another shout from that faraway place.

"She's in shock!"

But none of that matters, not with the warm glow in my mother's eyes, eyes so like my own, filled with the same longing swimming through me.

"You're so strong," she says through the tears. "You're going to be okay."

I try to lift a hand, can't.

"I love you so much," she murmurs.

My own eyes fill.

"But I can't stay," she says as new sensations rush through me, little streaks of warmth firing through my body like electrical waves.

Fading, she pulls back.

"No!" I try to lunge for her. "Don't go . . ."

Something stronger holds me in place. "Come back, damn it! Come back!"

"I love you," my mother whispers again, and then she's gone, leaving only the endless wash of white. Crying, I keep searching—frantic, desperate—and bring the sweep of dark hair into focus.

"Easy," he murmurs, as he always does, as he always did, and then his hand's there, the rough pads of his fingers easing against the side of my face, down my neck.

Everywhere he touches, warmth streaks, and pain ebbs.

But still I'm floating, and when I try to speak, my voice won't come.

He cradles me closer, his face a whisper from mine. "Just hold still and breathe for me . . ."

And I do. I did. Always. I breathe for him.

"I love you."

The words, quiet, ripped apart, echo through every cell of my body, and the spinning stops.

I hung there trying to breathe, looking from the hypnotic sway of the swings and the trees with the first green of spring, to the dark glow of silver burning from Dylan's eyes.

I was on the ground. So was he. He sat along a dark copper stain, with his back against the hub of the ride and me sprawled in his lap. I could feel him, all of him, the warmth of his body and the rip of his breath, his hand against my arm, the other tangled in my hair. But I felt something else, too, a tightness, like a cord pulled taut and straining against every line of his body.

It was like he was holding himself back, holding himself with every ounce of strength he had.

"W-what happened?" I asked, confused.

He spoke, his voice as restrained as his body. "You blacked out."

Each breath scraped like sandpaper. I swallowed and tried to pull up, but he wouldn't let me go.

Grace dropped down beside me. "Are you okay?"

"I—" Everything inside of me felt raw, like I'd been pummeled by rocks and some critical piece had broken away, revealing new places inside of me, soft and tender, not yet ready.

"Did you remember something?" she asked.

Dylan's hold on me tightened, as if he was scared to let go. And that confused me even more.

Dylan Fourcade wasn't afraid of anything.

Except of me.

"It's this place," I whispered, looking around, *remembering*. "It's like I walked through this invisible door and suddenly I was there again, back in time and reliving what happened with La-Salle."

Dylan's eyes went a little wild.

"And you." The warmth from his fingertips still streaked through me, as if by touch alone he could infuse me with the will to live.

His will to live.

He pulled back, twisting toward the front of the play area.

I heard it, too. Footsteps. Running.

Dylan turned back, holding a finger up to his mouth as he gathered me into his arms. And then he was carrying me, running toward a collapsed stage as Grace slipped in behind us.

Seconds passed. Ten. Fifteen.

"Police! Stop!" Jackson shouted, and my heart kicked hard.

"Oh, my God, *Will*," I breathed. I struggled to pull free, but Dylan wouldn't let me go. "He's scared. That's why he's running," I cried. "We have to tell Jackson not to hurt him!"

"I've got a visual!" Kiki called, running close.

Dylan's eyes met mine. Something silent passed between us. "Stay here!" he said, pressing a warm object into my hand.

Then he was gone.

Grace inched closer as I stared down at the switchblade against my palm. And I couldn't do it. I couldn't sit there in the shadows and wait, not with my heart slamming a million miles an hour. I staggered to my feet and took off around the stage.

The park sprawled in all directions, one path veering into another, each winding in different directions and, ultimately, forming one great big circle.

Against the rush of the wind, I listened, but no longer heard voices or footsteps. I took off anyway, darting back toward the concourse with Grace behind me.

Three quick pops stopped us cold.

Gunshots.

We spun around, searching. Nothing moved.

"Where'd they come from?" The open park made it impossible to tell. *"Oh, my God, Will,"* I whispered against the tight squeeze in my throat. Dylan.

Someone was down.

I tried to breathe. My whole body shook. In the distance, sirens wailed.

Closer, more footsteps sounded.

Grace grabbed my hand and dragged me back to the rusted water fountain between the bathrooms, flashing me a quick look that said wait.

We did. Four seconds. Six. Seven. And then we heard the shouting, and saw two uniformed officers sprinting past a second roller coaster, toward the back of the park.

I broke after them. "Come on!" I called to Grace.

Beyond the rides and gift shops, dirty concrete stretched into a parking lot, and an old metal building sat alone. At an open docking bay, the cops vaulted onto a platform and vanished among the heap of shipping boxes. They lay all over the place, torn open in a

sea of ruined stuffed dolphins and cartoon figures, beads, and even
T-shirts.

The sirens screamed closer, and Dylan stepped from the shadows.

Relief blasted through me. I ran to him, my heart pounding
so hard I could barely breathe. "Dylan!"

He jumped down and reached for me, crushing me in his arms
a long second before pulling back.

The second I saw his face, I knew something worse than des-
ecrated toys waited inside.

"Oh, my God," I whispered. "Will?"

Dylan shook his head, turning to lead me to a series of steps
leading inside what looked like a warehouse. Grace followed.

The body lay amid a spill of concrete boxes, with a dark
stain spreading from beneath. Jackson and Kiki stood nearby.
Cowboy hat gone, dreads hanging against his face, Jackson had
a hand to his partner's shoulder. Her eyes were dark, trained straight
ahead of her.

I stepped closer, and everything wobbled.

Dylan slipped an arm around me.

The guy lay at an angle, his body twisted one direction, his
head the other, revealing the inked "A" at the bottom of his neck.
His hair was dark, chin-length, and slightly greasy. His eyes were
closed, but if they'd been open, they would have been narrow
and intense.

"He was at the parties," I whispered, seeing it all over again,
Friday night when he'd come up to me and offered me a drink,
Sunday night when he'd crowded me against his body and asked
me to dance, then stood watching while my world fractured and

I ran out the glowing door. "He's the one who followed me into the woods."

"License gives a name of Shane Mitchum," Jackson said, crossing to us. He pushed out a rough breath, his eyes finding mine. "The name on your friend's wall was Sean Mitchell."

Will. "He knew," I said, wrapping my arms around myself.

Jackson held up a bag with a little device in it. "My guess is this is what he used yesterday."

"A Taser," Dylan said.

Jackson nodded. "Kieks and I saw him slipping in from the back and followed. He was watching you—"

I stiffened as a few more cops ran in, followed by the paramedics, who weren't really needed.

"—when you were over by the swings. We called for him to stop, but he took off running."

So many questions hit me at once. "You think he's behind all this?" I asked. "You think he's the bliss guy?"

Jackson shook his head. "I've got a unit en route to his apartment. We'll know more . . ." His words trailed off, his gaze locking beyond my shoulder, where the sunlight spilled in from the open doors of the dock, and Aunt Sara stood with Julian.

THIRTY

"Trinity, oh, my God, Trinity!"

She was there before I could move, running through the maze of spilled boxes and pulling me into her arms, holding me like she couldn't get me close enough. And my heart jumped into my throat, because I couldn't remember, I had no idea of the last time she'd hugged me like that, with warmth and emotion, so real and raw and *unprogrammed*.

"It's okay," I said, hugging her back. Her whole body shook, her very *thin* whole body. "I'm—"

Okay.

But the second she pulled back, the word died in my throat. Her eyes. For the first time in weeks the façade slipped, the suit of everything's–okay–armor she'd been wrapped in, and the pain bled through.

Julian slipped in from the other side, casting me a quick look as he slid a hand against my aunt's lower back. Slowly she turned from the body on the ground, staring off behind us, toward the gravel drive leading into the park.

"Aunt Sara," I said, reaching for her without thinking. "I know this is hard."

She pulled back so fast I froze. "Hard?" she repeated, her voice matching the word. "Is that what you think this is? You think it's *hard* for me to get a phone call from DeMarcus telling me you're here, *here* of all places, and that you got Tased yesterday, and now someone's dead?"

I winced.

"You think it was hard to look up and see Julian, because De-Marcus called *him, too,* and for Julian to tell me you're having visions again, but they're not real visions, because you're too emotionally devastated for your psyche to allow real visions to come through?" She pulled even farther back, wrapping her arms around herself and pulling her lavender dress—the one she'd worn that morning for church—so tight you could see the outline of her ribs. "But you never thought to tell me anything, not a word? You think that's *hard*?"

I looked at her standing there, with the long, side-swept bangs blowing around her face and the glassy sheen in her eyes, and something inside of me slipped. Because I could see *her* in there, through all the devastation and shadows, the aunt who'd welcomed me into her home and given me not only the pieces of my past, but unconditional love.

"Why didn't you say anything?" Her voice thinned on the question. "Why didn't you tell me?"

My eyes filled. "I couldn't."

"Why not?"

Tears spilled over. "Because I didn't know how!" I said, and then it was my voice that was thinning, cracking. "I didn't want you to worry. I wanted you to move forward, and I thought if I told you about the vision trying to form or the guy I was trying to help, the roller coasters I was seeing in my sleep, it would drag you back, and you'd see him again. And I couldn't do that to you. I couldn't bring him back into your life."

She froze. "What are you talking about?"

"LaSalle." Saying his name made me sick. "I brought that monster into your life. I didn't know! He creeped me out, but I didn't see the truth until it was too late—"

Her eyes closed.

"And he hurt you," I said. "He hurt you bad."

"Trinity, no."

"Yes," I said, feeling it, the fast, violent swelling deep inside, all the emotion I'd tried to chain away, rising up and slicing to the surface. "He did," I said. "He hurt you."

I'd tried. I'd tried to do this her way, living in that pretend world where everything was okay. But it wasn't okay. She wasn't okay.

Neither was I.

"And I just want you to be happy again," I said, and now the tears were coming, hard, fast, streaming in a free-for-all down my cheeks. "I want you to smile and dance around the condo, to sit on the kitchen floor with me and splurge on pralines, to hum while you work and laugh when Delphi jumps on the table and scatters your beads. I want you to let Julian in and I want—"

I broke off, swallowing a quick breath.

"You," I said, quieter now, softer, because she was crying, too, looking at me like she had no idea what I was talking about. "I want you to be you again," I managed. "The you who took me in last summer." Hesitating, I searched her eyes. The words were there, right there, burning against my throat. Once they'd been so hard to say.

"The you I love," I whispered. "The mother I never had."

The wind kept blowing. I could feel it rushing in through the open dock doors and swirling around us. And everybody else was still there, Julian beside her while Dylan and Grace stood off to the side. Jackson and Kiki were talking to two men in suits. But none of that mattered, only my aunt, and the amazing transformation of her face, like the sun rising up after a bitterly cold night and shimmering against frozen tundra.

"I don't like the paint," I said quietly.

Her shoulders rose and fell on one of those breaths she called deep and cleansing, the kind she used when meditating, back when she'd done that.

"Neither do I," she said, watching me, watching me so very closely, as if studying or trying to figure something out. "But I thought if I changed things up," she said, more quietly now, "if I made everything new again, you wouldn't be reminded of him, that you wouldn't see him every time you walked inside."

Me? The word shot out of me.

She smiled. It was crazy and insane and amazing, but even through her tears and still-perfect makeup, I saw her, more than just a glimpse. I saw my aunt.

My aunt from before.

"You," she said, and then she was moving toward me again, moving as she had so many other times, stepping into me and lifting her hands, sliding them along my cheeks to smooth the hair from my face.

"Because I wanted *you* back," she said quietly. "The *you* from

before, who darted in from school and threw your stuff everywhere, who sprawled out on the sofa and started texting, who
laughed when Delphi jumped on your chest and spent an hour
fooling with you hair before Chase would come over . . ."

Her eyes met mine. "The you I should have trusted." Her
words were quiet now, fragile but strong. "The you who told me
over and over that Aaron LaSalle creeped you out."

My throat tightened.

"The you who knew," she added. "The you I took away."

The devastation in her voice, her eyes, rocked me.

"Because I'm the one who trusted that man, not you. I'm the
one who threw myself into a relationship with him just to prove
Julian didn't know . . ." She broke off, closing her eyes.

Julian stepped closer, sliding an arm around her waist.

She twisted toward him, looking at him a long moment before
turning back to me.

"To prove he didn't know what he was talking about," she
said, and I could tell the words hurt. "That I wasn't hiding from
the past or myself. That I *could* have a relationship."

I watched them, blown away by the obvious intimacy zipping
between them, an intimacy I'd always suspected, but they'd both
worked hard to deny.

"I should have listened to you," she said, shaking her head.
"*Trusted* you. If I had, none of this would have happened. You'd
be okay and Chase would still be—"

Alive.

The word hung between us.

I wished it were that simple.

"No," I said, catching a quick blur of movement out of the
corner of my eye. "You don't know that. You *can't*. Do you really

think if you'd pushed that psycho away, he would have said, *'Oh, well,'* and forgotten all about his sick little game?"

Her mouth tumbled open. I could tell she'd never thought about it like that.

"I want the bricks back," I whispered as Jackson and Kiki turned from the guys in suits. "I want *you.*"

The remains of robo-Sara crumbled. "Oh, sweet girl." And then she was closing me into her arms like she used to, full and hard and tight. "That's what I want, too. That's *all* I want."

I hugged her back, feeling so warm and wonderful and connected, and wishing it could last.

When we pulled apart, Jackson was stepping toward us. His face was tight, his gaze dead serious.

"Got a call from the unit at Mitchum's apartment," he said as Dylan returned to my side. "The kid's definitely been dealing bliss, and it looks like he's cooking it, too, like a meth hybrid." He hesitated, looking like he hated what he was about to say.

"We also have reason to believe he was keyed in on you," he said, looking directly at me.

Dylan took my hand as Aunt Sara surged forward.

"There were pictures," Jackson said, "of you at parties and in the shop. Internet searches about psychic abilities and how they work, how you busted LaSalle."

Cold. It slammed into me like shards of ice. I felt myself sag, felt Dylan move from holding my hand to sliding an arm around my waist.

"And Will Ingram," Jackson said. "Mitchum had pictures of him, too. The history file from his laptop shows he spent a couple hours Saturday researching the kid. There were pages about the four-wheeler accident and near-death experiences."

"But why?" I said as Dylan took my hand. Me I understood. My precognitive abilities were no secret. "No one knew about Will. He was just a guy. Why would anyone key in on him?"

Kiki stepped in. "When you're breaking the law, it doesn't take much to make people suspicious. Maybe Ingram looked at Mitchum funny. Maybe he said the wrong thing. People with secrets go to great lengths to hide them."

I let out a slow breath.

"There's more, isn't there?" Dylan asked.

Jackson frowned. "Phone records. He made a lot of calls to a prepaid cell. And there's no record of where or how he got the bliss. It's a high-powered drug found mostly in Europe. There's no way some random nineteen-year-old would have access to it, unless from someone else."

"The person with the prepaid cell," Dylan said.

Jackson nodded. "Until we know more, I don't want anyone going back to the condo, or being alone."

The big Siamese cat watched me.

With the shadows of evening slipping in through the kitchen window, I sat on a bar stool, drumming my fingers against the TV tray, waiting. I stared at my phone, waiting to hear back from Will. I stared at my sandwich, waiting for the peanut butter to look appetizing. I stared at the insanely still animal perched on the fridge, waiting for Bakta to blink. I squeezed my eyes shut, waiting for the X-ray flash to form into a vision. I listened to the silence, waiting to hear noise from the front of the long, narrow apartment.

Waiting.

Aunt Sara went back to Horizons with Julian. Jackson had a unit at the condo, and Kiki was pretending to be an employee at Fleurish! Will, in his own hiding spot, was working on a list of every name and every place he could come up with. When last I'd talked to him, he was on his seventh page.

Waiting. Everybody was *waiting* to see what happened next.

Dylan wanted me to eat. He'd made me the sandwich and poured a glass of milk, then dragged the stool from the small window, the window with the shade pulled down and bars that had not been there last fall. Neither had the bars along the front window, or the twin, double-cylinder dead bolts on both doors. And the security system. That was all new.

But everywhere I looked, time rolled backward, and I could see him again, the night last fall after he'd pulled me from the river, coming to stand in the doorway after his shower, with a white towel slung around his bare shoulders and his jeans unfastened, dragging me to him and pushing me away, sitting on the side of the bed with a cup of hot tea in his hands, and leaning over me after a bad dream. I hadn't been thinking clearly that night. Actually, I hadn't been thinking at all. I'd just needed . . .

Comfort. That's what I'd told myself afterward. Security.

But just because you wanted something to be true, didn't mean it was, and what I'd felt that night, the soul-deep restlessness, had nothing to do with comfort.

I squeezed the sandwich, sending peanut butter oozing from wheat bread. Old jeans and soft T-shirts were comfortable. Dylan Fourcade was not.

With Bakta still watching, I brought the sandwich to my mouth, but even the small bite stuck in my throat, and the pale green walls closed in on me.

Restless, wondering if Dylan had any more of that magical dream tea, I stood, and the cat jumped to the counter.

I stepped toward the doorway, he leapt to the floor.

I moved quietly down the hall.

He slunk after me.

I stopped.

He stopped, too, keeping the same distance between us, like my own personal feline bodyguard, or, I thought with a silly smile, Dylan's sergeant at arms.

Squatting, I held out my hand, like I did to call Delphi. The big Siamese didn't move, didn't even blink.

I tried again.

Nothing. Not even a twitch of a whisker.

Sighing, I was pushing back to my feet when he took one slow, cautious step.

I hesitated, waiting. With cats, the move had to be theirs.

He moved slowly at first, one cautious step at a time. Then he was there, pushing his pointy face against my palm, tentatively at first, then harder, stronger.

"Good boy," I murmured, rubbing his black ears. Without really thinking I scooped him into my arms, and the ferocious guard cat started to purr.

Triumph made me smile. With a quick nuzzle of his wiry fur, I turned back to the front room. No sound came from within, only the muffled music leaking in from the bar downstairs.

The apartment was long and narrow, with three rooms the same size in a straight line and a hallway running along the side. The boxy bedroom was still utilitarian with a beige blanket pulled over the mattress, no shoes on the floor, the tall dresser alone against the wall. And yet everything seemed different, because I was different. Dylan was different. Six months ago he'd been a stranger, and now he was—

I still didn't know. I knew little more than his age and the fact he'd had to drop out of college, that his best day had yet to come and his scariest day involved me, and that Native American blood ran through his veins.

But that wasn't true, either. There was so much more to a person than basic facts like birthday and education, hobbies and interests and career goals. Those were the surface things, the clothes we put on to face the world. What defined someone ran way deeper.

And in *those* ways I knew Dylan better than I knew anyone.

Anyone.

He sat on the floor of the front room with his back to the wall and his legs bent, his feet flat against the hard wood. He'd showered and changed, but he still wore faded jeans and a black T-shirt. He held a stick in one hand, curved into a circle. With the other, he worked white yarn.

He knew I was there. He knew I was watching. He didn't need to look up for me to know that. I also knew it was no coincidence that he sat out of the line of the window and opposite the front door.

Against the adjacent wall, his laptop glowed from atop two milk crates. An old sofa sat opposite the television. Black-and-white photographs hung on two of the four walls. It was all the same, exactly the same as before.

"I think he likes me now," I said, ignoring all the big, life, death, and destiny stuff gaping between us and focusing on something simple: his cat.

Against the dream catcher he was making, his hands stilled. One second dragged into two, three. At first I thought he wasn't going to look up.

Then he did.

I'm not sure why my breath caught. Maybe because it always did when he looked at me like that, with that hot, slow burn in his eyes. But there was something else this time, a watchfulness, part protective, part predatory.

"He's always liked you," he said.

"Oh, okay," I said, rubbing my thumb along Bakta's cold nose. "That's why last time he watched me like he was trying to decide if he should scratch my eyes out."

"That's not what he was doing."

"No?"

"No." Dylan's hands worked the yarn again, but he never looked away from me. "He was waiting."

I laughed. "To see if he should scratch my eyes out," I persisted.

"No." Same word, but this time his voice was thicker, smokier. "To see if you recognized him."

"Recognized him?" Pulling the big cat back, I peered into the blue marble of the cat's eyes, as if we were old friends. "Why would I recognize—" Then it hit me.

"How old *is* he?" I whispered.

"Fourteen."

I did the quick math. Bakta was born when I was two.

"I knew him before," I realized, looking at the big beautiful Siamese as if seeing him for the first time. He watched me the way Dylan had at the Greenwood party, guarded, protective almost but with something else, a longing that made me want to pull him close and never let go.

"You named him," Dylan said quietly.

I looked up, didn't understand the sudden glow in Dylan's eyes. "I named your kitten?"

"No," he said. "You named *your* kitten."

THIRTY-ONE

Bakta stared up at me, the recognition of a thousand lifetimes swirling in his eyes. "Mine?"

"Yours."

My throat got stupid tight.

"Why didn't he go with me?" I asked.

"We couldn't find him after the fire." His face a tight collection of lines and angles and memory, Dylan looked down at the dream catcher. "We thought he was gone, too. Then Dad and I were out there with the demolition team, and I was kicking around where your room used to be, and I heard something."

I couldn't stop running my hand along Bakta's fur. *My* cat. That Dylan had been caring for all these years.

"How long had it been? Since the fire?"

"A couple of weeks. I didn't see him at first, because he was so little. But then I walked toward the trees and sat down, holding out my hand."

I could see it. I could so see it.

"And he knew you were safe," I said.

Dylan looked up.

"Like I did," I said before I could talk myself out of it. Always before the moves had been his. He'd been the one to come to me, both when my eyes were open, and when they were closed. He'd been the one who knew what to say, and when to say it. How to touch me. Kiss me.

Shatter me.

But it wasn't the destroying kind of shattering. I knew that now. It was the kind that made ice break away, and let healing begin. The shattering that cleared away debris, like the demolition crew that had cleared the remains of the house after the fire, to make way for something new.

"I knew that from the first time I saw you," I said, watching the light of a single lamp play against his eyes. "I felt it, that there was something there, some kind of connection. But I was with Chase, and you were a stranger, so I ignored it."

Ignored him.

"Until you pulled me from the river." And gave me the heat of his body and his breath, and reignited a forgotten dream. "That's why I kissed you," I said, remembering it all. Feeling it all.

Missing it, missing *him*.

"Because part of me recognized you, even then." I crossed to him and went down on my knees, holding Bakta there between us, the cat I named but he raised.

"No matter which road I choose, it always takes me back to the same place."

Him.

Us.

"Living the same moment over and over." Unable to stay away from each other, but unable to be together, either. "Stuck in a weird time loop like a scratched DVD that keeps circling back, but never goes forward." Heart in my throat, I lifted my hand from Bakta and brought it to the wide line of Dylan's cheekbone.

He ripped away so fast my hand froze there, in midair. "It's late," he said in a raspy voice, one I *so* recognized.

I also recognized what was coming next.

"You should get on to bed."

I sigh-laughed. It was either that or shove him as hard as I could. And I was so tired of that. Tired of shoving him away, when what I really wanted was to find a way back to before, when all the doors were open, and with nothing more than a look or a touch, he made the shadows go away.

"Did that used to work?" I kept my eyes playful, even as they challenged. "When I was two? Did I do everything you said just because you said it?"

The way *his* eyes got all dark drove me.

"I don't get you, you know that? I ask you to stay away, and you follow me. Now, here we are, alone in your apartment, and you try to send me to bed like a babysitter."

Something fierce hummed through me, a confidence I hadn't felt before. "Well, guess what?" I leaned closer, lowering my voice. "I'm not a little girl anymore."

It was amazing the way he could take stillness to a whole new level.

I watched his eyes, feeling the burn, feeling the hot, slow in-cineration deep inside me, and wanting more. "And I know what I need."

Taking his hand, I brought it to my chest, where my mother's dragonfly dangled.

"This," I whispered, feeling a different kind of warmth. "For you to touch me, like you did before."

He tried to pull back. "Trinity."

The wall stopped him, and I wouldn't let go. "Like you did when LaSalle tried to kill me," I rushed on, "but you wouldn't let him, because you wouldn't let go."

Dylan didn't move, not even with breath. But I knew he breathed. The warmth feathered against my neck.

"I *remember*," I said, watching him. "Being there today, at the park, it was like a door opened, a door I'd hammered shut because I didn't know how to handle what was on the other side. But I remember now. I remember you—and my mother."

The confusion and discovery, the warmth, the pain.

"That's why when everything else went dark, I kept seeing the roller coaster." Like a bookmark dragging me back to something important.

Not a memory, I realized now. Not something I could look away from. "Because somewhere inside, I knew the only way I'd ever move forward was to go back and find what I left there." What I lost.

Somehow he went even more still.

"My mom was touching me and crying," I remembered, "telling me how much she missed me and loved me." Exactly like she'd done all the other times I straddled the line between my world and hers.

"And all I could think was I never wanted the moment to end." Because it had been beautiful and perfect. "But then I heard you, shouting my name." And a different kind of beautiful and perfect had whispered through me.

They were my memories, but they played in the burnished silver of his eyes. "You were in shock."

Maybe. But that didn't change the truth.

"Part of me wanted to stay with her, but then I felt your hands on me, the heat that streaked from them." I leaned closer, searching. "Like invisible missiles firing through every nerve ending."

His chest strained against his T-shirt.

"And I looked into your eyes." Silver. Tortured. Like that exact moment. "And I knew it wasn't time for me to go, that this is where I'm supposed to be, with *you*."

It's what I'd been fighting all along.

"It's why I'm here now, why I asked Jessica to take me to you Sunday night, despite the fact I told myself you were the last person I wanted to see."

His breath was slow, rough. "Because of Chase," he whispered.

My eyes filled. "Because every time I think of you, there's this horrible stabbing inside me, and I see Chase again." The night of his uncle's party, after he walked away and Dylan stepped from the shadows. "The way he looked at me when he found us together." It was the moment I'd realized Chase and I were over.

"And at Six Flags," I added quietly. "When he told me to go with you."

Finally Dylan moved, lifting a hand to finger my hair.

"It was like he knew," I said. "Like he knew our paths were separating, that he was going in one direction, and I was going another."

With Dylan.

I'd known it, too.

I'd been fighting it for months, since the moment Dylan pulled me from a river and unlocked another inside me, one that had been hidden, but once exposed, ran hard and deep and strong.

Because Dylan Fourcade was not a stranger, and he never had been. I'd known him long before I knew his name. Long before I saw his face. He'd been in my dreams as long as I could remember.

That's what I'd been fighting, telling myself I was being foolish, creating some big romantic fantasy out of the flimsiest of dreams.

But they weren't flimsy, and I no longer had the luxury of writing off what I saw behind closed eyes as simple dreams.

"So you torture yourself," Dylan said quietly. "With all the things you could have done differently."

I didn't know how to stop. "He didn't deserve to die."

Dylan's hand slid from my hair to my neck. His fingers skimmed. Heat streaked. And all those quiet, fragile places inside me slowly began to reconnect.

His words were simple. "Neither did you."

My throat worked. I could feel it building, all the emotion I'd shoved away, that I didn't want to feel, swelling inside me, like floodwaters rising against a failing dam.

"But part of me did die," I said.

His hand slid lower, to the dragonfly at my chest. "No. You're still you, and you're still here."

Around me, everything glistened, as if a light had suddenly come on, shining so bright it blinded.

"Because you pulled me back," I realized, reliving it all over again, the need firing through me, the life force.

His.

"Like you always do." In so many ways.

"No." His voice was unnaturally quiet now, devastatingly hoarse. "I didn't pull you back."

A single tear slid over my lashes.

"I didn't *let go*," he whispered. "I didn't let *you* go."

My chest tightened, one last valiant stand before the dam crumbled. "You never do."

A rough breath shredded from him. *"I can't."*

I don't know who moved first, all I knew was suddenly I was in his arms and he was holding me, and I was holding him, holding him like I'd wanted to, *needed to*, every second of every minute of every hour since I'd seen him at the Greenwood party.

Before that.

Always.

And he was doing the same.

And it was just us again, finally, the us from before, without time or boundaries or explanations, without logic, or hurt, or pain. The us that burned so bright.

The us that just was.

Because he never let go, and forever was so much more than a throwaway word. So much more than the here and the now. The real forever lay beyond the frailties and limitations of this world, beyond the hurt and the cruelty and drama, beyond the trees, the sun. Beyond everything that we let shape our realities.

Forever was bigger than that.

It was that most sacred place in all of us, the part that bound us together, that kept us together. There were no beginnings or endings, just befores and afters.

"It's always been you," he said, running his hand along my back and pressing me against him. "It killed me staying in the shadows, waiting."

The rhythm of his heart pounded through every cell of my body. "Then why did you?"

"Because you were happy," he said quietly. "And I didn't want to take that from you."

I had to make myself breathe. He'd stayed in the shadows, because he didn't want to hurt me.

"But that's why your dad sent you to watch over me, isn't it?" I murmured against the warm flesh of his neck. "Because he knew if I got hurt, you wouldn't let me go."

Dylan stilled, and I knew I was right.

"And Julian." I didn't want to let go, either, but needing to see his face, I pulled back. "That's why he told you about me being blocked."

That dark sweep of hair fell against Dylan's eyes, hiding and revealing at the same time.

"I know," I told him, and with the words I lifted my hand to the line of his jaw.

Only a touch, that's all it was, but the warmth fired through me with the force of a thousand shooting stars.

And I smiled, real and bright and glistening. "I know it's not the salve."

The silver of his eyes darkened. He still held me, still had his hands to my body. I could still feel the reverberations, fainter now, but there.

Always there.

"Is it just me?" I asked quietly. "Or can you hold on to everyone?"

THIRTY-TWO

Life doesn't always lead you where you think you're going. Straight roads can suddenly branch in wildly different directions, wide paths can narrow, and unexpected dead ends can stop you cold.

But they can also make you turn around and see what you missed the first time through. And in that moment I saw what had been right in front of me all along.

Life had an amazing way of coming full circle.

Dylan had done way more than hold onto me in an emotional or metaphysical sense.

He'd held me in every way imaginable.

"You're a healer," I said as the wisdom of his ancestors flickered through his eyes. I didn't know much about the concept, but I knew there were many gifts beyond precognition and telepathy and clairvoyance. There were those who could move things with their minds, and heal with their hands.

And that's what Dylan had done for me, time and time again.

But now he looked as if I'd backed him against a wall, and lifted a knife to his heart.

I didn't get that.

"It's so clear now." An incredible sense of rightness drifted through me. I'd always known that about Dylan, even before I'd understood. It wasn't the salve. It was him. He had the ability to heal. *That's* why I'd ended up at his father's place Sunday, because deep inside I'd known I needed to heal.

And he was the missing piece.

I think I'd always known that, even when I resisted.

"Why won't you say anything?" I asked.

His hands remained against my hips, still sending warm, electrical currents pulsing through me.

"It doesn't work with everyone," he finally answered, his voice so phenomenally quiet it was no more than a whisper through my blood. "There has to be . . ."

"A connection," I breathed before he could.

"And trust."

"And we have both." We'd always had both. *"From before."* Always.

Forever.

I lifted a hand to his face, needing to touch, to memorize—to remember.

His eyes darkened. "Love makes it stronger."

Everything inside of me rushed, rushed hard and fast and deep. For the past few days, I'd only seen the differences in him. Now the wall was gone, and I saw the real Dylan. He was still there, had been all along.

"In this lifetime," he murmured hypnotically, "the last, and all those that lay ahead."

The rhythm of my heart deepened. Words. That's all they were. But that wasn't true. They were confirmation, and they were forever. "Because you find me," I whispered.

The breath ripped out of him. "Always."

"Why didn't you want me to know?"

"I never kept it from you."

That was true. He hadn't. He'd never made any attempt to keep his ability or our connection a secret, not even after the car accident in Belle Terre.

I need to touch you, he'd whispered.

Now I knew why.

"Then will you do it?" I asked. "Will you touch me like you did before, and make the darkness go away?" I lifted my hands to his. "Or is it only physical?"

The silver of his eyes took on a slow, dark, gleam. "It's more than physical."

"How does it work?"

Never looking away, he eased me down to the rug and twisted toward the iPod dock against the wall.

Bakta wandered over as the sound of drums and chanting drifted around us, and Dylan kneeled beside me. "Close your eyes."

Something dark and dangerous swirled through me. "What if I want to watch?"

"You can try." He almost sounded amused. "Deep breaths," he said. "Slow, steady."

Then he closed *his* eyes.

Fascination streaked to a whole new level.

Normally when someone closed their eyes they disengaged from the world around them. They tuned out. But Dylan became more aware, as if by shutting out the interference of his eyes, he slipped into an alternate dimension where his other senses took over.

Kneeling beside me, he spread his fingers and swept his hands along my body, not touching, not physically, but everywhere he skimmed, warm pulses skittered through me, slow and soothing, like a touchless massage.

"I can feel you." His hands hesitated over my chest, his fingers moving faintly, as if playing a piano only he saw.

Within seconds the rhythm of my heart, my breath, slowed.

"I feel you, too," he said quietly.

Another wave washed through me, thicker, stronger.

"What do you feel?" I asked. Or maybe I didn't. Maybe that was only a thought drifting through my mind. I had no conscious awareness of moving my mouth, only of the question, and anticipation.

"Strength." The quiet word moved through his hands, his breath.

"What else?"

He paused over my chest, my heart, and his hand started to shake. *"Nilch'i,"* he murmured.

The heaviness intensified, throbbing through me like a slow caress. "What's that?"

He started to move again, slowly toward my neck, reverently, as if touching something infinitely fragile.

"Your life force," he said. "The divine breath."

New tendrils of warmth feathered like the first kiss of spring.

"Stop fighting." The words were so, so quiet, without texture or tone, and I had absolutely no idea if they were mine, or his. Because everything liquefied, dissolving into a soft haze. Conscious thought swirled away, and dreams melted into memories.

Or maybe it was the other way around. Maybe it was memories that became dreams. Or maybe they were all the same, two sides of the same life.

But nuances like that didn't matter. Understanding didn't matter. There was something clinical about trying to define everything, to attach logic to the mystical. Of thinking I had to understand before I could accept.

"Please." This time the word was mine. I knew that, felt the need rise within me, just as I felt my hands reach for Dylan's and bring them to the fluttering at the base of my throat. It didn't matter that I couldn't see the glitter of his eyes or line of his cheekbone, the fullness of his mouth.

None of the mattered. None of that was even real.

All that mattered was the quiet river inside me, the one that flowed with memories and dreams and awareness, the *promise* that forever wasn't some obscure, distant place. It wasn't in the future. It was now. And it was real.

Vaguely I was aware of the drums and the chants carrying me to some other place, some other time, where glimmers of light broke the darkness, and fear fell away.

And then it was just us again, no longer standing alone in the after, but together in a new before. And without thinking I inhaled deeply and opened my eyes to a field of waving grass dotted by daisies.

"Better run!"

I spun around to find a boy with dark shaggy hair running toward me. His clothes were old, faded cutoffs and a white T-shirt, and in his hands he held a garden hose.

Then I was running, too, twisting around and hurrying not away from him, but toward something. I could feel it, the swirl of anticipation, the awareness that I had only to get through the tall grass, and something amazing would be there. Waiting.

"A promise is a promise," he calls.

Suddenly I'm at the door, the one that had not been there before. And I'm opening it and rushing back into the unknown. But there's no fear, only the promise of silence. I stand there, my heart in my throat, my soul on fire, waiting . . .

"I'm here." He is, too. I can't see him, but I know.

I always know.

The darkness won't give me detail, but I don't need that anymore.

"I'm ready." I breathe, and then he's in front of me, and he's moving and so am I, and I can feel him even before his arms close around me.

"I missed you," I try to say, but the words are more breath than voice.

He doesn't need them. He knows. "I always find you," he murmurs against my face. "Always."

"Forever." Lifting my mouth to his, I come alive with the remembered kiss, the breath we've shared so many times.

"You don't need to be afraid anymore," he promises.

"I'm not." Drawing back, I see his eyes, the silver gleam that's always there.

"I'll find you," he promises. His voice is lower now, hoarse. "Trust me."

Reaching for him, my hands slip through air. "No!"

Around me the night swirls. I run anyway, run without the chains of fear, knowing I can't let them hold me back. Not this time. I have to find him.

The silver stops me. Not his eyes, but a lattice of steel. It glows against the night, a bridge from one side of the darkness to the other.

I run toward it, but the wind pushes me back, and a scream rips in from behind me.

I spin around, toward the sudden throb of music, and everything stops. Everything but the scream of the electronic rhythm. They're strewn every-

where, grotesquely twisted, frozen where they lay, as if they'd been danc-ing when the world ended.

But they're not shadows.

"Oh, God," I cry, and then I'm running again, toward the bodies. They're everywhere.

Then I see the beanie. "Will," I breathe, running, running so fast. He's lying near the water, as if he just stretched out and went to sleep.

"No," I whisper, dropping to my knees. But already I know there will be no flutter at the base of his neck.

Numbly I pull myself back, and see the man standing across the canal. Watching. He's tall, well-dressed, and something familiar nudges at me.

"Trinity!"

I twist around, searching. "Dylan!" I start to run toward the bridge, but the body on the other side stops me.

It's not moving.

"No!" I shout, but the bridge begins to lift, a horrible grinding sound ripping into the night. I run anyway, run until the ground falls away, and the world goes white.

"Trinity."

I hung there frozen in the cold grip of terror, trying to breathe. "Dylan—"

"You're okay," he said in that low, hoarse voice of his, the one from an instant before, when everything had been so incredibly okay. "You're safe."

He was okay. *He* was safe, right there beside me, with his hair falling into his face and something I didn't understand burning in his eyes.

My hands shook as I lifted them. "You weren't moving." I touched him, needing that, the feel of the stubble at his jaw and the softness of his hair.

Blinking, I brought my surroundings into focus, the white sheets and pillow, the big Siamese and small boxy room and Dylan on the edge of the mattress beside me, leaning over me with his hands so steady and sure on my shoulders, holding me.

Not letting me go.

"You fell asleep," he answered before I could ask.

He must have carried me into his room. "How long?"

"About an hour."

Everything inside me raced, as if I was running still, running always. "I saw them." My breath stabbed. "The twisted shadows. It was like a party. They were all there, on the ground in the moonlight by a bridge, except . . ." The memory made me sick. "They were bodies."

I struggled for detail, but already the images were retreating. "You were there, too," I said. "But I couldn't get to you and the bridge was lifting."

His eyes darkened. "A drawbridge?"

The room kept spinning, tilting, but I made myself scramble from the bed and find the wall, using it to guide me to the milk crates with his laptop.

My fingers shook as I fumbled with the keys, entering words into the search engine:

New Orleans Drawbridge

"There weren't any cars." That confused me, the absolute darkness, as if we'd been alone in a postapocalyptic world. But I could see it now, finally, the image that had been trying to form since the Greenwood party.

"What else?" Dylan leaned over me. "What else did you see?"

"Will," I whispered. "He wasn't moving."

But then the bridge was there, not in my mind or memory, but in a small box on the computer screen.

"That's it." I clicked the YouTube link, and the image came to life, a huge, hulking steel structure lifting toward the sky.

"A railroad bridge," Dylan said.

It made sense, why there weren't any cars crossing it.

"Whatever you did worked," I whispered. My eyes flooded. "You helped me see again."

His eyes met mine. "No," he said quietly. "I didn't."

"You unlocked that place inside—"

His smile was slow, soul melting, and it changed everything. "What I do doesn't happen that fast."

"But I dreamed. I saw the bodies and the bridge and Will. It was all so clear and real."

"You," he said in that steady, unnerving way of his. "You saw, because you were ready to. Because it was time."

So much hit me at once, shock and confusion and happiness, relief, but there was no time for any of that, not after what I'd seen.

I looked at Dylan. "Something bad's going to happen there."

A quiet knowing came into his eyes. "You want to go."

"I *need* to," I said, remembering the man in the shadows. "I need to see what else I can pick up."

We called Detective Jackson. To be safe, he was sending a patrol to the bridge. Then I called Jessica and asked her to check on Amber, to try to keep her from going out for a few days, until we figured out what was going on.

When I called Will, he didn't answer. I kept trying, but the phone kept ringing. Kendall hadn't heard from him in hours.

"I don't like it," I said, staring straight ahead. "He's supposed to be working on a new list."

"We'll be at the bridge soon."

Jackson called a few minutes later, telling us the patrols had swung by and found nothing going on. That made me feel a little better.

"It hasn't happened yet," I said, putting down my phone.

Dylan slid me a quick look. "Only a few more minutes." We sped past a collection of new houses sitting next to the remains of long-abandoned neighboring homes, the well-traveled road deteriorating into a collection of potholes. At first there were streetlamps, then there were none, leaving the headlights to cut a path through the darkness.

And all I could think was here we were again, me and Dylan, racing toward the unknown. Except this time was *different*. This time we were ahead of the game. We were trying to *stop* something from happening, instead of figuring out what had already happened.

I wanted to be there. I wanted to walk around and breathe the air, to be where I'd seen the bodies strewn, to see if I could bring the vision back, to see more, even faces this time. The man. I wanted to make the nightmare end before it fully began.

Headlights cut through the darkness, the shadows giving way to steel beams and concrete against the desolate stretch of the Industrial Canal.

I grabbed the door handle before Dylan had the car stopped. "This is it."

THIRTY-THREE

"It's so quiet," I whispered as Dylan rounded the car, "like everything's holding its breath."

He stopped beside me. "You sure you want to do this?"

I looked at the play of moonlight against the silver of his eyes, and smiled, despite everything.

"I have to," I said.

He seemed to know that. Because we'd been in this moment before, so many times.

Maybe that's why I didn't feel the tight, cold fist of fear, because Dylan and I had faced uncertainty before. We'd faced danger. And we'd survived.

Or maybe it was the calm that always settled around me when he was near, the way scattered pieces drifted quietly into place.

The healer in him, that logical place of my brain tried to explain. But all those other places, the ones I'd locked away, been scared of, that had made me feel things I'd never felt before, knew it was far more than the Navajo in Dylan that settled me. It was him.

Us.

Slowly, hypnotically, he lifted a hand to slide a long tangle from my eyes.

"I know," was all he said.

Never looking away from him, I took his hand and curled my fingers around the width of a palm I knew to be square, and squeezed.

"This is right." It was what Madam Isobel had said a few days before, about the tapestry. "This is how it's supposed to be."

"I know," he said again.

I tugged him toward the bridge. "Come on."

He handed me a flashlight. He had one, too, and together our beams slashed against the old, wooden ties of the railroad tracks.

The hum was quiet at first, barely more than an undercurrent to my breath. But with each step I took, the vibration intensified, and I moved faster.

"What?" Dylan asked.

I lifted my face toward the night, inhaling deeply, as if I could pull the cool, hushed whispers inside me, as if I would know then, understand the darkness yet to unfold.

"I feel something." I hurried onto the bridge, searching, waiting. "An energy." A presence.

Dylan stayed close, the glow of his flashlight scanning the bank along the other side, where reeds and rocks tumbled down to the steady dark current of the water.

Shadows fell, slipped . . . *danced*. And on the breeze, music throbbed. I kept moving toward the other side, faster with each beat of my heart, until I was running, and the vision became people. They twirled in small groups along the edge of the canal, laughing and drinking, every movement in perfect time with the electronic pulse of drums.

The screaming ripped through me, had me running faster, running as the dancing changed into writhing, the laughing into shouting. I tore toward them as everything flashed, dropping them to the ground, exactly as they'd stood.

"Oh, God," I whispered, running among the sea of bodies. It was dark now, clouds blotting out the moon, leaving shadows drifting across faces.

But I would have recognized the rail-thin body and stringy brown hair anywhere.

"Amber," I whispered with a hot surge from somewhere inside me. I had to warn her, to make sure she never came to the bridge, and that she understood how dangerous bliss was.

But there were others, so many others who needed to be warned. It wouldn't matter, though, not unless I could stop the man. I twisted back toward the expanse of the canal, searching the overgrown tangle of grass and shrub, except then they weren't grass or shrub anymore. They weren't anything. They were dissolving, slipping back into the darkness, and taking the bodies with them.

"No!" I screamed. "Not yet!" Not until I saw the man. He was the key. Angling my flashlight in front of me, I started running, running again, running as fast as I could, until the sickening grind of metal against metal ripped into the night.

I twisted around, and somewhere deep inside I started to scream. Because I knew. This, too, I'd seen.

The bridge, big and massive and steel, folded in on itself, lifting toward the night.

"Dylan!" I started to run. He should have been behind me. He *had* been behind me.

But he wasn't now.

"Where are you?" I called, praying, praying so, so hard. *Not again,* was all I could think. *Not again!*

Gears grinded. Each crunch tore into the night as the steel steadily angled higher.

I fought my way up the incline, steep now, fought for every step, every breath, as if the air had thickened into something hot and vile and viscous, something shoving me back, trying to stop me.

I was so beyond being stopped.

The bridge angled higher, forcing me to grab onto the rail so I didn't fall backward. I pulled forward, toward the edge, and felt everything inside me go horribly still. Across the widening void of darkness, in the exact spot where Dylan and I had stood a few minutes before, he lay without moving.

My knees buckled, but I clung to the cool steel of the rail, knowing I couldn't let go. That I had to get to him. Get help. *And that someone else was there.*

Trying to breathe, I fumbled for my phone and stabbed a finger to Jackson's number.

"You're early."

I stiffened. The voice came from behind me, deceptively benign, friendly almost. But I knew whoever stood behind me wasn't a friend.

Sucking in a sharp breath, I wedged the phone back into my pocket and slowly turned around.

He stood at the base of the bridge, a tall man with thick dark hair and sharp, distinguished features, the kind of presence that made you take notice. He stood there so casually, in a crisp crimson button-down and khaki slacks, watching me as if watching a child's soccer game.

And with a punishing slam of my heart, all the remaining pieces sliced into place.

He'd been there from the start, from the very first swirl of unease at the beautiful mansion in the Garden District. I'd seen him inside the house, and out on the patio. I'd seen him with the police, and in the family portrait hanging in the darkly paneled room where I'd looked into Dylan's eyes and first realized how much remained between us. And how badly it hurt.

"Mr. Greenwood," I said, hoping and praying that Jackson had answered my call and was listening. That he'd alerted the patrol that had been here before. That *someone* was coming.

Mr. Greenwood smiled all casually, like he had the week before, the perfect host greeting a guest. "Next party's not until Friday night, sweetheart."

My stomach twisted. *Here.* There was going to be a party here, exactly like I saw in my vision. People were going to dance. They were going to die. Here.

Will.

Amber.

But I needed time, and calling him out wasn't going to buy me any.

"What party?" I asked, pretending I had no idea what he was talking about. He didn't seem to be in a rush, and I didn't want to create one.

He took a step up the incline, his movements as deceptively mild as everything else about him. It's what made him such a successful businessman—*salesman.*

"No games, sweetheart," he said. "I'm done playing, and so are you. We both know why you're here."

My throat convulsed. Bile surged.

"We also know there's nowhere to go," he said, tracking me one slow, methodical step at a time.

I inched back anyway. The bridge had stopped at a 45-degree angle. With one hand in a death grip around the Maglite, my only possible weapon, I kept the other on the rail.

"We tried to keep you away," he kept on in that sickeningly parental voice. "We tried to make you understand we were serious. But here you are anyway."

The wind pushed from all directions, harder, stronger.

I made myself breathe. I made myself think. "You don't understand," I tried, stalling. "Something bad's going to happen here, to my friends! That's why I'm here!"

Another step. "Something bad happens every day, everywhere." Another. "But you're right about here. This is where it all ends for you."

Another.

Time was draining, second by second. Breath by breath. And with it everything inside of me was twisting, screaming. I inched backward, acutely aware of how close I was to the edge, that Dylan lay on the other side, unmoving, and that only a few feet remained between me and Mr. Greenwood.

That if I screamed, no one would hear.

If I ran, there was nowhere to go.

"It might be awhile before they find you and your boyfriend," he said as if discussing antiques and not life and death. "The canal can be cruel like that, and no one will know where to look. But in two short nights, they *will* find Will right here."

With an exaggerated sigh, Mr. Greenwood shook his head. "The perfect place for the introduction of a new way to have fun, don't you think? Isolated, moonlit. And poor Will Ingram will be nothing more than another kid to make a bad choice. No one will think twice when they find him in the reeds."

Like I'd seen in my vision.

The reality of that chilled me to the bone. "You have to find him first," I gritted out.

He laughed. "Already taken care of that, sweetheart. You kids and your phones make things so easy."

A quick blast of horror went through me. That's why Will hadn't answered his phone.

"You're wrong," I said, edging back until my heels dropped off. "You can get rid of me and Will, but it won't change anything. The police are onto you. They already have everything they need."

"Then where are they?" he mused. "Why aren't they here? At my house?" Smiling, he pulled his hand from his pocket, lifting a hypodermic needle between us.

My heart kicked. Adrenaline raced. There were only two ways off the bridge: down into the dark swirl of the water, or past Mr. Greenwood, toward the woods. If I could push past him, the angle of the bridge would increase my momentum. But it would increase his, too. Then it would be a footrace, me against him.

"What is that?" I made myself ask, in case anyone else was listening.

"It's what's coming," he said. "What everyone is waiting for. Faster. More escape." Lovingly, he smiled. "Liquid bliss—there's nothing else like it."

Disgust blasted me. He was talking about a lethal drug like it was any other random merchandise.

"Didn't you hear what I said? People are going to die!" I shouted, horrified. "How can you do that? How can you put something on the street, knowing what it does? You have kids."

His eyes, warm and mild a moment before, flashed. "It's called free will, sweetheart. I taught my boys how to make smart choices. I don't make anyone do anything they don't want to." Another step. "If people want escape, that's their choice, not mine."

"But it *is* your choice!" I threw back. "*You're* choosing to put a dangerous drug on the street. *You're* making it more dangerous."

"And you, sweetheart, chose to ignore warnings." He hesitated, lifting the syringe to the moonlight. "Like I said. We all have choices."

Only three steps separated us.

With a hand to the rail he took one. "Drop the flashlight."

Curled around it, my fingers tightened. "What?"

Smiling, *smiling,* he lifted the syringe between us, and took the second-to-last step.

"Poor Trinity," he mused. "No one will be surprised, when they find your body, either, will they? After everything you've been through, you simply couldn't take the guilt and the grief anymore."

I realized it then.

He wanted me to jump.

THIRTY-FOUR

The night stilled.

"Drop the flashlight," Mr. Greenwood said again. "Or your friends won't be the only ones with a date with destiny."

I scanned the darkness. My options were limited. "What are you talking about?"

His eyes, nowhere near as placid as they'd been, met mine. "Funny thing about buildings in the French Quarter. They're old, bad wiring. When a fire starts downstairs, it all goes." He snapped his fingers. "Fast."

Aunt Sara and Julian.

"I have someone outside Horizons right now," he said coldly. "All I have to do is say the word, and it's bye-bye to New Orleans's favorite quack shop."

A thousand screams tore through me, but none of them found voice. I twisted to my right, toward the other side, but darkness and the hulk of steel stole everything.

I was out of time.

"Please don't hurt them," I whispered, pretending to play his sick little game. Doing my best to look like I was giving up, I dropped the flashlight.

What appeared to be my only weapon rolled down the incline.

"It's not me," he said. "You're the one who didn't mind your own business. You're the one who had to play superhero."

Choices. Mr. Greenwood liked to blame them on everyone else. I wanted to shout that at him, but the words were too strong, and I needed him to think I was weak.

"Now climb."

The time for stalling was over. Knowing I would only get one chance, I detached myself from all emotion and lifted my other hand to the cool steel of the trestle.

The night wind slapped at me, cool and sharp, *alive*. I stared out over the dark swirl of water, holding myself still as Mr. Greenwood took that final step, the one that brought the tip of the needle to my side. Then I came alive, ramming my elbow back as hard as I could, straight into his nose.

He recoiled with a shout of pain, staggering back. Momentum and gravity sent him sprawling. The syringe flew from his fingers.

Heart slamming, I pushed from the rail and fumbled for the hypodermic, not thinking, not planning, just grabbing it as fast as I could and lunging for him before he realized my intent.

The needle penetrated the sleeve of his shirt.

He swung toward me.

I stabbed the stopper down and quick-stepped away.

"You little bitch!" he roared.

But already I was running, gravity pulling me down the steep incline with the out-of-control speed of a downhill sprinter. My legs flew wildly, but I refused to fall. I had no idea what liquid bliss would do, but with any luck it would work fast.

"Stop or they burn!" Mr. Greenwood slurred.

I stumbled.

"I'll make that call! I swear to God!"

Darkness fell in a thick shroud, the faint light of the moon showing the dance of shadows among the tall, waving grass. My flashlight lay in the scrub, more than two body lengths away, and Mr. Greenwood wasn't down yet.

I darted toward it, and with a quick slip of the shadows, felt everything inside me start to race, hard and fast, like a waking dream.

"Good girl," Mr. Greenwood sneered, misinterpreting my sudden stillness as compliance, but I didn't care, not with Dylan rising from the water's edge with his switchblade in his hands and murder glittering in his eyes.

Quietly, he lifted a finger to his mouth.

Wordlessly I looked into his eyes, and told him that I understood. That I trusted. Because I did.

I swung back toward Mr. Greenwood. He was at the base of the bridge now, staggering like I had Sunday night through the woods. It seemed like a lifetime ago. In many ways, it was. Life was so much more than simply a collection of moments. It was each and every moment, each bursting with its own heartbeat.

Out of the corner of my eye, movement slipped against the far side of the bridge.

"What are you going to do now?" I challenged. Cautiously I glanced toward the shadows, where Jim Fourcade lifted his gun toward Mr. Greenwood.

"Maybe you should make that call," I suggested, standing

taller. Then I smiled. "Because you really don't have much more time."

Mr. Greenwood swayed and at the exact same moment Dylan and his father swung into view, one on each side of the bridge, me in the middle.

There was nowhere to run, even if Mr. Greenwood could have. Which he couldn't.

Liquid bliss was fast.

Mr. Greenwood's eyes widened as he stumbled back, and then he was twisting around and running, or at least trying to run. But he was beyond coordination now, beyond the control he craved.

Jim sprinted after him. "Freeze!"

I ran forward, too, but then Dylan was there, reaching for me, and this time when he pulled me into his arms, I didn't fight him.

"You're okay," I breathed, hugging him as tightly as I could. As tightly as I'd wanted to for so very, very long. I held him against me, loving the feel of him, so strong and solid, of his heart slamming against mine. *"You're okay."*

The damp heat of his body soaked into mine. The warmth of his breath feathered against my neck. Almost savagely, he pulled back and lifted his hands to my face, revealing the dark drench of horror and relief and something else, something *timeless,* gleaming in his eyes.

"Did he touch you?" His voice shook. "Did he hurt—"

I pushed up on my toes and pressed my mouth to his. "No," I whispered against his lips. "No."

He crushed me against him, his mouth moving against mine with a ferocity that fired through me, and a fever that seared through to my soul.

He was safe.

Jim's shout stopped everything. "Don't do it!"

Simultaneously we twisted around.

Jim stood with his gun pointed toward the high angle of the bridge, the edge beyond which nothingness gaped, and where Mr. Greenwood stood clutching a steel rail.

Then he jumped.

THIRTY-FIVE

We found Will in Mr. Greenwood's trunk.

"He was tracking us," Will told me after the doctors cleared him and I was finally allowed to see him. He sat propped up in the hospital bed, with Kendall curled up beside him, her hand protectively against his chest. "That's how he kept finding us. He put something on our phones."

"Sunday night," I realized, when both of us had been given bliss.

Will nodded. "I was hiding in an old mall," he said. "I thought I was safe. I was working on the list, when . . ." He slid Kendall a quick tentative look.

She smiled. "I told you," she said, widening her dark expressive eyes. "I *don't* think you're crazy. I think it's cool. I mean, how many boyfriends can talk with your grandfather on the other side? That doesn't happen every day."

But it might now, I thought with a quick smile of my own.

Will pulled her closer, sliding a kiss to her cheek. "I was behind the counter in the food court when like ten different people started shouting for me to get out of there." The confused terror of the experience lingered in his eyes. "I ran, but Mr. Greenwood had one of those Tasers like that guy used on you, and I went down."

I squeezed his hand. "I'm sorry." Greenwood had tied Will up and locked him in his trunk. In two days, he would have been given a lethal dose of the new liquid bliss and dumped at the party by the canal, where he would have been written off as yet another overdose.

It was a diabolically perfect plan. Mr. Greenwood was right. No one would have suspected foul play.

Of course it wouldn't have been that simple, not when *everyone* at the party collapsed. *That* wasn't the kind of new product launch he'd planned. Death didn't do a lot for demand.

"I should have known," Will was saying. "I mean, it was the party at his house where everything started getting freaky."

I'd felt it, too. "Sometimes it's hard to know, especially at first. With time, you'll learn what to pay attention to."

"So your vision . . ." He hesitated, his eyes searching mine. "You finally saw what was trying to form?"

I pulled back, looking toward the window as the image flashed all over again, the grotesquely twisted bodies, frozen where they lay, as if they'd been dancing when the world ended.

Because they would have been.

"Yeah," I said, filling them in on liquid bliss and the upcoming party. "The name that you wrote yesterday on that wall?

Brandy? That was a girl I go to school with, Amber." The memory of her unseeing, doll-like eyes haunted me. "She would have been there, at the railroad bridge, like you wrote."

Dancing.

When her world ended.

But it wasn't going to end now. Instead she was getting help. Everyone was. Jessica and Kiki had approached Amber's parents, the police issued a broadcast alert to all media, ten cases of bliss were confiscated, and the man behind it all was dead. The police found the older man's body within half an hour, trapped by a fallen tree. He'd drowned, like I was pretty sure he'd intended as soon as he realized he was facing the rest of his life in prison, or worse.

He'd chosen the worse.

Once Jackson and Kiki started looking, the illusion of refined antiques dealer that Paul Greenwood had built for the community quickly came crumbling down. His money was old money, and he'd lost most of it in the stock market. In debt, his business failing, and on the verge of losing his house—*and his standing*—he'd been experimenting with more lucrative merchandise. His frequent trips to Europe gave him a constant source, and a solid alibi. No one had ever suspected him. Hosting a party at his house was all part of the pretend world.

"Hey," came a quiet voice from the doorway, and then Will's parents and little sister were slipping back into the room with four cups of steaming hot cocoa and a big Mylar balloon in the shape of a puppy.

Realizing they needed time alone, I eased back from the bed. "Give me a call when you're ready," I said. Now that his secret was out of the bag, he had a ton of questions. "I've got some people I want you to meet." Like Julian and Grace.

Will grinned. "I was born ready."

Smiling back at him, I turned to leave, but hesitated when I noticed the little girl watching me.

"Hi," I said.

Her eyes widened. "Thank you," she said, all fast-like. "Thank you for helping my brother."

Will's mother glanced back. "Yes," she said as her husband slid in next to her. "Thank you."

"You did a very brave thing," he said. "We'll be forever grateful."

A few seconds later I opened the door and slipped into the stillness of the hall, with the buzz of fluorescent lights and the sparsely manned nurse's station.

It was a few minutes after midnight.

I walked through the silence, not sure where I was going or what to do next, until laughter drifted from the television in the lounge, and I turned to see them, see them all: Aunt Sara, with her soft wavy hair falling loose around her face and Julian by her side, a hand at the small of her back; Detective Jackson sprawled in a plastic chair two sizes too small for him, tapping out something on his phone; Grace in her grandmother's arms and Victoria in Trey's; Deuce and . . . *Jessica* rising from the sofa; and Jim Fourcade with his silver ponytail turning from the window.

And the tears spilled over.

They were all there, all except—

But then the softest hum moved through me, and with it I turned, and saw him, too. Saw Dylan standing by himself, cleaned up now, his hair dry and falling against the big white bandage at his brow, his jeans and T-shirt fresh, and . . . the little stuffed puppy in his hands.

———

"I don't want to go inside, not yet."

At the door to the condo, Aunt Sara turned back toward me. From inside, the red and brown of brick shone through the scrape of white.

"Are you sure?" she asked.

I nodded, and after one last lingering look, she and Julian went inside, and I went to the stairwell, and climbed. At the top, I turned my key in the dead bolt, pushed open the metal door, and stepped back into the night.

Clay pots sat everywhere, big and small, some with purple-and-gold pansies, some empty. A few round tables and chaise lounges sat scattered around, along with a telescope.

And with a quick thought of the dragonfly in my bedroom, the one of blown glass, I walked to the edge of the rooftop patio and breathed in the night.

A moment. A breath. The blink of an eye.

That was all it took for life to change.

And you never knew when that moment, that breath, was going to come.

"Your grandfather was right," I said, turning back to find Dylan standing by a beautiful cobalt planter. "You can't yank the sun from the sky just because it burns."

Shadows slipped through the soft play of accent lighting, emphasizing the stillness to him.

"But that's what I was trying to do," I whispered. Creating an ending where there wasn't one, because moving forward hurt.

"I see it now," I said, holding out my hand.

Eyes burning, he stepped toward me.

"If every time you're afraid, you turn on the lights, you'll never see the stars."

But I saw them then, saw them finally, an endless sea of white twinkling against the darkness.

Forever.

Epilogue

We drove through the night.

In the stillness of predawn, we parked, and I reached for the door handle. But I didn't open it, not at first, not without turning back and lifting my eyes to his.

He didn't say anything, and neither did I.

We both knew it was time.

Turning, I let myself into the soft swirl of the wind, warmer now with spring fighting off winter, stronger here so close to the surf. Louder.

At the end of the path, where the weathered boardwalk ended, I kicked off my sandals and stepped into the sugary white sand.

Fading glimmers of moonlight played against the waves, bringing a soft glitter to the ebb and flow of darkness. For a moment, I stood quietly by a big dune, curling my hand around the leather at my wrist as I looked at the Gulf of Mexico for the first time.

It was like stepping into a dream.

I'm not sure how much time passed. Vaguely I was aware of the first song of the birds as I finally slipped past the tall, waving sea grasses. In a few hours sun worshippers would pack the beach, but at that moment, alone at the edge of one world, a fragile intimacy swept in with the tide. That's why I'd come with the night, before the day swept away the quiet.

At the water's edge, where the surf gently broke, I waded into the waves.

"I'm here," I said against the salty spray to my face. Lowering my arms, I skimmed my fingers along the water surging up around my thighs. "It's even more beautiful than I imagined."

Behind me, a dog barked. Glancing over my shoulder, I smiled at the big muscular Lab galloping against the play of the waves.

When I turned back to the night, faint streaks of silver played against the darkness.

"I know you're here," I whispered. "Just like you've been there all along, trying to help me be okay again." Because that's the way life played. Nothing was random. There were no coincidences. Each experience, each encounter, *each breath,* built toward the next. You couldn't stop. You couldn't turn away. Grace, Madam Isobel, Julian, Will, Jessica, Chase . . . they'd all played a role in making sure I didn't stop, that I kept moving, that I opened my eyes to all that lies ahead.

"I've been writing you a letter," I said, wading deeper into the shimmery water. "But you know that, don't you?" I smiled. "You've been writing me back."

Another wave broke, this one shattering up against my face. I laughed, bracing myself for the next, and realizing for the first time that the heavy, crushing feeling against my chest that I'd been living with for weeks was gone.

I don't know how long I stood there like that, waist-deep in the rhythm of the surf, but when streaks of white against the horizon became seagulls, and a lone pelican emerged, soaring high before dipping majestically for the water, I slipped back into the moment, and knew it was time to go.

"Tell my mom hi," I whispered, instead of saying good-bye. Because those didn't exist. I knew that now.

Every after was simply a new before.

With the wind slapping damp hair against my face, I smiled as the first shimmers of coral streaked up from the horizon, and turned back to the beach.

Dylan stood at the water's edge, tall, barefoot, waves crashing against his jeans as the wind whipped long streaks of dark hair against his face.

I smiled and started toward him.

He smiled back, and waded toward me.

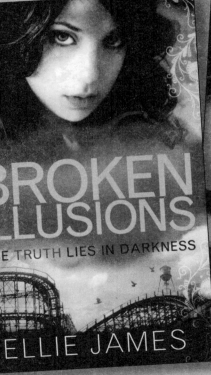

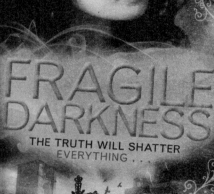

For special offers,
chapter samplers,
competitions
and more,
visit . . .

www.quercusbooks.co.uk
@quercuskids